Praise for Murder by Candlelight

'Brilliant characters that leap off the page' *The Sun*

'Faith Martin has created a wonderful Wodehousian world of intrigue and suspicion and a tricky puzzle to solve' Helena Dixon, author of the Miss Underhay Mysteries

'Amuses and intrigues in equal measure ... a splendid start to what promises to be a long-running series' *Daily Mail*

'All the ingredients of a classic mystery – engaging characters and an impossible crime. The story races along like a runaway locomotive . . . enormous fun' Orlando Murrin, author of *Knife Skills for Beginners*

'We devoured this whodunit in one sitting!' *Bella*

'The perfect village mystery. A golden-age world with an energy that is totally contemporary' J.M. Hall, author of *A Spoonful of Murder*

'With murder, intrigue, and ghostly happenings, this will satisfy cosy crime fans' *Heat*

'A charming and clever take on a locked room murder that left you guessing how and why the victim snuffed it! I enjoyed the clever plot, original ideas and the idyllic setting very much!' Sarah Yarwood-Lovett, author of The Doctor Nell Ward Mysteries

'Her knowledge of the genre and easy writing style makes this an effortless and fun read' *My Weekly*

'A clever mystery' *Woman's Own*

'This engaging and energetic mystery hosts an abundance of engaging characters and is great fun' *Platinum*

Also by Faith Martin

The Ryder and Loveday series
A Fatal Obsession
A Fatal Mistake
A Fatal Flaw
A Fatal Secret
A Fatal Truth
A Fatal Affair
A Fatal Night
A Fatal End

The Val & Arbie Mysteries
Murder by Candlelight

THE LAST WORD IS DEATH

FAITH MARTIN

HQ

ONE PLACE. MANY STORIES

This novel is entirely a work of fiction. The names, characters and incidents portrayed in it are the work of the author's imagination. Any resemblance to actual persons, living or dead, events or localities is entirely coincidental.

HQ
An imprint of HarperCollins*Publishers* Ltd
1 London Bridge Street
London SE1 9GF

www.harpercollins.co.uk

HarperCollins*Publishers*
Macken House, 39/40 Mayor Street Upper,
Dublin 1, D01 C9W8, Ireland
This edition 2025

1

First published in Great Britain by
HQ, an imprint of HarperCollins*Publishers* Ltd 2025

Copyright © Faith Martin 2025

Faith Martin asserts the moral right to be
identified as the author of this work.
A catalogue record for this book is
available from the British Library.

ISBN: 9780008590130

MIX
Paper | Supporting
responsible forestry
FSC™ C007454

This book contains FSC™ certified paper and other controlled sources to ensure responsible forest management.

For more information visit: www.harpercollins.co.uk/green

Set in Meridien LT Std by HarperCollins*Publishers* India

Printed and bound in the UK using 100% Renewable
Electricity at CPI Group (UK) Ltd

All rights reserved. No part of this publication may be reproduced, stored in a retrieval system, or transmitted, in any form or by any means, electronic, mechanical, photocopying, recording or otherwise, without the prior permission of the publishers.

This book is sold subject to the condition that it shall not, by way of trade or otherwise, be lent, re-sold, hired out or otherwise circulated without the publisher's prior consent in any form of binding or cover other than that in which it is published and without a similar condition including this condition being imposed on the subsequent purchaser

For my sister Marion

SEPTEMBER 1925

CHAPTER ONE

The black Alvis saloon swept jauntily around the narrow bend of a country lane, allowing its driver to catch his first appreciative glimpse of the sea. And a very nice glimpse it was too, he mused. A small bay with a crescent of pale sand next to a vast expanse of silver-gold sunlight reflecting off azure water, it made a chap fairly yearn to take a dip.

It was early September, and jolly old England seemed intent on having one last hoorah of wonderful weather before settling down into the more tempestuous season of autumn – a circumstance which suited one Arbuthnot Lancelot Swift (known far and wide as Arbie to friends and foes alike) right down to the ground.

In the distance and overlooking the idyllic bay, the handsome youth could see his ultimate destination, the seaside village of Galton-next-the-Sea sunning itself like a contented cat as it spread and straggled its way along the coastline and up one side of the hill. It looked every inch the up-and-coming holiday destination that sundry tourist posters had promised, and he felt his spirits positively lift.

As he nervously pointed his faithful steed's metallic nose downhill to begin the somewhat precipitous descent into the village proper, he could only hope that the only hotel, newly bought and redeveloped from its former existence as a large country house, would likewise be as billed in the advertising. Private bath, hot and cold running water, good grub and a fine wine cellar hit the ticket all right!

Not that Arbie was there solely to enjoy himself, as his publishers would insist on reminding him, far more often than he felt was needed or, indeed, was comfortable. He was also there to research the resident ghost in these parts for the last chapter of his current book, the much-anticipated follow-up to a previous effort of his, which had been an unexpected sensation and runaway best seller, *The Gentleman's Guide to Ghost-Hunting*, a travel guide whose holiday destinations came complete with a spectre or ghoul. For those who liked that sort of thing.

He stopped the car as he spied an old man sitting on a bench beneath a giant chestnut tree, placidly smoking his pipe and regarding, with amusement, a very fat black-and-white cat that was attempting to stalk a robin. The robin, naturally, was having none of it.

Poking his head out of the window, Arbie called amiably across to him.

'Good afternoon, sir. I take it I'm on the right road to the hotel?' A clean-shaven man of some twenty-six years or so, with plentiful amounts of dark hair and wide, seemingly innocent-looking grey eyes, he smiled affably. Smiling affably came easily to Arbie. As did loafing.

The old man regarded him judiciously for a moment, then slowly removed his briar pipe. 'Yerse. You be after the old Dashwood House then?' the ancient worthy asked, with the slow, pleasing drawl of the local accent.

'Be I?' Arbie reflected unhelpfully. 'Blast if I can remember the actual name of the place, now that I come to think of it. I've been invited down by Captain George Penderghast and his lady wife?' he offered up hopefully. In his experience, villagers knew absolutely everything about absolutely everyone within a country mile.

As expected, the old man began to nod wisely. 'That'll be the Dashwood place. They say they installed electricity and everything in there when they were doing it up and makin' it all fancy for these here guests they reckon they got coming.'

Arbie gave him a nod and a thanks and a cheerful wave as he drove off.

In less than a minute he spotted a very nice Georgian house, set a little up the hill and surrounded by seaside-type planting and looking reassuringly spic-and-span. Crisp white new paint had been applied to the exterior woodwork, the stonework had obviously not long been repointed, and the roof looked to be in reassuringly good repair. A rather self-effacing sign, painted on a discreet white wooden board, did indeed proclaim itself to be **The Dashwood House Hotel, Prop. Capt. And Mrs Penderghast**. The small print underneath apologetically added that rooms were available only to the discerning guest.

Wondering absently what undiscerning guests were supposed to do if, after travelling all the way here they found themselves to be distinctly de trop, Arbie turned off the village road and up the slight incline beside the hotel where he spotted a raked gravelled driveway leading off to the left. This had been squared off in one corner to provide parking, and with a sigh of satisfaction, he nudged his machine into a shady spot and turned off the engine.

As he climbed out, he glanced around to get his bearings. Directly behind and below him was the sandy beach with its inviting stretch of water, and he hoped that he'd been given a room with this most desirable of views. And since he had been invited down with the tacit understanding that he would be treated to the best of everything (gratis, naturally), providing that he gave the new hotel an excellent rating in his next travel guide, he had every reason to suppose that this would be the case. If his past experiences of writing his first *Gentleman's Guide* was anything to go by, proprietors of pubs, inns and other such domiciles could be very accommodating indeed when it came to keeping influential guests happy.

Leading off to either side of the house, impeccably mown and trimmed lawns with lush flowering borders promised yet further gardens to the rear. Didn't he have a vague idea from the Penderghasts' letter that there'd be ponds and water fountains, not to mention a well-stocked fruit orchard? He hoped so – he was rather partial to the odd freshly picked plum or two . . .

His happy speculations were abruptly brought to a halt when a truly appalling and ear-shattering noise brayed very loudly in his ear. Not surprisingly, he smartly commenced to shoot about six feet into the air, whilst simultaneously spinning around, his fight-or-flight instinct fully present and correct. Quickly, his eyes scanned the vicinity for the source of the assault on his ears.

On the border of this side of the hotel, a small paddock stretched away to the hotel's nearest neighbour, a rather ramshackle farmhouse that nevertheless had centuries of authenticity on its side, lending it a paradoxically patrician charm. Surrounding this paddock was a two-rail wooden fence and having just thrust its head over the topmost barrier, a handsome grey donkey was regarding him hopefully.

'I say, old man, you nearly gave me a heart attack,' Arbie admonished him, grinning widely. And the boy in him (which in Arbie's case was never very far away, as any of his chums could attest) had him wandering casually over to stroke the rather dusty snout and outlandish, velvety ears. 'Don't happen to have a carrot for you on me, old bean, not being in the habit of going about with root vegetables stuffed into my pockets and whatnot. But I promise I'll see what I can do about finding something for you later.'

The paddock's only other resident, a snooty-looking fat white pony, raised its head to sneer at him, as if saying she'd heard it all before, and resolutely turned her back. The donkey nudged Arbie's arm hopefully. Rather tall for a donkey, he wore no bridle and went unshod, but in the soft mud and grass of the paddock, he looked healthy and happy enough, so clearly somebody loved him. 'I might even be able to stretch to the odd apple or two,' he added loudly. That would teach the pony a valuable lesson.

Going back to his car, he undid the leather straps that secured his two cases to the back of the Alvis and set off towards the open front door of the hotel, which was to be a home away from home for the next two weeks or so. As he did so, he whistled a cheery couple of bars from the latest ditty doing the rounds at the music halls (something about a cobbler's daughter and her problems with a pair of oversized clogs or some such) and hoped that the village of Galton-next-the-Sea truly was as haunted as the Penderghasts had assured him in their letter. Otherwise, he'd be forced to head off early in search of a more accommodating ghost.

*

The reception hall was reassuringly cool and tranquil. Black-and-white tiles underfoot led to several open doorways, through which Arbie could detect a lounge, a reading/writing room and – best of all – a cosy private bar. A grandfather clock ticked ponderously against one wall, and several easy chairs were scattered around small tables, littered with fishing magazines and such fare.

A reception desk stood half in the alcove created by a wide, sweeping semi-circular staircase, a giant vase of bronze chrysanthemums providing a magnificent splash of colour at one end. Behind it was a wooden board hung neatly with keys. A telephone booth was set up nearest the door to the bar. There was a smell of furniture polish in the air, and although he could hear a murmur of faint voices coming from somewhere, he was all alone. But then, Arbie supposed, a Monday afternoon betwixt and between lunch and teatime was hardly likely to be a particularly lively time for any hotel.

He put his bags down in front of the reception desk, noting that there was a tray marked 'Post In' and one marked 'Post Out' loitering on the surface, along with a leather-bound register, pen and inkwell set, and a brass bell. He duly plonked one of his digits on the bell and heard it give a loud and satisfying 'ping'.

Instantly, there came movement from somewhere within one of the three rooms leading off the hall, and a moment later, a short, slightly plump and very pleasant-faced woman with blonde hair and friendly brown eyes appeared from the lounge.

'Oh, I'm so sorry, I didn't hear you arrive,' the lady said by way of apology, moving adroitly behind the reception desk. 'And you must be our famous author too! The Captain will be vexed that we weren't front and centre to greet you. What must you think of us? I'm Millie – Millie Penderghast. Welcome to the Dashwood House Hotel, Mr Swift. It *is* Mr Swift, isn't it?' she asked anxiously.

Arbie modestly admitted to being Mr Swift.

'I do hope you had a pleasant journey down. Did you come by train? It's so convenient to have a train station in the next town to us.' As she chatted pleasantly, a young lad appeared from somewhere and made off with his bags, and Arbie found himself effortlessly swept away and into the bar by his charming hostess.

'We're expecting a large party of guests who are celebrating an engagement, which is always nice, don't you think?' Millie said with an arch smile.

Arbie nodded uncertainly. Like most eligible bachelors who had been remorselessly stalked by any number of mothers intent on marrying off their daughters, he found that the mere mention of such things tended to make his nerves decidedly jittery.

She proceeded to introduce him to the man behind the bar, a sandy-haired, blue-eyed chap, well set up if leaning a little towards fat, who turned out to be her husband. His eyes lit up with pleasure and perhaps just a hint of anxiety as he gleaned the identity of the newcomer. Running a nervous finger across his moustache, George Penderghast asked him what he was having. Arbie accepted a pint of the local brew, and after his first sip of the ale was glad that he had. He then parked his posterior on the nearest bar stool and glanced around approvingly.

The room was charmingly decorated, with a small potted palm in one corner and seascapes from a good artist dotted about on the walls. The chairs looked comfortable, and the view out across some more colourful gardens was cheery and pleasant. Over in one shadowy corner, he spied an older gentleman and presumably his wife sitting at a table, genteelly sipping sherry. He looked like a retired solicitor, or bank manager or some such, and his wife, dressed in an impeccable, lightweight twin set and pearls, and sporting a mop of curly white hair, matched him in respectability. Catching the direction of his gaze, his host smiled jovially.

'That's Mr and Mrs Babbacombe,' he said, making sure he spoke loudly enough for the other couple to hear him. 'They're with us for another week. This is the gentleman I was telling you about, the famous author, Mr Swift.'

At this, Mrs Babbacombe sat up and took proper notice, and a slight flush came to her cheeks. 'Oh, Mr Swift! We both so loved your travel guide, didn't we, dear? My husband couldn't put it down, could you?'

Her husband nodded obediently. *'The Gentleman's Guide to*

Ghost-Hunting, wasn't it?' he said affably enough. 'Jolly good fun, that. The information about good holiday spots looked solid enough, and your little exploits with the local spooks and whatnot had us fellows at the club chuckling, I can tell you. Good idea of yours, that – to combine a tour guide with, er, local folklore and so on.'

At this, the only other resident in the room, a thickish-set middle-aged man with thick blond hair and pale blue eyes, who was seated on a bar stool a little further down the length of the bar, looked up from the contemplation of his half-empty glass and regarded Arbie with vague curiosity.

'I'm glad it amused you, sir,' Arbie said, tipping his glass to the older man in salute. 'I tried my best. Not that I can lay claim to being a very able psychic investigator, doncha' know. Oh no – there are proper johnnies for that, if you're seriously interested in the subject. I'm strictly an amateur and just potter about with my trusty camera and try and see if there's anything to the local ghosts and whatnot. Some of the tales I get told can stand your hair on end, I can tell you.'

'Mr Swift is here to write us up in his next book,' Captain Penderghast said hopefully, vigorously polishing a pint glass. 'If we come up to scratch, of course!' He gave a slightly nervous laugh, and Arbie was quick to put him at ease.

'Oh, I'm sure the Dashwood will be perfectly splendid, Captain,' he said, looking around. 'I've only been here five minutes and I already approve.' Especially, he mused silently, since he expected to be cossetted like a rich maiden aunt on her last legs, surrounded by hopeful relatives.

As Arbie and the Captain nodded at each other in happy mutual understanding, the blond man down the bar raised his hand for another drink. 'Another, Captain, if you please.' And as the Captain hastened to oblige, the stranger turned and nodded amiably at Arbie. 'I take it then that there must be some tale of a local phantom hereabouts to have brought you to this neck of the woods, Mr Swift? I'm Charles Morris by the way. Former man of business, now one of mostly leisure. How do you do.'

'How do you do. And yes, I have it on good authority that the ghost of a highwayman can be found in these parts,' Arbie responded.

Over in the corner, Mrs Babbacombe squeaked in excitement. 'Oh, how awful. What, right here in the village, you mean?'

'So I understand, Mrs Babbacombe.' Arbie nodded, smiling. 'Roger "Red-Dog" Briggs, I believe the gentleman was called.'

'How thrilling. Oh, do call me Gillian, Mr Swift, and this is John.' She indicated her husband with a vague wave of her hand. 'Jack and Gill, our friends call us,' the lady said with a giggle. 'Do tell us more about him,' she encouraged.

This innocuous request put Arbie at something of a disadvantage, however, for he knew very little about Galton's ghostly resident.

When he'd received the Penderghasts' letter offering him a free holiday at the Dashwood, they'd mentioned the local legend only in passing and strictly as a lure to bring the author of *The Gentleman's Guide* to their newly opened hotel. Now he racked his memory for the little they had written about the spectre in question.

Luckily, and perhaps sensing his difficulties, their host spoke up for him. 'From what I've heard from the locals,' the Captain said, taking up the story with relish, 'Red-Dog was hanged in 1774, I think it was, for robbing the stagecoaches to London. Alas, on his last foray, he'd been betrayed by some doxy or other, and the soldiers were waiting for him, resulting in him and his horse making an ill-fated dash along the coastal road in an effort to get away. But they caught him here in good old Galton. Now they say that on certain nights you can hear him and his ghostly steed galloping hell for leather along the roads hereabouts.'

'Far more likely they're just hearing their fellow villagers on horseback on the way home from the local pub,' Charles Morris said with a smile. 'I doubt there'd be a headless horseman or a hanged robber or what have you amongst the lot of them.'

Arbie grinned at him in secret agreement but felt obliged to shake his head. After all, a chap had to hold up his end and, what's more, his publishers were expecting a suitably chilling and thrilling last chapter to his book – along with a glowing review of Galton and the environs for would-be holidaymakers in search of a new spot for their summer holidays.

'Oh, I don't know,' he said amiably. 'I think most men, if they'd had a drop too much, would tend to wend their way home very carefully, what? And their steeds would tend to be ancient or placid horses who know the way to their master's door blind-folded, neither of which is exactly known for their turn of speed,' Arbie argued reasonably, turning to the Babbacombes. 'What say you, Jack and Gill? If you heard a speeding horse in the middle of the night hereabouts, would it give you a case of the shivers?'

'Oh yes,' Mrs Babbacombe said at once. 'Especially now I know about the ghost! Oh, I do hope you include us in your next book, Mr Swift. Won't it be fun, John, to tell our friends that we were right here at the time he was actually writing about it? It'll put the village on the map too, which would be nice. It's quite picturesque here, isn't it, dear?'

Again, her husband nodded obediently, and Arbie got the distinct impression that it was something he'd done a lot during the years of their marriage.

'Glad to hear it,' Arbie said. 'Otherwise, my publishers might not approve of either my choice of locale or my chosen ghost and ditch the whole chapter and make me write another one!' And here he shuddered – quite genuinely in horror – at the thought. Arbie was not a man who liked to work at the best of times (as his friends and relatives could readily attest) and the thought of working and then not being thoroughly recompensed for it was something of which nightmares were made. Then, catching the look of concern on his host's face, added quickly, 'Not that that will happen. I'm here as much for my own holiday as to do a job of work, and I'm sure I shall thoroughly enjoy everything you have to offer here and will say so in print.'

As the Captain visibly relaxed, Charles Morris gave a small grunt. 'You wouldn't find me combining pleasure and work like that. When I work, I work, and when I go on holiday I like to go on holiday and not think about anything else but relaxation and enjoying myself. Can't see the point of combining business and pleasure m'self.'

'Oh? What line are you in?' Arbie asked, not really interested, but willing to make an effort.

'Antiques nowadays,' Charles said vaguely. 'I used to dabble on the stock market, but got out once I'd made my fortune, as they say. Retirement bored me however, so I've recently turned my hobby of collecting antiques into a minor business. Nothing major you understand, just enough buying and selling to give me something to do, and all that. And every now and then, if I see a good thing, I'll dip my toe in the financial markets.'

'Interesting,' Arbie said, thinking the exact opposite. Working in the 'city' was another thing that gave him nightmares.

'It is, rather. I was a sapper in the army but didn't fancy taking up engineering as a lifelong career.'

'Been here long?' Arbie tried again.

'No, just a few days. It's a nice spot though, right enough. I might see if I can't get one of the local fishermen to take me out in a boat and see if I can't land myself a few bass.'

'Now there's an idea,' Arbie said, bucking up instantly. 'I might just do the same.' The talk turned from ghosts to fish, and from thence (by some curious, random meanderings) to the merits of the local golf course.

Arbie ordered another pint of the local brew and sipped it happily, and the Babbacombes excused themselves to take an afternoon stroll along the beach.

All in all, the various residents of the Dashwood Hotel had good reason to be a contented lot.

*

The following morning, after a good night's sleep in a decent bed, freshly shaved and bathed, Arbie went down to breakfast looking forward to his bacon and eggs.

As he strolled into the dining room, the Babbacombes and a few other guests were taking their seats also, whilst Charles seemed to have finished his breakfast already and was loitering over the morning papers and the crossword puzzle. Obviously, an earlier riser than the rest of them.

Arbie could never understand the appeal of rising with the lark himself.

'Good morning, Mr Swift. We're expecting the engagement party in later this morning,' Millie Penderghast said by way of greeting, as she met him at the entrance to the dining room and escorted him personally to his table, where a somewhat nervous-looking waitress hovered, waiting to take his order. Arbie instantly had her pegged as a local village girl who was in the process of being trained-up by their vigilant hostess, who watched her closely.

'Oh?' Arbie asked. On the one hand, he supposed the hotel could do with some lively company – and he could quite see how Millie, as the owner, would want it to be as full as possible. But on the other hand, he had found himself appreciating the quieter and more somnolent ambience of a large and comfortable hotel that was barely half-full, right at the end of the season.

'Yes – a charming group of people. They're holding a fancy-dress party here on Saturday night, and some of their people are arriving today to have a bit of a holiday in advance as well. Isn't that nice? I'm so glad the weather is holding out for them. The Hythe-Gills are something big by way of mills and manufacturing and things,' she added vaguely. 'Their daughter Beatrice – a charming girl, I met her when she and her mother came down to make the preliminary arrangements – is marrying a Mr Samplestone. His family are something big in transport, or so they said. Or was it shipping? Margaret, pour Mr Swift his tea,' she said to the waitress, who flushed and did – very carefully – as she was told.

Arbie smiled his thanks, somewhat astonished to see the girl blush fiercely at this. Millie gave a slight sigh at this sign of gaucherie. 'All right, Margaret, go and fetch some hot buttered toast for the gentleman whilst he makes up his mind what he wants.' Watching the girl's retreating back, Millie shook her head slightly. 'I can recommend the kippers,' she then advised brightly.

And because he was an obliging sort of chap, Arbie ordered the kippers to start with and then the bacon and eggs to follow. Never let it be said that he couldn't be a good trencherman when the occasion called for it!

CHAPTER TWO

Martha Van Dyne congratulated herself on having the good fortune to bump into Mona Rice-Willoughby at the train station, as it meant that she could leave it to the decrepit old so-and-so to pay for the taxi to the hotel. As the old woman duly did so, Martha glanced up at the Dashwood House Hotel and cautiously approved.

When her cousin Alexander Hythe-Gill's gilt-edged invitation to attend his daughter's engagement party on the south coast had first arrived, she'd been inclined to write a polite note thanking him but coming up with some excuse not to attend. That is, until she'd read his accompanying letter stating that family members could arrive at the hotel a few days early for a short impromptu holiday, courtesy of the father of the bride-to-be, if they were so inclined.

And, naturally, Martha was.

Although born into the same family as her wealthy cousin, Martha – as a girl – had not inherited much, save a small annual income courtesy of her now deceased mother. And that lady had always somewhat bitterly maintained that Alexander's side of the family had unjustly received the lion's share of the family business on the death of the original founder.

And since Martha's unwanted divorce some years ago, much to her distress, she soon discovered that the pitiful amount of alimony she'd been awarded hardly stretched to the luxuries of life. Hence, she had no compunction in taking advantage of any largesse that might come her way – be it from any member of her large and extended family, or her wide circle of friends. As an involuntarily single woman used to a certain way of life and now forced to make deplorable concessions, she'd sponge off anyone who's conscience was pricked or who's generosity was on offer. And do so with enviable aplomb.

Her mother, a Gill by birth, would no doubt have been appalled by this behaviour, but having had the misfortune to die relatively young, she had no say in the way her daughter now chose to conduct herself.

It was not as if she could have foreseen that her marriage would end in the way it had, she thought now grimly. Bad luck could happen to anyone after all – and often did! Just look at what had happened to her friend Myrtle Orpington. What a rotter *she* married! Ran off and deserted her the moment he realised she wasn't anywhere near as independently wealthy as he'd first thought and was never seen or heard of again. Leaving poor Myrtle to move back to her parents' country estate in humiliation and raise English setters.

At least after her own marital faux pas she'd had more spunk about her than to disappear, shame-faced, into darkest Berkshire and live the rest of her life like a nun! Not on your nelly! She had been determined to face down society and get back onto the social ladder and enjoy all that life had to offer.

So it was that Martha sighed now with some satisfaction at the thought of staying for a few days in a new and hopefully luxurious hotel, allowing her to make the most of the last of the summer weather.

'Looks like another country house has fallen by the wayside, then,' Mona said dryly, watching the taxi driver struggling to unload their combined luggage. 'If many more old families lose their family seats to the tax man we'll soon have nobody left worth visiting.'

At seventy-seven years of age, she was a small, slightly stooped-back old woman with white fluffy hair and rheumy grey eyes. During the last few years of her life, she'd become a little deaf, very forgetful, and prone to taking violent likes or dislikes to people and things, and stubbornly refusing to listen to reason when her opinions were challenged. She was also well-off in her own right, so had no need of the begging bowl herself.

Now she sniffed disdainfully. 'What do you know about these Penderghast people anyway? Are they at least related to the Bristol Penderghasts? That would at least be something.'

Martha (who liked to give the impression that she was somewhere in her late thirties but was in fact now in her mid-forties) tugged her old but carefully cared for and impeccably tailored dark green jacket down a little to sit more perfectly on her fine shoulders and gave an elegant shrug. 'I doubt the Bristol Penderghasts would acknowledge them if they were,' she said airily. 'I hear *this* Penderghast still uses his title of Captain, although Alexander was too lazy to find out which regiment he was in. At least Susan was a little more observant when she came down to inspect the place. She was telling me over tea the other day that she believes it's the wife who is the one with all the money and most of the breeding, and you know Susan. She's seldom wrong about people.'

Mona wheezed gently at this and then gave a surprising and rather unpleasant little cackle. She was a great-aunt of Beatrice, the girl whose betrothal they were to celebrate at a fancy-dress party on Saturday, and had been known – of late – to make the odd embarrassing scene at social functions.

Martha could only hope the old girl would not get too sozzled on her favourite tipple to cause a rumpus this time.

Now the old lady nodded wisely. 'Ah, well, that's because Susan was a Copperton before she married Alex,' she mused. 'And you know the Coppertons – they always make it their business to know everything about everyone. Bertie Bainstock always maintained it's how they made their money in the first place, by knowing who they could bribe, and who they couldn't,' she said carelessly, too old to worry about the repercussions of passing on scandalous – and possibly slanderous – confidences anymore. 'And you're right, she said much the same thing to me. She's convinced the wife is the brains and the driving force behind the setting up of this place,' the woman nodded at the building in front of them, 'and is determined by hook or by crook to put the hotel on the map. I hear it's got electricity in every room.'

'Well, let's hope it's as good as they're trying to make it sound,' Martha said, who made it a point of honour never to be impressed by anything if she could help it. Certainly her ex-husband had never managed it. 'At least the beach is literally on their doorstep, as advertised,' she added grudgingly, casting a look at the beautiful vista behind them.

They watched the taxi driver deposit the last of their luggage through the open door of the hotel, and then return, touch his cap at them, bid them a polite farewell and then drive off. Mona must have tipped him well, Martha thought. And why not? The awful old trout could well afford it.

'Well, let's find out what we're in for,' Martha said cheerfully and set off across the short gravel stretch towards the front steps. 'It does look as if it once used to be a nice family house, so let's hope they haven't butchered it too much.'

Inside, they found themselves in a large hall and seating area, which was sparsely populated, but their hostess wasn't tardy in welcoming them. She slipped out from behind the reception desk with a wide smile and vague wave of her hand. 'Hello, it's Mrs Rice-Willoughby and Mrs Van Dyne, isn't it? Welcome to the Dashwood,' Millie Penderghast said. 'I'm so pleased to meet you both. Mrs Rice-Willoughby, we've put you in the Harrington Suite, and Mrs Van Dyne, a room with the best view of the bay.'

Martha kept her smile on her face, but she knew she had just been put in her place. Mona, as a wealthy relative of whom Alexander probably had expectations, had been allocated a suite. Whereas she, a mere room with a view. Not that she believed the proprietor of the establishment was aware of this fact, for Millie Penderghast showed no sign of embarrassment on Martha's behalf.

With a detached gaze she swallowed her anger and watched her bags being swept upstairs by a young lad who at least appeared to be efficient, and told herself that, with a little luck and some careful handling, her days of petty humiliations would soon be over. That is, if she could just bring Michael to the altar sometime soon. So far, the successful racehorse breeder and trainer was proving just a bit difficult to net – like a wary salmon that had nearly taken the bait too many times to be easily landed. And the fact that she was obliged to make the effort at all still had the ability to make her furious.

Not for the first time, Martha silently cursed her ex-husband, Malcolm Grainger. She had reverted to using her maiden name in a fit of pique, sniffily telling all her friends that the Van Dyne name was, after all, a much more illustrious one. For indeed, her mother *had* married a Dutchman of some aristocratic – if poverty-stricken – lineage, who had been something minor (*very* minor) in the art world.

In truth, however, she'd still been smarting over the humiliation of losing him to a younger version of herself, and what's more one who had, within a year of his re-marriage, presented him with the heir he had demanded. An heir that she herself had been singularly careful not to produce.

Ever since a contemporary of hers had died in childbirth when she was twenty, Martha had vowed never to risk the same fate, and she had always bitterly resented Malcolm for not bowing to her wishes on this matter.

Paradoxically, given her hatred of her former husband, she'd refused to drop the title of 'Mrs', as the term 'Miss' in her opinion was a derogatory one and implied that a woman was incapable of finding herself a husband. Consequently, she now habitually – if somewhat confusingly – called herself 'Mrs Van Dyne' wherever she went. Those who knew her circumstances found it either amusing or appalling, according to their natures, and strangers of course simply took it at face value.

Michael Tanter, as a widower of some years standing, she had been careful to ascertain, already had three grown sons and thus wouldn't require her to give him more.

As Mona, with as finely a tuned homing instinct as you could wish for, unerringly made her way to the bar – rumour had it that the little old lady could drink a navvy under any table you cared to choose – Martha found herself watching the progress of a handsome young man as he stepped through the door from the lounge and into the hall. Tall, lean and dark, he was dressed casually in Oxford bags and white shirt, and instantly made her wish that she was ten years younger.

Arbie, who was on his way to change into shorts for an hour or two's loafing about on the beach, became almost instantly aware that he had become the object of curiosity. And in the way of admired young men, he returned the older woman's gaze with a polite smile and an inclination of his head. And, naturally, made a rapid inventory of the hotel's latest discerning guest.

Petite, at only five feet two inches or so, she had auburn hair of a lush shade that, had he been female, would have roused instant suspicions of hair dye in his mind. Dressed in a well-tailored dark green outfit so severe that it only served to emphasise the delicate nature of her slight figure, she looked striking enough to make him stop slouching and stiffen his shoulders.

Martha, noticing this, gave a satisfied smile and inclined her own head in acknowledgement of the non-verbal compliment, before passing on serenely through the door to what was a small reading or writing room. Glancing through the open door, Arbie noticed that Charles Morris, who was the room's only other inhabitant, glanced up from the modern novel he'd been reading, before both were lost to his sight as he continued on his way to the stairs.

In the bar, Mona Rice-Willoughby was regarding Captain Penderghast with vague suspicion. But at least he served good gin, which meant the old lady was willing to give him the benefit of the doubt. For now.

*

Mid-morning on the following day – Wednesday – brought with it most of the family members of the engagement party, their noisy entrance en masse bringing the Penderghasts out in force. Arbie, who was in the garden pretending to write notes in his notebook, sank down even lower in his sunchair, and hoped that he was rendered invisible behind the late-flowering rose bushes.

The amount of feminine chatter, interspersed with only a few male voices, made him vaguely uneasy. Women tended to expect a chap to dance attendance on them at the drop of a hat, and he'd grown rather used to being left unmolested these last few days.

He was not altogether surprised then when, just a few minutes after the mass arrival, a shadow fell across him, and a female voice interrupted his peace. He *was*, however, considerably taken aback by the note of brusque surprise in the voice, and that its owner already knew his name.

'I say, you aren't actually *working*, are you, Arbie?'

'Eh?' he asked, scrambling to get to his feet. And putting a hand over his eyes to shade them from the dazzle of the sun, he peered wildly at the young woman who was regarding him with a mixture of amusement and disbelief.

As she turned away from the sun's glare, and he was able to make her out properly, he felt his mouth fall open. *'Val?'* he managed to squeak. His brain scrambled to process what was happening, but – not altogether surprisingly – failed to come up with anything that made sense. 'What on earth are *you*, of all people, doing here?' he finally demanded.

The tall, fair-haired Amazon, dressed in a plain white frock and sensible sandals, regarded him levelly from blue eyes that, as ever, seemed to be accusing him of something.

'And why shouldn't I be here?' Valentina Olivia Charlotte Coulton-James demanded right back. Vicar's daughter and lifelong resident of the same village as Arbie, she looked at the man she'd known all her life with her usual mixture of aloof resignation, mixed with a touch of pleasure and seasoned with a dash of superiority. 'If you must know, I'm here because I'm going to be a bridesmaid at Beatrice's wedding. She's an old school chum of mine.'

'Who?' Arbie could only mumble helplessly.

'Beatrice Hythe-Gill. She's newly engaged to a nice man called Ernest and they're having a party this weekend to celebrate,' Val informed him. 'She introduced me to him last Christmas. I'm sure I must have told you about them. He's a rugby player when he isn't adding to his family's fortune. Broad shoulders, chestnut-coloured hair. A smashing chap.' She sighed a little enviously, then regarded Arbie, in his rumpled shirt and Oxford bags.

Arbie blinked. 'Oh. Righty-oh. Jolly nice.'

Val sighed again.

'Well, old girl, it's a small world, isn't it?' he tried again. 'I have to say, little old Galton-next-the-What-have-you is the last place on earth I'd have expected to run into someone from the old homestead.' Although he was trying his best to sound pleased, he was, in fact, silently lamenting his rotten luck. Just what was it, he wondered morosely, that the Fates had against him, to send Val, of all people, crashing into his serene little holiday hidey-hole?

Val regarded him solemnly as he began to fidget nervously on his feet, and bit back the urge to tell him to stand still. 'I ran across your friend the other week, you know, the one who publishes you? He told me you were down here, working on your next holiday-cum-ghost-hunting guidebook. I thought the name of the place sounded familiar for some reason, and then it came to me. I'd not long had a letter from old Draughty Dottie telling me that our old school pal Beatrice was throwing her fancy-dress engagement bash here.'

She had then lost no time in contacting her old school chum, and after a few happy hours of reminiscences, shopping and gossip, had easily managed to wangle herself an invitation down here for the party. Not that she'd ever tell Arbie she had gone to all that trouble. He might just get a swollen head.

'So, tell me about the ghost then,' she said cheerfully. 'I'm sure I can help you with it, just like I did that last time,' she added. 'And I can probably help with the research too. Make sure you don't slack off. Your friend mentioned that you had a deadline to meet,' she concluded firmly.

Her blue eyes met his, and her pretty face smiled winsomely.

And right then and there Arbie had the good sense just to mentally throw up his hands and admit to the Fates that this round had gone to them.

*

Teatime was bringing some of the scattered newcomers together again in the lounge. Arbie and Val, seated by a pair of large windows overlooking a paved terrace, had just ordered tea and scones when the first of the party members entered, looked around and took a seat.

'That's Randolph Harrington,' Val remarked casually, pointing out one in particular. Arbie glanced across the room. About his own age – twenty-five or so – he stood around six feet tall and had fair hair and pale eyes, which when he got close enough to see them properly would probably turn out to be blue. 'He's a great chum of Ernest, Beatrice's intended, and will be their best man at the wedding,' Val added obligingly.

Randolph Harrington had the look of a scholar about him, rather than that of a sportsman, and Arbie hoped he wouldn't be buttonholed to talk about modern poetry or ancient Greeks, or – worse yet – mathematics. Or newts or something. As an Oxford man, he wouldn't put anything past a proper scholar.

As the new arrival smiled blandly at the approaching waitress and murmured his order, Arbie saw the smile freeze on his face as somebody else walked in through the door.

A quick turn of his head brought Charles Morris into view, and Arbie was just in time to see the older man enter with his usual confident stride. Then his head swivelled casually around the room, passed over himself and Val, then stalled for a moment on Randolph as his progress across the room was momentarily checked.

The next instant Charles was once more making his way towards a table in the far corner, where he sat down and casually opened up a newspaper. During the few days that Arbie had been at the hotel, he'd hardly seen the older businessman without one broadsheet or other. Either doing the crossword, reading an article and – once or twice – studying the racing form.

The next one through the door was the very attractive red head that he'd seen yesterday out in the hall. Today, seeing her in the bright sunlight filtering through the windows, he mentally added a few extra years to her age, not that the lady need have been concerned. Dressed in a severely cut grey summer dress that suited her hair and sherry-coloured eyes to perfection, she looked as if she could have graced a movie screen. Her eyes lingered on Arbie for a moment, but then noted his young companion with an eye-flick of regret, before passing him over.

Val, by his side, naturally noticed this little by-play and gave a small sound that could have been amusement or could have been anger. 'And that must be the infamous Martha that Beatrice has told me so much about,' she said archly. 'I've known Beatrice for years, ever since we were at school together, and she's often mentioned her, but our paths have never crossed. She's a cousin or something of Beatrice's father, and rather notorious.'

'Oh, and why is that exactly?' Arbie murmured, distinctly interested now. Not only was the lady a picture to delight the eyes but was apparently a genuine femme fatale as well. Things *were* looking up!

He turned curiously as no reply was forthcoming from his companion and saw that Val was giving him a gimlet gaze. He swallowed hard, knew that he was probably now flushing with guilt under those familiar mocking eyes and tried to brazen it out. 'What, is it a state secret or something?' he asked as nonchalantly as he knew how.

'She's a divorcee,' Val said primly. 'And Beatrice and her mother are convinced she's on the hunt for a rich husband.'

'Ah,' Arbie said, considerably sobered. And then had a nasty thought. Did *he* qualify in this category? His *Gentleman's Guide* had been a runaway success and had topped up his coffers nicely – coffers that, thanks to a healthy family inheritance, had never been that distressed in the first place. And he was still very much a bachelor.

Val saw the alarm cross his face and almost laughed. 'I don't think you have anything to worry about, old bean,' she said dryly. 'You're far too young. She'd be accused of cradle-snatching if she set her sights on you. Besides, from what I've overheard from listening to some of the other party members on the way here, she has her sights set on someone in Berkshire.'

At this, Arbie relaxed but again silently cursed the Fates that had brought Val here. When a chap grew up in the same village as a girl, she knew him inside and out – whether he liked it or not.

Now, he tried not to be obvious as he watched Martha Van Dyne select a table in one of the prime spots near a window on the other side of the room. For a femme fatale, she didn't seem all that keen to catch anyone's eye or make much mischief, for she merely seated herself at the empty table and ordered a pot of tea – Indian, not Chinese.

The next invasion came in a pair – two women, one of about twenty -one or -two, a tall, slim brunette with brown eyes and wearing a summer dress of gold and silver; and one a little older, slightly shorter woman with a very daring cap of raven hair that had been bobbed in the latest fashion, and greenish hazel eyes. She was dressed in a fashionable outfit in peacock blue that made Val heave an envious sigh.

It was the taller girl who noticed them first, and with a smile of happiness, said something to her companion that had them both approaching Arbie and Val's table.

Arbie instantly rose.

'Val, here you are! I was just saying to Clarice that I hoped we'd have time for a proper chat. What with the journey down yesterday – which was exhausting, I do so hate motorcars don't you? – and then being seated at different tables at dinner, we never got a chance to have a proper chinwag. And then this morning we both had breakfast in bed, didn't we, Clarrie darling, so didn't get to see you at brekkers, but I bet you were up with the larks, weren't you? You always were, even at school. Clarrie darling, I *did* tell you all about your fellow bridesmaid-to-be, didn't I?'

The chatterbox, Arbie presumed, was the girl whose engagement was to be celebrated in such style on Saturday, and was proved right, as Val introduced them. 'Beatrice Hythe-Gill, this is Mr Arbuthnot Swift, and Miss Clarice Fotheringham. Beatrice, Clarice, Mr Swift.'

'Oh, he's your *author*,' Beatrice said, gaily slipping into the chair and casting a winsome glance at the menu. 'The one who solved that ghastly murder in your village last year? Oh, how clever you must be. I am so glad to meet you, Mr Swift. Oh, they have strawberry scones. I really do love strawberry scones, but Mummy would have a fit if she saw me eating one. And I dare say she's right – I'd never fit into my wedding dress.' She gave a happy giggle, and Arbie couldn't help but smile back at her. It was nice to see a pretty girl so obviously happy with her lot.

Now that he thought about it, Val rarely giggled, he realised, with a little inward sigh.

'Ah yes, that funny little book that combined hotels and resorts and places to stay and whatnot, along with ghost-hunting opportunities for those who like being given a case of the shivers,' the woman said, finally managing to slip in a word or two.

She had scarlet-painted lips that matched her scarlet-painted nails, and the greenish eyes that looked at Arbie were cool and slightly amused. 'Some of your accounts of those episodes where you almost run afoul of a ghost or two are really rather funny. Of course, it's all rubbish, there's no such things as spooks and ghouls,' she added dismissively. 'So, tell me, how do you expect to actually *prove* one of them exists?'

Arbie tipped his head gallantly. 'I don't claim to know the secrets of the occult, Miss Fotheringham. I only hope to introduce those with an interest in such things as to the best place to find them, whilst at the same time, being very comfortably accommodated whilst they do so.'

'And a jolly clever idea of yours it was too, so Daddy says,' Beatrice Hythe-Gill gushed. 'He says you cornered a market or something, and good luck to you. I suppose I'd better just stick to tea,' she added as the waitress converged on them to take their order.

Once the orders were given and the waitress had departed, Clarice hunted in her fringed and intricately beaded silver bag and extracted an elegant ebony-and-silver cigarette holder. Arbie's hand gallantly went into his own pocket for a cigarette lighter in order to oblige. He was more of a pipe man, when he bothered to smoke at all, but a chap found it handy to have a lighter.

But as he put the flame to the tip of her cigarette, he saw her cat-like eyes suddenly narrow – and it was nothing to do with the smoke from her newly lit cigarette. Following her gaze, Arbie saw that she was observing Martha Van Dyne, who was just pouring out for herself a cup of tea.

'I wasn't surprised to learn that *she* got here early,' the raven-haired siren observed archly, causing Beatrice to make frantic shushing sounds. 'I wouldn't put it past her to stay on for three or four days after the rest of us have left, either, given that her "dear cousin" is footing the bill.'

'Oh, don't! She'll hear you,' Beatrice whispered.

Clarice shrugged. 'Who cares, dear heart? She's got the skin of a rhinoceros. She must have, the way she carries on. Did you know she's making a fool of herself, pestering an old pal of mine?'

Val shifted a little uncomfortably on her seat. She wasn't a vicar's daughter for nothing, and whilst she was happy to catch up with her friends in private, she didn't like to see – or hear – bad manners in public, and abruptly changed the subject. 'Arbie's here to research a chapter in his next book, aren't you, Arbie? Apparently, the village has a resident ghost,' she said, tossing the little verbal bomb into the mix, sure that it was bound to divert the conversation onto less personal lines.

As it did.

Beatrice instantly gave a little squeak of excitement. 'Oh no, that's awful! How wonderful,' she exclaimed, paradoxically. 'Do tell us. What is it? A white lady, I expect. They're usually white ladies, aren't they? A poor soul who committed suicide over some wicked man or other. Or else got herself murdered by a jealous husband or some such.'

'Ah, not this time, Miss Hythe-Gill,' Arbie corrected her. 'This spook is male and is only to be found on horseback, and late at night.'

'Oh no, not a headless horseman!' Clarice said dryly. 'How trite. I read that American story – you know, the one about a sleepy hollow or some such, when I was at school. It scared one of my classmates into a fit of the vapours. A silly ass called Mary Dewhurst. Do you know the Devonshire Dewhursts?'

As the women's talk turned to mutual friends, Arbie let

his eyes wander around the room. He wasn't quite sure why, but something didn't sit very well with him. He was not the sort to get 'premonitions' or other such nonsense, and in spite of his national reputation as a psychic investigator, he had no truck with clairvoyance or fortune-telling, or any of that rot.

And yet, as he sat in that perfectly ordinary and sun-lit lounge, drinking fine tea and eating even finer strawberry scones, he felt himself give just a little shiver of foreboding.

CHAPTER THREE

'So, are you going out tonight to hunt for your ghost? And if you catch one, what do you actually do with it?'

It was just over four hours later, and Arbie was once more seated at a table in the dining room, but now more formally attired for dinner. The old lady opposite him regarded him thoughtfully as she awaited his reply.

'I don't think I'll be out and about tonight, no, Mrs Rice-Willoughby,' he said, carefully avoiding Val's disapproving eye, 'and I've never actually "caught" a spectre, so I have no idea what one is supposed to do with it. But I think asking it politely to leave and stop haunting innocent bystanders would be a good place to start.'

It had been Val who had invited the old lady to dine with them. None of the others of Beatrice's large party had seemed in any hurry to claim her for their own tables, and one sight of the old dear, peering around the room in search of company had had Val going instantly to her rescue.

Now Val gave a small sigh of reproach. 'I'm afraid Mr Swift has a rather lackadaisical approach to his work, Mrs Rice-Willoughby,' she informed her archly. 'He should, of course, be haunting the lanes himself every night, but . . .' She gave an elegant shrug of her shoulders.

The old lady wheezed a chuckle. 'Can't say I blame him,

m'dear. Why do more than you have to? That's always been my motto. And please, you pretty young things, do call me Mona.'

Arbie instantly brightened and began to take a shine to the old girl. She was, after all, a woman after his own heart! 'Thank you, Mona, I agree. I've known Val here all my life, and I've tried to teach her that life is for the living, but she insists on taking things like duty and honest toil horrendously seriously. I despair of her, I really do.' He grinned and shrugged helplessly.

Mona eyed him with favour. Most young men nowadays had no idea how to be charming and amusing, and it did her good to know it was not a totally forgotten art.

Val, who'd always been immune to Arbie's charm, merely shot him a sweet smile. 'And I, Mona, you can rest assured, have taken no notice of him at all.'

The old lady, looking from one of them to the other, let out another delighted cackle. 'I do so like to be around the young, it keeps me young at heart myself. Mind you, there's some I'd rather avoid like the plague. Killers, and the like, you know.'

At this, Arbie nearly choked on a mouthful of his very fine wine. Even Val's normally wide blue eyes widened yet further, and she shot Arbie a speaking look. Arbie, having known the fair damsel all his life, instantly read her silent message. Had she just heard what she thought she'd just heard? And, naturally, it was up to him to find out!

Arbie gave a feeble smile. 'Sorry, Mona, I could have sworn you said killers,' he repeated weakly. 'I must have misheard you.'

'Oh, no you didn't,' the old lady contradicted emphatically. 'See that young filly over there f'r instance?' She stabbed a silver fork which she'd been fiddling with in the direction of a table nearby. 'She got away with murder just a few months ago.'

Arbie blinked. 'Er, did she?' he mumbled, giving Val a speaking look of his own. And just as he'd had no trouble interpreting her unspoken message, she had no trouble translating his.

He now wanted her to take charge and get him out of the mess he'd got himself into. As usual! The fact that she'd been the one to invite Mona to join them in the first place was neither here nor there.

'I say, that sounds intriguing,' she said, careful to keep her voice light and amused. Turning her attention to the old lady she smiled gently. 'But I think you might be exaggerating just a little?' she added encouragingly.

'Huh,' Mona said petulantly. Putting her fork back down, she shook her head so vigorously it made the white curls on her head bounce. 'Looks like butter wouldn't melt in her mouth, doesn't she?' she added, shooting fulminating looks across the room.

Arbie glanced at the table in question where six people were dining, three of them women. He thought he recognised the mother of the bride-to-be and doubted that she could be the object of Mona's displeasure. He'd seen them earlier in the day talking amiably enough together. The other woman was their companion of the afternoon tea, Clarice Fotheringham, and the third woman he'd never seen before.

'Dressed in her fancy ruby-red Parisian gown! It should be scarlet – scarlet for a killer,' Mona continued to mutter alarmingly.

Arbie swallowed hard, cast a quick and frantic look around to see if anyone else was close enough to overhear the old lady's slander, and ran a hand under his collar which was beginning to feel just a little tight. Fortunately, nobody was staring their way, so for the moment at least their bizarre dinner conversation was being strictly kept among the three of them.

Val, after a quick glance at the group concerned, spotted the only woman wearing red. 'Do you mean Miss Fotheringham? Clarice?'

'That's the one. She killed my Monty. Bold as brass. Then had the cheek to say it was his own fault. I ask you! That's the kind of heart she has. Can't think why she's so popular with everyone. Cold as the North Pole that one,' Mona said, then visibly perked up as the soup was served.

As Val and Arbie exchanged frenzied glances, Mona picked up her dessert spoon and began to slurp happily.

Val found herself wondering, a shade hysterically, if she should point out her cutlery mistake, then supposed that the proper use of a soup spoon was probably the least of their worries.

'Er, this poor Monty chap,' Arbie ventured bravely, taking up the baton once more. 'Was he . . . er . . . your husband?' She had, after all, called him 'my Monty'.

Mona's rheumy eyes goggled a little, and she looked at him as if he'd grown a second head. 'Don't be silly, young man,' she rebuked crossly. 'Monty was my dog.'

'Ah,' Val and Arbie said, almost at once, both relaxing somewhat.

'Ran him over, she did, in that fancy car of hers, and not so much as a by your leave,' the old lady swept on savagely. 'Didn't even sound very sorry about it. She said she hadn't seen him, and that he'd ran out in front of her car, or some such nonsense. Monty would never do something so stupid. Jack Russells are known for their intelligence, doncha' know?'

'Oh, that must have been heartbreaking for you. Had you had him long?' Val asked sympathetically.

'Nearly seventeen years. I was just getting used to him,' the old lady said philosophically.

Arbie just managed to stop himself from laughing at her rather off-hand resilience, and felt Val give him a warning kick under the table.

'I'm so sorry to hear all this, Mrs . . . Mona. Do you know Clarice well?' Val asked. 'She's Beatrice's friend more than mine, so I haven't got to know her until now.'

'Lucky you,' Mona sniffed. 'And no, I don't know her well either. I was just visiting Beatrice and her family at the time, and that woman happened to be there as well. Heartless hussy.'

Seeing that the old lady was not going to be mollified over the death of her beloved pet, Val very deliberately changed the subject, and Arbie felt himself begin to relax again as the ladies' talk turned to women's tennis. Val, naturally, was a veritable Amazon and could play tennis like nobody's business, along with golf, croquet, hockey and archery. Arbie had always felt exhausted just watching her, sometimes, during those long summer afternoons of their childhood when she would sweep all before her.

Having successfully steered clear of some choppy waters, Arbie made a mental note of Mrs Rice-Willoughby's eccentricities and vowed to try to avoid the old girl in the future. Meanwhile, he let his eyes roam vaguely around the dining room. He should, he supposed, be making notes on both it and the quality of the food for his guidebook, but he could always do that later.

Instead, he let his gaze wander over those of the other guests nearest to him. Beatrice, the charming chatterbox, was gazing in adoration at her fiancé. Or at least, Arbie supposed that the chap opposite her must be the fiancé, otherwise the young girl was heading for a ruckus of some sort! His eyes moved on to the table next to them and saw a man who looked as if he had the weight of the world on his shoulders.

Somewhere in his mid-fifties or so, he had brown hair and eyes and was beginning to gain some weight around his middle. He looked the epitome of a prosperous businessman, but one who'd just found a fly in his soup. And after studying him for a while, Arbie realised, with a bit of a start, that the identity of the stranger's particular fly was none other than Charles Morris, whom he scowled at regularly.

Morris, who was dining alone and seemingly content to do so, seemed oblivious to the dark looks being cast his way, and Arbie wondered, yet again, why the poor chap seemed to have been singled out for the cold shoulder by yet another member of the engagement party.

'I say, Val, do you know who that man is, the one in the rather nifty suit with the white carnation?' he asked casually.

Both Val and Mona looked, but it was the old lady who spoke first. 'Oh, that's Alexander. The father of young Beatrice. He looks a bit down in the dumps, doesn't he? Can't think why. That young man of Beatrice's is a good catch.'

'He does look a little grumpy,' Val conceded.

'Mind you, he is paying for all this,' the old lady said, with a vague wave of her hand. 'Not just the party, but the accommodation here. Alexander likes to make a big show now and then. Perhaps he's begun to realise the size of the bill he's going to be landed with come Monday morning.' This seemed to amuse Mona greatly for she cackled happily and then catching Val's puzzled eye, winked outrageously. 'Between you, me and the gatepost, poor old Martha is on her uppers, and grabs any chance she can to live it high on somebody else's money. *She'll not be leaving here in any hurry once the party's over, I can tell you* – not if she can fit in a few extra days and make a proper holiday of it. Still, that nephew of mine can afford it.'

In fact, had they been able to read his mind, they'd have known that Alexander Hythe-Gill was feeling far more than grumpy – and that the cost of his daughter's engagement celebrations had nothing to do with it. He was, in fact, feeling distinctly put-upon. Of all the places to run into that bounder Charles Morris!

It wasn't even as if Galton-next-the-Sea was a hot spot of

high society. It might be trying to turn itself into the next Bognor Regis, but so far, very few of their set had discovered it. No, it must just be sheer bad luck. But one thing was for certain – the man's presence was in danger of ruining the whole party for him, and the thought made him as mad as a hornet.

As if the cad hadn't caused enough trouble in his life as it was.

His eyes went to his daughter, who was the apple of his eye, and her young man. Ernest was a good match for her, and his wife was looking forward to their engagement party being the social highlight of all their closest friends who had travelled down here to celebrate.

He was relieved that neither of the women in his life had any idea of how close to disaster he'd come. Or how very nearly the engagement might never have happened. For the Samplestones would never have consented to their boy marrying the daughter of a bankrupt, that was for sure.

Yes, it had been close, but he'd just managed to avert calamity. Of course, Morris had made a killing at his expense. And now, just a couple of years later, here he was looking like he didn't have a care in the world, damn him.

How, Alexander wondered, could he possibly enjoy himself now that there was such a snake in the grass right under his nose, and spoiling everything?

Oh, Morris was making out like nothing had ever happened, and was ignoring him as if he had no idea who he was, but Alexander was sure the swine was silently laughing up his sleeve at him.

He heard his dreadful relative, Mona, give a coarse cackle and hid a wince. She was becoming more and more of a worry for the family. Her uncensored words and wayward behaviour were beginning to cause offence to their friends, and it could only be a matter of time before she became a public laughingstock. Or worse! If the old trout weren't so well-off, and everyone wasn't so keen to inherit her fortune, they would have moved her into a 'rest home' long before now.

*

Clarice Fotheringham studied her dessert course with an eye for complaint and was rather disappointed not to find one. The syllabub she'd ordered was a perfect balance of tart, sweet and creamy, and the shortbread that came with it crumbled with buttery perfection.

Catching the knowing eye of one of her dining companions, she gave more of a grimace than a smile. 'I must say, Susan, you did well to find this place for Beatrice's bash,' she conceded. 'One does so worry when leaving the city for pastures more bucolic and where standards are bound to be lower. But so far, I'm pleasantly surprised.' She gave a vague wave of her hand to indicate the charming dining room and its surrounds. 'Did you know the Penderghasts from before somewhere? Is that why you chose this charming little spot?'

Susan Hythe-Gill shook her head. 'Oh no, I saw the place advertised in one of the better home and country magazines and it looked like just the ticket,' she admitted modestly. Unlike some, Susan didn't enjoy playing the game of one-upmanship. It had always struck her as being both unkind, and requiring too much effort. 'And when I came down with Beatrice and we saw it for ourselves, we agreed it would do nicely.'

'I still don't know why you didn't want to celebrate the engagement in London,' Clarice said, a distinct touch of condescension in her tone. 'Surely, Ernest's people would have preferred it? It is rather out of the way here, isn't it?'

'Oh yes, but that's just the reason why everyone in the immediate family was so keen on it. We all felt we wanted a change and to do something a bit different for the young couple. London can get so old, can't it? Besides, Alex and I hadn't had a holiday this year – he's been so busy working all hours over the last couple of years – and has looked so tired that now he's finally surfaced, as it were, I wanted him to have a real rest. And then Beatrice said she'd love to dance with Ernest overlooking a lovely beach, and, well . . .' Susan shrugged a shoulder and attacked her own dish of strawberries and meringue.

A rather short and plump woman with mousy brown hair, Susan didn't much care that she was hardly the kind of society hostess that people such as Clarice Fotheringham was probably used to patronising. Indeed, if her husband hadn't done so well by way of business, she would have been content to stay in their small market town and lead a life of relative anonymity. But there, Alexander had been so clever and had expanded his business so much and so quickly, that before she knew it, she had become a woman of substance. And, she had to admit in all fairness, their daughter hadn't suffered from the move to the capital when she'd been just ten years old.

Attendance at a minor but very well-respected private girls' school had quickly erased all trace of Lancashire from their daughter, and Susan knew that Beatrice would never have made a catch of Ernest Samplestone's calibre had they stayed in the place of their birth. So all in all, she was content with her lot.

Still, there were times when Susan felt a little out of her depth and could wish – just a bit – that her husband hadn't become *such* a successful self-made man. She suspected that she never quite 'measured up' to her high-flying husband nor fitted into 'society' as well as she might have.

And people like Clarice only reinforced her feelings of inferiority.

Why this socially eminent social butterfly had befriended her daughter in the first place, Susan couldn't fathom, but she suspected it hadn't been out of the goodness of Clarice's heart. Susan, for all her inherently placid temperament, was nobody's fool when it came to understanding human nature. Perhaps Clarice's own impeccable family lineage sparkled just a bit more brightly when contrasted to that of the more plebeian Beatrice? Or maybe it was that her tall, slim, brown-haired girl's nondescript prettiness only served to throw into greater effect Clarice's more startling and 'modern' looks?

Whatever the reason, Susan had never much appreciated this particular friend of her daughter and wished that she hadn't been invited down to the coast. Now that nice Val, the daughter of a country vicar, was real, proper class, but with none of the arrogance or sense of entitlement that cloaked Clarice Fotheringham.

Still, Susan knew, in life you had to take the rough with the smooth. And if, as she'd long since learned, a glass or two (or three) of very good sherry, brandy, wine or port helped to smooth over the bumps, what did it matter?

She took another healthy drink of her wine as Clarice watched her, a knowing smile seeming to lurk on her red-painted lips.

'Shall we take coffee in the lounge?' the other woman at their table asked brightly. Everyone agreed, and abandoning the dining table, they swept out.

*

Seeing them leave, Martha Van Dyne also rose from her table and drifted out, an action that was slowly repeated by most of the diners as the last remnants of the meal were cleared away by the attentive waitresses and waiters. The few unattached male guests who weren't part of the engagement party contingent tended to drift towards the bar, except for 'Jack and Gill' Babbacombe, who retired to their room early, and Charles

Morris, who sauntered out onto the terrace to light his first pipe of the evening.

In the lounge, Martha favoured a comfortable settee and was not particularly pleased to be joined there by Mona. Val and Arbie were joined by Beatrice and her intended in a nest of armchairs by the fire which, given the current clement weather, remained unlit. Susan and several of the older members of the engagement party very promptly organised a game of bridge and set about fierce battle.

As Charles Morris sauntered back into the lounge with his lit pipe, he was passed by Clarice on her way out into the hall. There, she must have checked the postal trays, for when she came back into the room only a few moments later, she was clutching a small pile of envelopes. These she took to her seat and began to open them eagerly.

Noticing, Beatrice momentarily abandoned Val and the others and went over to her, where she leaned over the back of her friend's armchair and watched the proceedings with interest. 'I say, Clarice, you've only been here a day,' she teased wonderingly. 'What's all this?' She nodded at the collection of papers gathering on her friend's lap.

'Oh, invitations from people down here,' Clarice said, waving a hand vaguely in the air. 'You know how it is, you mention you're off on a short holiday somewhere, and everyone and their grandmother knows someone in the vicinity of where you're going, and then they write and ask them to show you some hospitality, and before you know it, you've got more invitations than you know what to do with. Oh, what a hoot – this one's from Bumptious Freddie. You remember him, Bea?' she asked with a laugh. 'That awful man, from . . . oh, where was he from now?'

The room was an intimate size, and each conversation taking place could be easily heard, should one be interested in it. Val saw several of the others in the room glance at Clarice with various expressions of boredom, amusement or mild annoyance as she spoke so confidently and indiscreetly.

'Bump . . . Oh, that chap who was begging you to marry him last year? Didn't you send him off with a flea in his ear?' Beatrice obliged.

'I certainly did, and it appears he went off in this direction. He now owns . . . oh, some gallery or other, from what he says in this letter.' She waved the offending article briefly in the air. 'He's asked me if I want to attend a show by some up-and-coming watercolourist. I ask you! Not on your nelly!' With a casual flick of her fingers she tore the missive in two, then pounced on another one.

'Oh, this is much more like it. The charming Admiral Withers wants me to dine with him tomorrow. He has a very wealthy son, as I seem to remember, and rather good-looking as well. Oh, *what is* his name . . .'

As Clarice's gay, inconsequential voice swept on, over on the settee, Mona felt her old grievances stir. 'Listen to her – bragging about all these people she has dancing on a string. She'll be hogging the writing room as if it's her own personal office, next. The rest of us won't get a look in – you mark my words.'

Martha lit a cigarette with vicious movements. The fact that the younger, attractive woman was so in demand wasn't something she cared to contemplate. 'I dare say – but I for one shall most definitely continue to use it! Mind you, if she's off galivanting somewhere every day being her sparkling self with all the local swells, then at least *we* will be spared having to see much of her.'

At this, the old lady cackled in approval and nodded vigorously. 'It's not as if she'll be missed. Susan doesn't like her, I can tell you that now. And the way she gives herself airs and graces, I doubt anybody here does much either. Perfectly good hotel, this, and yet you can tell that madam over there thinks anything less than Claridge's or the Ritz isn't good enough for her. I can tell that the Penderghast woman doesn't like it, and who can blame her?'

Charles Morris, who'd been standing and puffing aimlessly on his pipe just inside the doorway, now wandered across the room and headed over towards Arbie and Val, nodding an acknowledgement at Arbie as he did so, and receiving the expected invitation to sit down and join them.

Martha watched him for a moment, sucked viciously on her cigarette and wondered how soon she could politely get up and leave the old lady to her own devices. Perhaps she could set up a rival game of cards with some of the other party members. Canasta, perhaps?

As she was contemplating likely candidates for a game, Martha felt a little warning twinge in her chest, and took a quick glance at her little gold-and-diamond cocktail watch. Time for her pills. She should have taken them ten minutes ago but had forgotten.

She reached into her bag, shook out a white pill from a small bottle and swallowed it without fuss, draining the remains of her coffee after having done so. Mona watched her and then nodded.

'Oh, yes, you've always had that bit of heart trouble, haven't you?' the old lady said loudly, with another of her unnerving cackles. 'I remember now, you have to take care you don't overtire yourself or get too excited about things and what have you. What a bore that must be. My own ticker is sound as a bell,' she added proudly. 'Nearly eighty, and still pounding away like a Trojan, so my doctor assures me.'

Most of the others in the room were generous enough to give her a brief smile at this booming piece of bombast. After all, it was marvellous (and rather reassuring) to see that a vigorous old age was perfectly achievable.

Martha, however, only sighed. 'Congratulations,' she said caustically. 'Some of us, however, don't have your luck!' And getting up, she approached a pair of bored-looking women and their equally bored-looking partners and began to talk card games. Picquet, possibly? She doubted that their conversation would be stimulating, but anything was better than listening to Alexander's most irritating relative droning on about her good health.

CHAPTER FOUR

The next morning, Thursday, dawned as warm and fair as had the week that had preceded it, and after wolfing down his usual breakfast, Arbie left the dining room in good spirits. Instead of heading straight out to the beach, however, or saunter about in the countryside, or even take his car into the nearby town, he made his way instead into the kitchen, where he cajoled an unpeeled carrot from the bemused cook.

Mindful of the promise he'd made to a certain individual upon his arrival, he made his way to the railed fence that separated the grounds of the hotel from the neighbouring smallholding.

In the thistle-rich paddock he immediately spotted the snooty white pony, who didn't even design to prick up its ears at Arbie's friendly whistle. However, the encouraging sound *did* bring his large, noisy grey friend trotting quickly over to investigate, as he'd hoped it would. And as the gangly donkey easily thrust his head over the topmost rail, his ugly-friendly face seeming to give a smile of welcome, Arbie grinned back at him and produced the carrot from behind his back.

'Here you go, old chap, I promised I'd find a treat for you,' he muttered, holding out the orange titbit, careful to keep his palm perfectly flat so as to avoid getting unintentionally bitten by the animal's tombstone-like teeth. The donkey then wasted no time in using aforesaid gnashers to demolish it noisily, and after Arbie had scratched his bony head, stroked his ridiculous ears and patted his dusty rump, the animal began to nudge his arm continuously and encouragingly.

'Nope, I've only got the one carrot, I'm afraid,' Arbie said, having no trouble interpreting the meaning behind the affection. 'But I promise I'll bring an apple next time.'

So saying, Arbie set off somewhat aimlessly. If he ever saw any tots from the farm round and about, he'd have to ask them the donkey's name. If he belonged to him, he'd have called him Don Quixote, or Quasimodo. But he'd probably find out he was plain old Ned, or some such.

And so, without a care in the world and idly contemplating fitting donkey names, Arbie set off to find a good hiding place for himself, where he could safely loaf away the morning and where Val wouldn't find him. Should such a fate befall him, he knew from past bitter experience that she'd only make him start some actual work on the notes for the final chapter of his book. And it was far too nice a day to do something so hideous.

*

As Arbie set about putting his wily plan into action, in the hotel, others were going about their own affairs.

In the entrance hall, Millie was busy putting that morning's just-delivered post into the 'Post In' tray on the reception desk, ready for their owners to retrieve them as they came down to eat. As she went through them, placing neat little bands around those who had more than a single letter, she noticed one was for Mr A. L. Swift, and bore the name of a London publishing house. As she slipped it into the tray, a small, satisfied smile played about her lips.

To her immense relief, the famous author of that amusing and informative best-selling book *The Gentleman's Guide to Ghost-Hunting* had turned out to be rather a sweetie. Which made things so much easier for her. For Millie, more than anyone, was only too aware of how much they needed to make the Dashwood House Hotel a success.

Born of wealthy but not exceptionally rich parents, she had been fortunate enough to inherit a good amount of money on the death of her remaining parent.

Knowing how lucky she was to be given such freedom – a freedom that few of her fellow women ever knew – she had thought long and hard about what to do with her windfall, and after a period of mourning for her beloved father, had finally decided on the purchase of a hotel. And one that was far away from her remaining tight-laced and disapproving relatives, some place where she'd have room to breathe and enjoy a new challenge in peace and without interference.

As Milly set about constructing a fresh flower arrangement for the front desk, her mind slipped back to the past. She knew that her choice of husband hadn't met with her mother's total approval, but liked to think that, before she died only two years after her daughter's marriage, that she had come to reconcile herself to Millie's choice.

Of course, there had been nothing actually *wrong* with George Penderghast. His family were respectable enough, and he'd done his bit in the Great War. But not even George's best friends could claim that he had much between his ears. Nor was he overburdened with ambition. He did, however, have an amiable and easy-going nature, which, in Millie's point of view, was a much more desirable commodity. For a man like that came with so many advantages.

A malleable man who would grow accustomed to letting her have her head suited her down to the ground. And her latest scheme, to purchase a hotel, run it and make it a success, was a case in point. How many men, after all, would have been amenable to their wife using her own money to buy and run her own business? Men of more ego and less bonhomie than that of her husband would have kicked up no end of a fuss.

Her father, she'd always suspected, had understood perfectly the reasons behind her choice, and although he had never said as much, she believed that he had heartily approved.

Anyone out and about that morning, had they been able to read their hostess's mind, might have been astonished, and left with the opinion that the lady could have had no real affection or regard for her spouse. And in that, they'd be wrong. Very wrong. For she was genuinely fond of him.

And she knew that serving behind the bar in a nice little hotel overlooking the sea and playing the part of genial host, whilst not having to do any actual work or share the onerous burden of any real responsibilities, would suit him admirably. As, indeed, it had.

And if that meant that all the toil and occasional worries fell solely on her shoulders, that was just how she liked it. Besides, she was having fun! Finding and buying the right property had been fun. Getting it renovated and seeing that all the latest modern conveniences were installed had been fun. Choosing fabrics and paint colours, and even re-designing the gardens to accommodate the wants of guests en masse, had been fun. Even finding and interviewing the staff had been fun.

And watching her guests enjoy the fruits of her labours was deeply satisfying. But, ever the pragmatist, she was mindful of the need to ensure that her entertainment paid for itself. And that meant the hotel had to succeed. And to this end, she had given herself just four years to recoup her initial outlay of expenses and ensure that the new venture was bringing in steadily rising profits.

To this end, she had written to Mr Swift's publishers, pointing out the ideal qualities of the hotel for the next edition of their *Gentleman's Guide*. Inclusion in that light-hearted but very widely read guidebook would, she knew, all but guarantee that the hotel would be booked to capacity from Easter until the autumn next year. And once the hotel's reputation was known, she would hardly need to advertise again.

Which was why Mr Swift was constantly on her mind. He, at all costs, must be kept happy. She had half-expected the author of such a runaway bestseller to be some little peacock of a man, puffed up with his own success, picky about everything and in need of constant flattery, and had braced herself to grin and bear it.

So the arrival of a young, rather good-looking, and affable individual had come as a very welcome surprise.

Naturally, it hadn't taken her long to get his measure, for Millie had always been a good judge of character. And Arbie Swift, she'd quickly noted, was basically a lazy but undoubtedly talented young man, with not an ounce of malice in him. And so long as he enjoyed himself and was treated to the best the hotel had to offer, she was confident that the Dashwood – and their local ghost, of course – would feature prominently in next year's book.

So far, she had yet to see him doing any actual writing or note-taking, which was a slight concern, but if needs be, she could always cajole him into sitting down with her one afternoon and spoon-feeding him all the best details about her hotel. The ghost, she had no interest in. She might even offer to help him write out the accommodation-based entry, thus saving him the effort.

Which would no doubt please him mightily.

She only wished that all her guests were so easily managed. For some reason, Millie was aware that there was some kind of 'an atmosphere' developing in her hotel, and she didn't like it. Once or twice she felt as if she could detect a general sense of vague unease rippling among her guests, a tenuous feeling of things not being quite comfortable somehow. It was nothing she could put her finger on yet – but its origin, she felt sure, was somewhere within the engagement party contingent.

Perhaps there were tensions within the two families? Either way, she'd have to keep an eye on things. She couldn't allow anything to ruin the next few days. Whilst Mr Arbuthnot Swift was here, she wanted nothing to spoil the pleasant atmosphere of her hotel. And if something did, she would just have to take matters firmly in hand and deal with it.

Millie, for all her pleasantly plump, pretty ways, always got what she wanted.

*

As Millie carried on about her duties, Randolph Harrington, having finished his breakfast, made his way onto the terrace and scanned the sun-lit garden for the man he was hoping to see.

His own thoughts were not particularly pleasant, but they were, in their own way, just as busy as those of his hostess, and – just like Millie Penderghast – Randolph was intent on getting his own way.

The sun was rising higher in the sky and gaining heat, a heat which was beginning to beat down on his unprotected fair head, threatening to give him a headache later on. He made no move to go inside to retrieve his Panama hat, however, since he'd just spotted his quarry walking towards the tennis courts.

He had no racket, and wasn't dressed in whites, but then, Randolph doubted that Alexander Hythe-Gill had ever played a game of tennis in his life. But from the sound of balls being whacked over a net, somebody *was* enjoying a game, and the father of the bride-to-be was probably intent on watching the match.

With a spurt of speed not usually associated with the aesthete young man, Randolph set off along the neatly trimmed grass paths, the glory of the roses and brightly coloured dahlias for once totally lost on him as he hurried to catch up to the older man.

Randolph, as a lifelong friend of the Samplestones and Ernest's choice of best man, wasn't all that familiar with the family of his friend's intended. But in the early hours of the morning, as he'd lain awake, twisting and turning and totally unable to sleep, it had come to him that there had been some rumour going about, a few years ago now, concerning Alexander, and he'd racked his brains to bring it to mind.

Although Randolph was not a man of business (he had been lucky enough to inherit stocks and shares that provided him with a regular income without his need to do much more than sign the odd paper or two provided quarterly by his accountants), he still inevitably picked up the odd bit of gen here and there concerning what was happening in 'the city'. And even if his own hobbies and pastimes were more devoted to writing academic papers of esoteric merit than in pursuit of Mammon, overheard conversations at his clubs and whispers at parties kept him informed of the various victories and defeats of the people in their set.

And as he gained on the unsuspecting Alexander Hythe-Gill, he was sure that one such account about this particular man concerned a very bitter defeat indeed. For, unless he'd totally got the wrong end of the stick, Hythe-Gill's disastrous investment in certain stocks had once nearly bankrupted him. And only after years of hard graft, and with a bit of luck and the help of some of his friends, had he managed to pull his fat out of the fire.

When Randolph finally caught up with him and put out a hand to touch his shoulder and thus halt their joint progress towards the tennis courts, he hoped he wasn't making a mistake. Or had mis-remembered the identity of the man who'd been at the root cause of his losses. Otherwise, he was about to make a prize ass out of himself. But he was willing to take that risk.

For it was possible that this man and himself could have a common enemy. And if that *was* so, and they could get their heads together, then it was just possible that a little idea of his might just come to fruition.

And revenge – a very sweet and apposite revenge for each of them – could be within their grasp.

*

By ten o'clock, most of the hotel guests had finished with breakfast and were setting out to enjoy their day. Beatrice and the majority of the 'bright young things' had opted to go into a nearby small town for a few hours and had all piled into the various automobiles on offer, as well as the one local taxi, which had been summoned to the hotel by the ever-obliging Mrs Penderghast.

Martha Van Dyne, however, was not among their number. She told herself that this was not because she hadn't been invited, but because she herself had preferred to do some sunbathing in peace and quiet and had said as much to everyone in her immediate vicinity.

And so, whilst Alexander Hythe-Gill and Randolph Harrington began a very unexpected but fascinating conversation over by the tennis courts, up in her room, Martha donned a thin-strapped top, which she paired with a light and floating skirt, and slipped on a pair of sandals. A few minutes later and carrying a large beach towel and parasol (with her colouring she wasn't actually foolish enough to sit in the sun for any amount of time!), she stepped onto the beach, noting without much interest, that the tide was slowly coming in. Seagulls called lazily overhead, and a pleasant sea breeze had picked up, making the coastal grass rustle gently.

Several families with children were already on the beach – day-trippers, no doubt, from the nearest cities, out to make the most of the last days of summer before the school term began in earnest. These, she did her best to avoid. Noisy, tiresome people were always such a nuisance, in her opinion.

But as she walked towards the dunes and their subsequent offerings of shade – she couldn't help but be a witness to a small act of larceny.

A couple were firmly holding the hands of their two young children, aged somewhere around four and six, and were paddling and splashing about noisily in the waves, having left behind them a bucket-and-spade set by their deckchairs. These play items, made of an eye-catching, bright red-and-yellow tin, had been spotted by three keen-eyed ragamuffin youngsters who were almost certainly residents of the village. Dressed in well-worn clothes and shoes that were practically disintegrating from around their feet, they didn't have the more affluent appearance of the other day-trippers.

After a bit of pushing and shoving by the trio, Martha heard one of the boys 'dare' their playmate to do something. Consequently, when one of them then made a sudden dash for the family belongings on the beach, the explosion of movement and shouts of encouragement from the other two boys caught her attention.

As she turned to stare, she noticed that two of the young lads were almost certainly brothers, sharing as they did toffee-coloured hair and very similar features. The other boy was a bit taller and thinner and had dark hair. But it was one of the brothers who ran across the sand to snatch up the bucket-and-spade set and make off with it. All three then ran off laughing. Martha, who was certainly no expert when it came to children, put all three of them at around ten to twelve years old, and she gave an angry shout at them as they made off with their booty.

At the sound, the one carrying their trophy turned and looked at her over his shoulder, his eyes going round with alarm.

The father of the young children also looked up at her warning shout, saw what had happened and began to chase after them, but very quickly gave up. They now had a considerable head start on him and were probably much fleeter of foot than himself anyway. He also no doubt felt foolish, a grown man being bested by children, and after raising a fist at the retreating boys and muttering a few half-hearted threats, he turned back to his family, shaking his head wryly. His youngest child began to cry piteously – and she heard the mother promise to buy them a new bucket so that they could make more sandcastles later.

No doubt the toy had only cost ha'pennies and could be easily replaced, but Martha, on principle, felt distinctly cross. And even though it was, strictly speaking, none of her business, she vowed to give a description of the children to Captain Penderghast when she returned to the hotel. Having lived in the area for some time whilst the hotel was being refitted, he'd be sure to have got to know the locals and would have a fair idea which of the village children were a bad lot.

She'd demand that he have a word with their parents and make sure the little thieves were brought to task. After all, the last thing his guests wanted, when trying to enjoy a holiday, was a disruptive element spoiling things. What's more, the proximity of the beach was one of the hotel's biggest attractions – and thieving could become a habit. It might only be a cheap child's toy today, but who knew what the little reprobates might be tempted by next? A swimmer's watch, carelessly left behind –

sunglasses, shoes? Why, they might make off with anything! And the better class of guest that they wanted to attract would quickly shun the new hotel if word got out that their valuables weren't safe!

No, Martha thought with a sniff. She'd do everyone a good turn and demand the Captain did something about keeping the beach free of riff-raff in the future. And with that somewhat self-righteous thought in mind, she made her way towards a shady spot, spread out her towel and lay down with a small sigh of pleasure.

CHAPTER FIVE

Half an hour or so before lunch, the younger element returned from their trip, with most of them deciding to head for the beach to stretch their legs before eating. Val, having unexpectedly failed to bump into Arbie that morning at breakfast, had joined their jaunt into town, and now likewise trailed them onto the beach, but was feeling rather lacklustre about the whole thing.

Oh, it was fun and all that to be with a crowd of people, and Beatrice and her group were a jolly lot, but Val was definitely beginning to feel a touch restless. Although she would never admit it, even to herself, she hadn't come to Galton-next-the-Sea only to enjoy a little holiday and catch up with her old schoolfriend and help her celebrate her engagement. It had only been when she had learned from Arbie's publisher friend, Walter Greenstreet, that Arbie was *also* staying at the village for research purposes that she had really sat up and taken notice.

Last year, in their own small village, she'd joined him in a ghost-hunt or two, the results of which had been entirely unexpected and had, in a rather ghastly sort of way, had a very exciting outcome. Not only had they solved how a particularly baffling murder had been done, but they had been able to unmask the identity of the murderer. Well, perhaps Arbie had put the clues together more so than she had, she had to admit to herself reluctantly. But that only went to prove that, when he could be induced to put his mind to things, Arbie Swift could surprise not only himself but those around him.

And although she didn't expect anything so bizarre to happen again, she *had* hoped that he and she might get together again and do a ghost-hunt here by the sea. But so far, her feckless friend was being aggravatingly elusive! She hadn't even been able to pin him down long enough for her to get all the details of the ghost – having to content herself with reassurances from Millie Penderghast that the ghost didn't frequent the hotel itself, and that 'Mr Swift knows his business, I'm sure'.

Val, however, was not going to be put off!

Listlessly plucking a wildflower and twirling it absently between her fingers, she sat down on the sand a little away from the others, but then watched with some interest as Clarice appeared, dressed in a bathing dress and robe, and carrying a large beach towel. She dropped the towel and slipped off the robe with enviable unselfconsciousness and headed determinedly into the sea.

Now Val knew herself to be a very good swimmer, but she'd cut her teeth on the placid, freshwater river that flowed through her village, and could only watch, impressed, as Clarice headed out fearlessly into the waves and began to move through the swells with clean, easy strokes.

'Quite something, isn't she?' a male voice said, somewhat dryly, making Val twist her head around and look up, shading her eyes against the sun. And discovered Randolph Harrington watching the aquatic show with a slightly mocking look on his face.

'Yes – I was just thinking how athletic she was,' Val confessed thoughtfully. She had packed her own bathing dress, unsure whether she'd have the chance to use it, but now, after watching Clarice's slim body propelling itself through the troughs and waves, she made the decision to give sea-swimming a go herself. 'I'll have to try it myself. It looks like jolly good sport.'

'Been in the sea before?' her companion asked, a shade sharply.

Val admitted that she hadn't.

'Be sure to stay close to shore then,' he advised. 'And check the tide timetables. And just bear in mind – if you're caught in a cross current and are swept out to sea, that might well be the last anyone sees of you,' the young man added flatly.

Val blinked at this dire warning, and instantly sobered as she glanced anxiously towards the receding figure of Clarice. She was wearing a bright yellow bathing cap, so she could be clearly seen, but she was now some way from shore. 'Do you think Miss Fotheringham is safe?' Val asked, beginning to feel alarmed.

'Oh, you don't need to worry about Clarice.' It was Beatrice who spoke, having wandered over with the ever-faithful Ernest in tow, and having just caught the tail end of their conversation. 'Clarice is part dolphin! She was school champion at practically every distance, and whilst the weather is warm, she'll swim every day and come to no harm at all. You'll see,' she added gaily, tugging on her fiancé's hand as they continued their private little stroll along the shoreline.

Val hoped she was right. But she made a mental note to make sure that Arbie was with her when she went swimming herself.

Which reminded her – she really needed to track him down and make sure that he buckled down to some actual work. Arbie's friend, Walter, had rather hinted that, so far, his publishing company hadn't received any reassuring noises from their best-selling author about the state of his final draft. When Val had told him she was going to be in Galton herself very soon and promised to tackle Arbie about his notes so far on his last chapter, he'd almost fallen on his face and kissed her feet.

Of course, Walter hadn't actually gone so far to *ask* her to chivvy him along a bit, but Val had easily read the essence of the appeal in the young man's eyes and couldn't resist coming to his rescue. Naturally, as one of Arbie's oldest friends, Walter was as aware as anyone of Arbie's rather lackadaisical approach to work. But as his editor, it was obvious that he was under some pressure from the senior partners to make sure that the next edition of *The Gentleman's Guide* was delivered on time.

Never one to renege on her word, she was determined to come up trumps for poor Walter but managing to pin Arbie down and find out just how much work he had actually done over the last few days had proved to be nigh on impossible. But she was confident that he would make an appearance for lunch, and then she'd pounce. He might look lean and elegant, but he had the appetite of a carthorse, and if there was one thing you could count on, it was that Arbuthnot Lancelot Swift never missed a meal!

Bidding Randolph farewell, she set off determinedly back to the hotel, where lunch must now be imminent.

*

As Val entered the shady, cool hall, she saw that it was the Captain, not his wife, who was on duty behind the desk, and that he was being lectured about something by Martha Van Dyne. The small redhead seemed to have a definite bee in her bonnet about something and was intent on making her feelings known.

Val hid a smile as she heard the Captain soothingly reassure her that he knew the lads in question, and would be sure to have a discreet word with their parents, and that she must never have any worries or concerns about the safety of her valuables on the beach.

Sailing on into the dining room, Val breathed a sigh of satisfaction as she instantly spotted her quarry. As she'd thought, Arbie, along with one or two other guests, was already seated at a table for two, and talking affably to an old couple at an adjacent table. As she got closer, she could have sworn that he was addressing them as Jack and Jill (surely not?) but he broke off when he spotted her bearing down on him.

'Oh, hello old thing,' he said, not quite meeting her eyes. Which, in Val's vast experience of him, meant that he was feeling guilty about something. He was dressed in his usual Oxford bags, which he purchased religiously from Walters of Oxford, and a plain white shirt, tieless and open at the neck. He looked relaxed and lightly tanned, and already one or two of the women that made up Beatrice's party had remarked upon his good looks and eligibility. One and all had also professed to have read his book and thought it a 'scream'.

For some reason, their silly gooey-eyed and speculative conversations about him irritated Val considerably. Now she cast a rapid glance over him and told herself that some women were very easily pleased.

'There you are. I was hoping to finally run you to earth,' Val said bluntly, seating herself opposite him, and pushing back her long, fair hair. 'It's almost as if you're trying to avoid me.' Again, his eyes didn't quite meet hers, and her lips twitched knowingly.

That morning, she had donned a pretty powder-blue summer dress which showed off her legs rather more than her mother would have liked – had she been there to notice – and which matched the colour of her eyes almost exactly. With her fair skin glowing with health, Arbie thought she looked as pretty as a picture.

Others obviously thought so too. Val vaguely noticed that a middle-aged man with fair hair was also watching her appreciatively and remembered him being pointed out to her as some kind of businessman called Charles something-or-other. Naturally, she studiously ignored him. Middle-aged men with an eye for the ladies were something Val seldom deigned to notice. Besides, her concentration was fixed solidly on Arbie.

'Now, tell me all about this ghost,' she said firmly. 'Have you done a vigil or anything yet?'

Arbie sighed woefully.

The older couple, clearly listening with fascination, hardly dared move in their seats, lest they fail to hear his response.

'No, not yet, Val. It's not going to be so simple this time,' Arbie hedged. 'It's not a haunting in a house, like it was that time before,' he said, referring to a previous 'haunting' they'd investigated back in their home village. 'This is an example of an outdoor haunting of the countryside round and about. So my trusty camera is going to be useless this time. As, probably, will be the recording equipment. I know from experience when writing the first book that all I'll get are foxes yelping and owls hootin' and cows munching grass and things.' He nodded knowingly, infuriating Val, who knew that he was, indeed, the expert when it came to such things.

Catching the fascinated eye of Jack and Gillian Babbacombe, he smiled over at them. 'Miss Valentina Coulton-James, Mr John and Gillian Babbacombe,' he introduced them. 'Miss Coulton-James and I are neighbours, and last year she was kind enough to, er, accompany me on a ghost vigil at a mutual acquaintance's house.'

He didn't mention the name of the house, for the murder

trial of the person responsible for killing someone there had been last year's sensation, and was the last thing he or Val wanted to discuss now. It was bad enough that the papers had got the idea that he had helped the police significantly in the solving of the crime, and that his publishing company had been cock-a-hoop over the free publicity for his *Guide*, which had then enjoyed a second spell of popularity, leading to a second and then a third reprinting.

'Oh, how fascinating,' the older woman said, looking at Val curiously. 'And is Miss Coulton-James a fellow psychic investigator?' she added, fishing for information gently.

'Miss Coulton-James is the daughter of our vicar,' Arbie said firmly, 'and was there at the request of the owner of the house, an elderly lady whom we had both known for all our lives.'

'Oh, I see,' Gillian Babbacombe said, a little abashed. 'I'm sorry, I must have sounded very inquisitive, but everyone here is all agog about having such a famous author amongst us. And to think you're going to put this hotel in your next book. And the ghost of course.'

'Yes, about the ghost . . .' Val began, a glint in her eye, but just then the waitress arrived with the first course, and Arbie determinedly turned the conversation to other things. But he could already tell by the look in Val's blue eyes that the reprieve from discussing work was only going to be temporary.

And so, as he tucked into his turbot, he waved farewell to his previous plans for a quiet afternoon fishing off the jetty and resigned himself to slaving over his notebook instead.

*

After lunch, Charles Morris was just pulling out of the shady parking area when he spotted Arbie and his lovely companion setting off into the village. It was not far to walk, but he couldn't resist pulling over his Crossley and leaning his head out of the window.

'I say, hello there. Want a lift as far as the harbour?' he offered.

As he'd hoped, Arbie instantly accepted and gallantly opened the passenger door for his lady. As Val smiled at him coolly and slipped in beside him, he surreptitiously admired her legs.

Charles smoothly introduced himself, forcing Arbie, somewhat reluctantly, to supply Val's name. During his few days at the hotel, Arbie had come to form the opinion that Charles Morris was something of a lady's man, and whilst Val's parents must have been satisfied that Beatrice's parents were competent chaperones for their daughter, he knew where his duty lay.

And he was not about to let some ageing Casanova get ideas.

Besides, if even the slightest whiff of scandal concerning their daughter were to reach their ears, Arbie was pretty sure that, somehow or other, it would all turn out to be *his* fault.

'So, where are you off to this afternoon?' Arbie immediately launched into conversation, determined to make all the running and give the older businessman no time to try out his charms on Val.

'Oh, I've got to nip into London on a little business matter,' Charles said. 'Bit of a bore, but there you are. I'll dine in town and come back on the late train.'

'What do you do, Mr Morris?' Val asked, sounding polite but not really interested.

'Oh, this and that. I've no real need to work, but I dabble a little here and there in antiques, just to stave off the boredom. Not that old artefacts and such are something that would interest a lovely young lady such as yourself,' he added gallantly. 'And now and then I buy or sell the odd stock or share, just to keep my hand in.'

Luckily the ride was so short that within a minute or two they found themselves by the small harbour, where the village's fishing boats could be found sheltering when they were not at sea, as they were now. 'This suit you?' Charles murmured, pulling up in front of the village's only public house.

'Perfectly, thanks,' Arbie said, and wasted no time in alighting. Nor did he fail to see the way Charles watched appreciatively as Val, with lady-like decorum, also exited the car. He shut the car door rather harder than was necessary, but Charles only gave a jovial wave in acknowledgement as he set off along the coast road towards the next town, where there was a branch line that would take him north and hence into the capital.

As the Crossley vanished from sight, Val reached into her voluminous rattan beach bag and came out with a large notebook and pen. 'So, where do we start?' she asked, genuinely curious to learn the ins and outs of Arbie's chosen profession. Although she had been on a ghost vigil or two with him last year, she'd never actually learned anything at all about what went into the process of producing a book, ready for publication.

As she looked at him with a mixture of eagerness and inquiry, Arbie glanced around a little helplessly. Normally, when starting a new case history, he'd go into the pubs and chat to anybody who had tall tales to tell, but he could hardly do that with a vicar's daughter in tow. Due to the deplorable state of inebriation to be found amongst one or two denizens of public houses, some of the tales he'd heard tell had very little to do with local ghosts, but instead concerned ladies with some odd ways about them indeed. And these were definitely not fit for ears such as Val's.

Before setting out from the hotel he'd had time to fill her

in on some aspects of the legendary highwayman who was said to plague these parts, but what he needed now was to get some quotes from people who'd met the chap – so to speak. 'Well, first we need to hear what the villagers themselves have to say about old Red-Dog,' Arbie said, glancing around hopefully for a likely candidate, and immediately finding one in a familiar figure sitting on the harbour wall and leisurely smoking a pipe.

For here, surely, was the same old man he'd spotted when he'd first arrived at the village, and who had been good enough to direct him to the hotel. 'Ah, this fellow will do nicely, I think,' Arbie said, walking over to join the man who watched Val's approach with much interest.

'Hello there, nice day, what?' Arbie said, by way of greeting.

The old worthy slowly took the pipe from his mouth to acknowledge the truth of that. 'Ah, so 'tis.'

'Mind if we join you for spell?' Arbie went on, jumping up lithely to sit on the wall next to the old fellow, whilst Val, with more decorum, contented herself with simply leaning her elbows on the wall and gazing out across the pretty little harbour.

'Don't mind at all,' the old man said, eyeing Arbie with an amused glint in his eye. 'You be the writer fellah then? Maud Jessop 'as been tellin' everyone you're here to put us in your next book. Gonna make our little village a place for tourists, then? That'll please some, but not others. The old biddy who runs the local shop has been cackling and crowing about it ever since she heard you wuz here – like a hen that had just laid a golden egg, she was. And the fellah who runs the taxi is almost as happy. Others are muttering about the place bein' overrun and people making a mess, though.'

'Ah, well, I don't know about all that,' Arbie said, anxious not to get caught up in local politics. 'I just go around visiting places that might give someone a good holiday, you know. And especially for those who are interested in ghosts and folklore and that sort of thing. Which is where I hope you can help me.'

'Oh, yuss?' The old man's pipe went back into his mouth, and he took a hearty puff. Val, turning her back on the harbour, opened the notebook properly and stood poised, pencil at the ready. Arbie hadn't actually *asked* her to take notes, but she wanted to make herself useful. And who knows, if she did a good job, perhaps she could become his secretary on a more permanent basis? It would save him from doing a lot of the mundane work, which should please him. And since her parents were making rather pointed remarks on her own bare engagement ring finger, getting a 'proper job' might just stave them off for a little while, and give her some much-needed breathing space.

But as she mused on the possibilities of her immediate future, she noticed that a tall, thin man with white hair and walking an Airedale terrier was heading their way. And from his quick glances, was clearly interested in their conversation.

'You talking about Red-Dog then? 'Im as you can hear sometimes of a night, galloping hell for leather along the lane up yonder, but when you stop to look, can't see 'ide nor hair of 'im?' the old man with the pipe was saying.

Arbie nodded eagerly. 'Yes, yes, that would be the one. You ever see him yourself?'

'No,' came the quick and uncompromisingly flat reply.

At this, Val felt her spirits droop a little, but Arbie merely shrugged philosophically. An old hand at this game, he knew better than to expect to hit the jackpot the first time. But the old man then went on to surprise him. 'You don't see old Red-Dog, young fellah-me-lad.' The old man pointed his pipe at Arbie and jabbed it in the air to emphasise his upcoming point. 'You hear him, see?'

Arbie blinked, then nodded knowingly. 'Ah, got you. People just hear hoofbeats then?' Although he smiled, he could already foresee the difficulties that lay ahead. Unless the Galton ghost did more than merely ride unseen through the countryside, he couldn't see how he could wring much entertainment value from it for his readers. Anyone would just assume that the locals were hearing any old mortal horse rider going about their business in the night.

As the old man with the handsome terrier drew closer, Val couldn't help but interrupt. 'But surely there's more to the legend than that? I mean . . .'

'Oh, it's not just the sound of hoofbeats.' The pipe was once more removed so that the oracle could speak. 'My granddad told me that folks, if they were brave enough to go out and about after dark on the anniversary of ol' Red-Dog's hangin' – then come midnight, they would hear the ghostly swinging of a body swaying from a gibbet.'

At this Val gulped and began making rapid notes.

Even Arbie perked up a bit at this. This was more like it – this was what his readers paid out their shillings for! 'When you say they could hear something odd, do you mean . . . ?' he trailed off hopefully, and the old man grunted obligingly.

'Granddad said you could hear the squeak, squeak, squeak of the rope against the hangin' tree branch,' he said, his voice lowering dramatically. 'What's more, he said that if you heard it, it could drive you mad.'

'No, no, you've got it all wrong, Sid.' The man with the terrier had now drawn abreast of them. As the dog instantly approached Arbie to be petted, his rear end swaying in friendly greeting, the dog's owner eyed them with obvious pleasure.

'Apart from anything else, notorious criminals were hanged in towns or cities to draw as large a crowd as possible, and Briggs met his end miles and miles away from here on Tyburn Hill. You'd have to have a pretty good pair of ears to hear that – even with the wind blowing in the right direction! Your old granddad was just blowing hot air.' The dog owner gave a loud guffaw. 'Besides, everyone knows it's not the highwayman himself who's the real terror of Galton, but his horse.'

At this, the old man on the harbour wall drew himself up stiffly. 'Now 'old on, Jeremiah. You don't know nothing – you'n your kin are incomers. You ain't bin here but five minutes.'

'My family came here in eighteen twenty-two,' Jeremiah spluttered. 'And everyone knows my uncle Frank knew more about Red-Dog than anyone, seeing as he wrote him up in his journals.'

Before the two old men could work themselves up into a proper argument, Val – ever the vicar's daughter – stepped into the breach to pour out the soothing oil. 'Oh, I'm sure you are both experts on the subject, each in your own way,' she said, turning a charming smile upon the newcomer to the group, then turning to the pipe smoker and laying a light hand on his arm. 'And I'm sure that Mr Swift is keen to listen to any and *all* details about the ghost, aren't you, Arbie?'

'Eh?' Arbie said, who was busy engaged in scratching the terrier's head and whispering sweet nothings into the mutt's hairy ears. He'd always loved animals, and they invariably reciprocated. 'Oh, yes, er, definitely. I'm sure my readers will want to know all you can tell us. So, er, what's this about the horse being the star of the show? We're a nation of animal lovers, aren't we? And I'm sure a ghostly horse will go down a treat with my readers.'

Val, who had been half-convinced that Arbie hadn't been listening to a word of any of it, had to acknowledge that perhaps, on this occasion, she had misjudged him. What's more, she suspected that he was right and that his readers would find a ghostly horse fascinating. She knew she did!

'Huh,' the man with the pipe grunted, unmollified, and began to puff smoke frantically to show his displeasure as his rival held forth.

'See, it's like this,' the terrier-owner began. 'When the soldiers who were chasing Red-Dog finally caught up with him, just above Galton on the upper road, they finally managed to drag him off Stalwart.'

'Stalwart's the name of the horse?' Val interrupted, writing busily, and not wanting to make a mistake. If she was going to impress Arbie with her skills as a literary assistant, she had to be word-perfect.

'Yes, young lady. A fine black stallion, they do say. Anyway, Stalwart, seeing his master's plight, tried to defend him by rearing up on his hind legs, and kicking out at the soldiers.'

Arbie, listening silently but attentively to all this, thought that scenario was very unlikely, but wisely kept his scepticism to himself. Besides, it would make for a colourful and dramatic account in his last chapter and would no doubt please Walter and the other fusspots at his publishing house no end.

'And they say he did manage to break the arm of one of them, and even kill one of the soldiers with a hoof to his head, but the poor beast was eventually overwhelmed by the sheer force of numbers. And as they all dragged poor old Stalwart to his knees one of his legs was broken, and the captain in charge used up one of the balls in his musket to put him out of his misery.'

'Oh no!' Val said. 'The rotters.'

'Indeed, though some maintained that the horse never did break its leg, and that they shot him purely in revenge for his killing one of their own.' The man gave a shrug. 'Now, on the anniversary of the sad event, villagers hereabouts started telling tales about how they could be walking home of a night, and hear ghostly hoofbeats. But no rider ever appears. Even worse, they say that when it's the dark o' the moon and you're under the trees with no light to be 'ad at all, if you're out and about come midnight, you might just feel the hot breath of a horse breathing down your neck. But when *that* happens,' the old man dropped his voice to barely a whisper and leaned in closer to them, so that even Arbie began to feel a little chill at the back of his neck, 'they say that *no* sounds of hoofbeats is ever heard at all. As if ol' Stalwart is making sure that you don't hear him coming and have the chance to run away.'

The dog owner stepped back, nodding wisely.

'Yerse. And there's worse to come,' the old man with the pipe, not about to let his thunder be stolen, piped up stridently to have the final word. 'They do say that if you're foolish enough, when you *do* feel the hot breath of faithful Stalwart on the back of your neck, to turn around to look to see what's there, you drop dead of fright at the sight of 'im. Four villagers over the centuries have been taken that way. They find their corpses always on the top road, dead of fright on the grass. Ar, you mind my words, young fellah, if you ever feel old Stalwart breathing down your neck, you just keep your eyes front and head for 'ome as fast as yer legs'll take yer, and never look back. That's my advice. Now then.' And he nodded so emphatically that his disreputable old flat cap nearly fell off his head.

'Gosh,' Val whispered, swallowing hard.

Arbie, with some effort, tried to shake off the heebie-jeebies that were threatening to overwhelm them all and bring the voice of reason to the proceedings. 'Oh well, I dare say these dead villagers really died of natural causes, don't you know,' he said robustly. 'The result of too much ale, late at night, and then they don't see a tree branch and bang their head, for instance, and brain themselves. Then there's heart attacks and whatnot. Back in the old days, remember, folks died all the time of this and that, and they didn't have the proper medical johnnies around then to say what really happened.'

The two old men looked at each other, then turned away, mutually unconvinced.

But Val nodded loyally. 'Yes, I expect you're right, old thing. I mean, nowadays, we can take patent medicine and pills and whatnot and recover from all sorts of things that did in our poor ancestors.'

'So, when exactly does Red-Dog and this faithful nag of his come out a-haunting?' Arbie asked, deliberately making his tone of voice cheery and light.

'Don't you know? Surely you've researched the date of his execution?' Val asked accusingly.

Arbie coughed into his hand. 'Oh, not yet, old thing. Er, the library's the sort of place to find out things like that, doncha' know? And I haven't got around to that yet.'

Val eyed him sceptically. Then, remembering her campaign to become indispensable to him, said brightly, 'Oh, that's all right, old bean. I can do all that for you.'

Arbie blinked at her. Somewhere in the back of his mind, a faint warning bell was beginning to clang away, but for the moment, he had no idea why. He only knew that the innate cowardice and venal cunning of generations of his Swift ancestors were now flowing through his veins and warning him to beware!

'Actually, the anniversary of Red-Dog's hangin' is this Saturday coming,' the old man with the terrier put in helpfully.

'Eh?' Arbie said, thoroughly taken aback. He'd had no idea that the anniversary of the night when the highwayman and his wretched horse had met their fate was as close as all that. If he had . . .

'Oh, Arbie!' Val said, distracting him, her eyes shining rapturously. 'We'll have to set up a vigil! At midnight! On the road and the very spot where it all happened. Then we're bound to see or hear something, don't you think?' she asked excitedly.

'Oh, er, yes. What ripping good luck,' Arbie agreed feebly.

CHAPTER SIX

That evening, the last of the remaining members who'd been invited to attend Beatrice's party arrived in the reception hall, causing a little flurry of greetings and much chatter.

Arbie, brooding over a pint of beer in the bar, looked up vaguely at the invasion of sound and movement, then went right back to his brooding. Ever since returning to the Dashwood House Hotel he'd been trying to come up with some excuse that Val would accept for not going out at midnight on Saturday.

It was not that he was afraid – or expecting – to meet up with either Red-Dog or his horrible horse, of course. During his time researching and writing the first *Gentleman's Guide* no ghost had ever been so impolite as to put in an actual appearance. And, indeed, it was an unspoken given that his book (and now its sequel) was there merely to inform its readers of the various good but little-known holiday destinations and accommodations there were to be found around Great Britain, whilst entertaining them to light-hearted accounts of local ghosts and any interesting snippets of folklore there might be in the vicinity. Arbie's literary 'investigations' of ghostly goings-on on behalf of his reader were meant merely to amuse and intrigue, and he was always at great pains to reiterate that he was not in any way an academic or scientist intent on serious study of the subject. Neither his publishers, his readers nor Arbie himself (it went without saying) would welcome any actual encounter with genuine paranormal activity!

No, Arbie was not *afraid* to go out on Saturday night, he told himself firmly. After all, hadn't he sat up, of a midnight, in country houses galore where 'white ladies' and ghostly nuns or monks were said to roam, without so much as turning a hair? (Well, there was that one time when the wind blew open a faulty window latch and made a vase crash over . . .) But no, apart from the odd few mishaps that might have put his heart in his mouth, he now considered himself to be a seasoned and hardened hand at this old ghost malarkey.

It was only, he told himself peevishly, that the idea of skulking about on country roads in the dead of night held no appeal. All of his previous 'ghosts' had had the good grace to haunt either inns, private houses or the odd church or two, where he could set up camp with a nice hot Thermos of tea and a deckchair, and while away the wee small hours of the night in relative comfort.

But walking for hours on end, out and about in the countryside? What if it rained? Or blew a gale? And now that he thought about it, this spell of exceptionally late summer warmth was bound to end in a rattlingly good thunderstorm at some point. Most heatwaves did, didn't they?

As this occurred to him, Arbie perked up a bit over his glass of beer. Yes, if it was stormy in two nights' time, not even Val would expect him to go and wander about on the upper road on the off chance of meeting the Galton ghost.

Would she?

Gloomily, Arbie suspected that she just might. At this, he heaved a sigh, and the Captain, sensing his melancholy and knowing that his wife would hate to see he-who-must-be-pleased-at-all-costs looking down in the dumps, approached him with the idea of geeing him up a bit.

'Another one, Mr Swift?' George Penderghast asked hopefully, nodding at Arbie's glass. 'Or something a bit stronger perhaps?'

Arbie obligingly drained his beer and indicated that he could set about another pint, then looked around the room. It was that rather dead hour just before dinner, and so far, he was the only one in the place. 'Bit quiet, eh?' he asked, not unhappily.

'Yes. Most of the engagement party are greeting the new arrivals, and even Mr Morris seems to have deserted us.'

'He had to go to London,' Arbie said vaguely. 'Between you and me, he seems to have a bit of an eye for the ladies. Is he married, do you know?'

'Widower,' the Captain said shortly, and gave a sly wink. 'From what I've been able to put together, his late wife was very well-off, and left him the lot. Which, just between you, me and the lamppost, is what I've heard a few people say is the real reason behind his business "successes". She died of the Spanish flu, apparently, and ever since then, he's been enjoying himself. Oh, hello, here they come,' the Captain added bracingly, abruptly changing the subject. And sure enough, the new influx of guests, along with the old hands, began to pile in and demand cocktails.

As he found himself surrounded, Arbie listened with only half an ear as Beatrice told everyone that they must go into the nearest town tomorrow, to do a bit of shopping and pick up any 'necessaries or fripperies' they had forgotten to pack. At this, a rather tall brunette became the butt of some joke or other for her awful packing. But it wasn't until Beatrice asked what a small, somewhat squat young man had brought for his costume for her fancy-dress party, that Arbie suddenly realised that he'd been worrying about nothing.

For, surrounded by bright young things discussing Saturday's upcoming celebrations, he realised that the perfect way to avoid a midnight maunder on Galton's sleepy lanes had been presented to him on a silver platter.

'Here you are,' Val said, sliding up beside him. 'I've typed up the notes I made this afternoon and slipped them under your door.'

'Oh, good-oh,' Arbie said vaguely. 'I say, Val, I've just realised – you can't come with me on the ghost-hunt this Saturday night after all,' he began casually. Which happy fact meant that he himself could just pretend to leave for his rendezvous with Red-Dog and Stalwart, but then nip back into the hotel by one of the side doors, and thus be tucked up in bed and happily in the land of nod with no one (meaning Val) any the wiser.

'Oh?' Val said, stiffening at once, and shooting him a deeply suspicious gaze. 'And just why is that, pray tell?'

'Well, because of them,' Arbie said, waving vaguely at the now buzzing bar. 'It's your friend's engagement party this Saturday, isn't it? And you'll be expected to attend, won't you? Being pencilled in as a future bridesmaid and all that. What a pity Red-Dog's anniversary isn't tonight or tomorrow night. Or even Sunday night. But as it is . . .' He shrugged helplessly in a fair imitation of commiseration.

Val's lips, which had been thinning ominously during this ingenuous recital, turned up at the corners and formed themselves into a wry smile. 'Oh, don't worry about that, old bean,' she said bracingly. 'That shouldn't be a problem at all. We don't have to be up on the top road until midnight, do we? I mean, that's when our ghostly highwayman is likely to be doing his thing, yes? So I can still attend for most of the party, and then change and meet you outside at, say, about half past eleven?'

'Oh, I say, Val, you can't do that,' Arbie protested. 'Won't your pal Beatrice think you a proper stinker for abandoning the festivities so soon?'

'Oh no, Bea won't mind. In fact, she'll think it a scream. She might even want to come with us! All of them might, for that matter.'

At this, Arbie went a trifle pale. 'Oh, good grief, that won't do! We can't have revellers dressed up as Marie Antoinette or Napoleon or what have you wandering around in the dead of night. If they're a bit squiffy they'll make an awful racket and if they're seen they'll give all the villagers heart attacks. Especially those dressed as dandies of the Georgian era. They'll think Red-Dog has not only come out to play but brought a selection of his ghostly cronies with him!'

'Yes. Yes, I can see that would be a bit awkward,' Val agreed reasonably. 'Oh well, I just won't tell them. It'll be just you and me – which is much better anyway. We're the professionals, after all,' she added placidly.

At this, Arbie's mouth fell open a little. '*We?*' he squeaked. 'What's all this "we" business?'

Val put her hands on her hips. 'Well, it won't be my first ghost vigil, will it?' she demanded.

'Er no, but . . .'

'And,' Val swept on, 'have you forgotten what happened last year? Didn't I help you expose a murderer?'

'Well, actually, no you di—'

'And didn't I keep a cool head throughout?' Val cocked her head to one side, her lovely blue eyes narrowing, and daring him to deny that she hadn't.

Arbie, forced to concede on this point, muttered something about her being as steady as a rock, a jolly good sport, and really, for a girl, had been quite decent about the whole ghastly business.

'Exactly. So, that's settled then,' Val said firmly. 'We'll slip out around eleven thirty and tell no one. Nobody will even notice – by then they'll all be blotto on champers anyway.'

But Arbie was not quite beaten just yet. 'Oh, I say, Val, it's still not really practical, is it? For a start, you'll be dressed up in fancy dress, won't you? Er, what are you going as?' he asked curiously.

But Val batted this away with an impatient wave of her hand. 'I can always nip upstairs and change into something more suitable first, you muggins,' she said, almost fondly. 'Into something dark, is that the ticket? A dark skirt and jumper, that sort of thing?'

'Er, so long as you wear sensible shoes,' he advised. 'And something that allows you to run. Fast. If need be,' he added in a mutter and under his breath.

'What was that? I didn't quite catch it,' Val demanded.

'Er, oh nothing,' Arbie said feebly. And bending his head over his beer, began to pray fervently for torrential rain in two nights' time.

'Oh, Val, darling, there you are.' Beatrice, dressed in a knee-length tiered silver cocktail dress, with strands upon strands of coloured beads that almost reached to her knees, fell on Val's neck and called gaily for the latest 'wallop'. The Captain, now aided behind the bar by his wife and one of the waiters, promised it would be coming right up. 'Everyone's going to town tomorrow. Want to come? Daddy!' she sang out as she caught sight of her parent. 'Are you coming with us?'

Alexander Hythe-Gill smiled but shook his head. 'No, darling. Randolph and I plan to motor to a place that a friend of his advised us to visit. There's a ruined abbey there—'

'Oh dear, how dreary that sounds,' Beatrice interrupted him with a laugh, and instantly turned away to seek out more interesting company.

'You can count me out too, darling,' Arbie and Val heard Clarice drawl a few moments later. 'I simply have to get some swimming done tomorrow. Once this lovely spell of sunshine is over, I won't be able to get into the sea for six months or more. Really, English seasons are so unreasonable, don't you find?'

As the noise and general gaiety continued to grow in volume, Arbie allowed himself to be jollied along by the infectious good humour of the others. And by the time they all trooped in to dine, he had regained most of his good spirits.

*

Martha Van Dyne felt quietly pleased with life as she walked up the wide staircase shortly after eleven that evening. Not only had she dined well, but she was in a buoyant mood – much more buoyant than she had been on the day she had arrived at this sleepy little backwater.

But then, who'd have thought that coming to Beatrice's engagement celebration would bring about such a change in her luck?

She was still smiling over this as she entered her bedroom and draped her light silk shawl over the end of the bed and musing happily on how good life could be as she moved towards her dressing table. She had her eye fixed on the little jar of her favourite night lotion, an exotically fragranced and very costly little pot she'd been given as a gift, and which had come all the way from Paris. Anticipating that sensuously delicious moment when she could sit down and apply it, she wasn't paying enough attention to where she was putting her feet.

The first hint she had of trouble was when she felt the toes of her right foot knock into something, checking her stride and forward momentum and sending her off-balance and lurching awkwardly forward. Trying to regain her balance, her other foot fell prey to the same obstruction, which, looking down with a short cry of alarm, she saw was the small footstool she had carelessly forgotten to stow back again under her bedside chair.

Unable to save herself now, she fell face forward onto the carpet, automatically throwing out both hands to break her fall. She felt a sharp pain lance through her right wrist, but at least she managed to avoid the indignity of having her face hit the Axminster. The footstool skittered comically away, as if trying to disavow any knowledge of the affair, and for a few moments, Martha lay where she fell, slightly winded, feeling foolish and cursing like a trooper under her breath.

When she felt sufficiently composed, she began to put her weight on her hands so she could first get her knees under her and then become upright again, but her right wrist protested so painfully to this she had to use only her left hand to accomplish a vertical state again. She took a few tentative steps, relieved to find her ankles were not sprained. Only her right elbow throbbed a little in protest, and she flexed it experimentally.

She gave the footstool a vicious kick then walked to the dressing table and slumped down. She scowled at her reflection in the mirror and absently rubbed her right hand, flexing the fingers and finding, to her relief, that nothing appeared to be broken. She suspected though that she'd bruised it thoroughly, and, from experience of such things, didn't doubt that in the morning it would feel far worse and stiffer than it did now.

With an angry sigh, she reached for her night lotion and set about her night-time routine, using both hands whilst she still could.

Her good mood of earlier had – not surprisingly – vanished, and by the time she'd washed, undressed and slipped into bed, she knew she'd never sleep without a little help. Reaching into her bedside table drawer, she extracted and unwrapped a small paper twist of powder, which her doctor prescribed for her whenever she needed help in nodding off. As she poured out a glass of water and swirled the mixture around in the glass until it dissolved, she cradled her now throbbing hand protectively.

She'd have to be sure to remember to lie on her left side tonight.

*

As the unlucky Martha finally drifted off to sleep, a few doors down from her, Mona Rice-Willoughby was also drinking something to help her sleep – but Mona far preferred good brandy to patent sedatives.

Smacking her lips over the last drop of amber liquid, she too pulled back the covers of her bed and lay flat on her back, staring up at the ceiling.

She was, once more, thinking of that floozy and dog-killer, Clarice Fotheringham. So far, the young madam had ignored her, trying to pretend she simply didn't exist. Clarice couldn't have known that Mona, too, had been invited to the party, otherwise she wouldn't have come. Or would she? The old lady scowled up at the ceiling, uncertain. Perhaps she had known all along, but just hadn't cared tuppence?

Mona wouldn't put such behaviour past her. She'd certainly made no overtures to try to apologise again for killing poor Monty. Was it possible the heartless chit had *forgotten* him? Last year, to her, might now seem decades ago, but to Mona it felt as if it was only yesterday she'd watched the gardener dig a hole in the back garden and lay poor Monty to rest.

The old lady thrashed her legs angrily under the bed covers. Right now, by rights, Monty should be on the bed with her, curled up and pressed against her side, snoring slightly.

And did the heartless wench *care* that he wasn't? Not she! Not a bit of it. The 'bright young things' of today, the old lady raged silently, thought they were a law unto themselves, that was the trouble. The Great War had eroded all their morals, every one of her own generation knew that! Nowadays, such things as duty of care, honour or moral responsibility had been tossed gaily by the roadside, washed away by cocktails and all this horrid jazz music.

It was intolerable!

Then, slowly, unseen by anything but the darkness of the night, Mona Rice-Willoughby began to smile. And then nod to herself. Of course, people who didn't care about the things they did could always be *made* to care. Couldn't they?

*

At some time in the dead of night, Valentina Coulton-James sat up abruptly in bed, her heart thumping.

Normally, as one could expect of a vicar's daughter, Val slept deeply and peacefully, her conscience untroubled by anything, and her mind free of thoughts of the wicked world. Well, mostly. So she knew that it wasn't to escape the toils of a nightmare that had brought her so abruptly awake.

She lay still for a moment, listening intently. For such a deep sleeper, she was nevertheless easily awakened by anything out of the norm, and, being possessed of very good hearing, it didn't take her long to detect the cause of her interrupted slumber.

Somebody was sneaking down the corridor outside.

Like the well-appointed hotel it was, Dashwood House was carpeted throughout, but there was inevitably a little give in even the most well-behaved of floorboards, and it was the slight squeaking of some of these that had awakened her.

For a moment, she was tempted simply to lie back against the pillows and go back to sleep. It was probably just someone who had been forced to rise in the night to visit the bathroom, after all. But now she was awake, she knew it would take her some time to drift off again.

With a small sigh of annoyance, she sat up, slid on her pair of slippers and wandered over to the window. On such a warm night it was open to allow in a breeze, which carried with it the heavenly efforts of the night-scented stock that had been planted in a nearby flower border. For a few moments she looked out over the gardens with pleasure. She hadn't been given a room with a view of the sea but didn't really mind.

After reconnoitring the layout of her surroundings on her first day here (it was the sort of thing Val, a girl guide leader, did automatically), she now knew that her bedroom was directly above the reading room and part of the dining room below. Lifting her gaze to look across at the elms and Douglas firs that screened the hotel from some parts of the fishing village, the church clock suddenly struck; a pleasant, mellow sound at this distance. She counted three, and then all was silent.

Having filled her lungs with good fresh air and the scent of the stock, she was just about to return to bed when a flash of light caught her eye. It wasn't a bright light, but it flickered, intermittently, shedding a small beam across some of the flowering borders below her. It puzzled her for a moment, for it was not the full, steady light of someone who'd switched on a lamp.

Then she realised what it was.

From one of the rooms beneath here, someone was flashing around a torch!

This, coupled with the sneaking footsteps which had just awakened her, had Val's curiosity ratcheting up considerably, and without really thinking things through, she reached for her dressing gown, donned it and tightened the belt firmly around her waist.

She walked lightly to her door, opened it slowly and looked cautiously out. Just enough moonlight was allowed to creep in through the windows so she could see to the head of the stairs. Nothing seemed to move.

Briefly, she contemplated going to Arbie's room and rousing him, but shied away from it. A young lady didn't go knocking on a man's hotel room in the middle of the night. And certainly not a vicar's daughter. It might be misconstrued. Besides, she thought grimly, he'd probably refuse to get out of bed and tell her she was just imagining things and to go back to sleep.

With her chin up, but her heart rate accelerating slightly, she set off determinedly – but quietly. She all but tiptoed down the main staircase, cautiously peering over the banisters as she went. Nothing stirred in the hall below either. No fleeting shadows or suspicious scuffling caused her alarm. Pausing halfway down the stairs, she stopped and listened for a few moments. Again, she heard nothing untoward.

Perhaps someone had simply used their torch to make their way outside for a breath of fresh air, or to smoke a cigarette? Somebody who was having trouble sleeping, perhaps?

Somehow, though, and as comforting as that thought was, Val wasn't quite able to make herself believe it.

She detoured to the door of the dining room and pushed it open. Unhelpfully, it gave such a high-pitched and loud squeak that it scared her almost out of her skin, and she had to slap a hand over her mouth to stop herself from squeaking right along with it.

Frozen in the doorway, she found herself holding her breath. But everything within the room was dark and nothing moved. She dared not turn on the light for a better look though, for fear of giving herself away. Someone besides herself was down here, after all, and quite suddenly she felt far more frightened than the occasion seemed to call for.

For all she knew, the person using the torch was halfway to the village by now. Or had gone back to bed by another staircase? One of the servants perhaps?

And yet, perversely, now she couldn't help but feel there was something *too* quiet about the place. As if something in the darkness had heard the squeak of the door opening and had frozen in place, listening, furtively waiting to discover what had been the cause of that sound.

She told herself not to be silly, and that she was just having a case of the jimjams. Nevertheless, she backed nervously out of the doorway to the dining room and did a quick survey of the large hall. If this were her own home, she would have checked every single room without fail, in case of burglars. What's more, she'd have picked up a heavy poker from the fireplace and would have screamed the rafters down had she encountered someone up to no good.

But she was *not* at home. This was *not* her house, and most of the people in it were strangers to her.

Suddenly, she felt unsure of herself and faintly ridiculous. What was it to her if a guest was wandering around after dark? Was it even her business?

Not sure if she was being sensible or had allowed some form of cowardice to influence her decision, she reluctantly climbed back up the stairs and returned to her room. She shut her door so carefully that it made not even the slightest of clicks. Instinctively and atavistically, she felt that if someone *had* been watching her, or been listening out for her in the dark, she didn't want them to know who it was who had shared that darkness with them.

She turned the key in the lock of her door as silently as possible, then crept back to bed. But as she lay under the covers on that warm September night, her hands felt cold.

It took her a long time to fall back to sleep.

And beneath her, this time unseen by anyone, the torchlight once again flickered intermittently in the darkness.

CHAPTER SEVEN

That Friday morning – the day before Beatrice's fancy-dress party – everyone seemed to be out and about early, with party members anxious to be off in search of last-minute items, either to tweak their costumes or to improve their appearances in general. One pal of Randolph's was bewailing his valet, who'd forgotten to pack the pomade, whilst another young lady simply must have a pair of diamante buckles to make her 'drearily dull' black shoes sparkle.

Only Arbie, Charles Morris and the few other hotel guests who weren't part of the engagement contingent seemed their usual relaxed selves over the breakfast table. Amongst these were Jack and Gill Babbacombe, who perked up visibly when Arbie entered the dining room and instantly invited him to join their table.

Val, coming in a few minutes later, was also instantly exhorted to join them, an invitation which each of the younger people politely accepted.

'There now, isn't there a jolly atmosphere this morning?' Gill began, sipping a glass of prune juice with every evidence of pleasure. 'I must say, this party your friend is holding sounds as if it's going to be the bee's knees,' she added. The phrase didn't sit entirely naturally on her lips, and Arbie wondered where on earth she'd picked it up, but she looked and sounded so pleased with herself for knowing it, that he couldn't help but grin at her and agreed that it was indeed 'the cat's pyjamas'.

Val saw the older woman gleefully mentally filing it for future use and couldn't help but throw Arbie a fond glance. When he wasn't annoying the Dickens out of her, he could often surprise her with such shows of random, good-natured, woolly-minded kindness.

'Eat up, m'dear, you know we need to get going in an hour or so,' her husband prompted her gently, and to Arbie, explained amiably, 'We're off to take the ferry to this beauty spot a friend of ours recommended, and we mustn't miss the sailing times. Then we're going to dine with some friends not too far from here, and they're going to drive us back later.'

'Yes, a nice full day,' Gill said happily, spreading her toast with Oxford marmalade. 'Galton is a lovely little place, but once you've seen the beach and the fishing boats and things, well . . .' She shrugged delicately.

'Yes, I know what you mean. The first few days by the seaside are all tickety-boo, but then you can have too much of sea and sand,' Arbie agreed. 'It's a constant worry when writing a travel guide, I can tell you! So, tell me all about this beauty spot,' he said, stunning Val by reaching into his jacket pocket and retrieving a small notebook and pencil. 'I'll have to check it out and see it for myself, but if it's worth seeing, I might include it in my chapter on Galton as a must-see excursion, and say it was recommended by your good selves. Especially if there's a boat trip to be had as well. Everybody loves a boat trip, don't they?'

Val, annoyed with herself for not bringing her own notebook and missing such a golden opportunity to show how useful she could be, listened vaguely as the Babbacombes, delighted at this chance of gaining some vicarious fame, eagerly gave the feted author the details he'd asked for.

Out in the hall, Millie – who had just left the kitchen after having satisfied herself that the chef and waiting staff had breakfast under control – slipped behind the reception desk and retrieved a folder from the long, slim central drawer. It was marked 'Hythe-Gill Party' and contained all her working notes on what still needed to be done to help facilitate the upcoming event.

She hesitated momentarily before opening it up and checking her list of outstanding tasks, though. Something, she felt, was subtly different or out of place. She glanced at the vase of flowers, but it hadn't been moved. The large leather register was still decorously closed. She frowned and it wasn't until she checked her 'Post In' and 'Post Out' trays that she realised what it was. The pile of correspondence that had arrived a half an hour earlier, courtesy of the first post, looked more depleted than usual. Normally, it took most of the morning for the guests to check the 'in' tray and pick up their letters.

Then she shrugged. It was just simply busier than normal this morning, and more people had come down early, that was all. Minor mystery solved, she opened the folder and extracted a list of names and telephone numbers.

Going over to the telephone booth situated between the doors to the reading room and bar, she stepped inside and began the laborious process of ringing up the tradespeople who were due to arrive tomorrow to make deliveries for the engagement party. It was marvellous nowadays how many people had had telephones installed in their premises. It made things so much easier than relying on messenger boys. This was her and the hotel's first big test at holding a large social 'event' and she wanted to make sure the Hythe-Gills would have no cause for complaint and would instead heartily recommend the hotel to all their friends.

She began with the florists, who assured her that the floral arrangements would arrive tomorrow late afternoon, pristine and as fresh as . . . well . . . a daisy. Laughing obligingly at the florist's little joke she hung up, crossing them off the list, and next telephoned the vintners and reassured herself that the champagne and wines she'd ordered would also be delivered on time.

As Millie began to dial the number of the region's most reliable butcher, back in the dining room, Arbie and Val bid the Babbacombes farewell as they departed to change and get ready for their day out.

The moment they had the table to themselves, Val leaned forward and tugged on Arbie's arm. 'I say, Arbie, something odd happened last night,' she whispered.

This, naturally, made Arbie blink in alarm. In his experience, odd things that happened in the night could prove rather tricky. But when Val went on to describe her adventures, he felt himself relax. 'So you see, *somebody* was up to no good in the early hours,' she finished, her eyes solemn as they watched him for his reaction. She expected interest, excitement and maybe a little admiration for her bravery.

Arbie merely nodded. 'Er, yes, I see,' he muttered, awkwardly. Looking, it had to be said, not particularly interested, excited or overwhelmed by her courage. In his defence, what he considered to be the obvious explanation of the night-time perambulations had occurred to him at once – and he was busy trying to find a way out of having to explain them to his companion.

He prided himself on being a man of the world and all that – and having stayed at various hotels during the writing of his first book, he knew all about the shenanigans that often went on in them. But how could a chap explain to a lady – and a vicar's daughter at that – the naughty comings and goings that occurred when normally respectable ladies and gentlemen were alone and away from home and the prying eyes of neighbours?

'Really? And what is it that you *do* see?' Val prompted archly, annoyed by his prolonged silence. And was astonished when Arbie Swift blushed like a schoolgirl.

'Oh, er, nothing, old girl. Just a figure of speech and all that,' he mumbled.

Val's eyes narrowed dangerously. She suspected he was feeling superior in some way, and that always infuriated her. 'So, you agree with me then, that someone was behaving suspiciously?'

'Oh, yes, undoubtedly,' Arbie lied manfully. 'But unless it was a ghost or something, it's not really any of my business, old bean. I mean, is it?' he demanded reasonably.

Val sighed heavily.

*

As Val bitterly considered the head-in-the-sand approach to life favoured by the male of the species, and Arbie tucked happily into a bloater, over at her own table, Martha chose porridge for her breakfast, knowing it would be easier for her to handle a spoon left-handed.

As she'd prophesied, her right wrist was now feeling very painful indeed and wasn't having anything at all to do with holding even lightweight objects, or in performing any fancy manoeuvrings. Her waitress, always a keen-eyed girl, noticed that 'madam' was having difficulties, and that the chic redhead's right hand and fingers were looking a little puffy, but she'd been too well-trained by Mrs Penderghast to do anything so crass as to make a comment on it or offer unsolicited sympathy.

Unaware that she had failed in her face-saving mission to fool everybody in the dining room that nothing was amiss, Martha kept her injured hand demurely out of sight on her lap and beneath the hanging white damask tablecloth. Too, too humiliating to admit to having clumsily injured herself! She only hoped the worst of its interminable throbbing would have passed by tomorrow night. She wanted to enjoy herself at this lavish entertainment her relatives were throwing, and it was hard to dance the night away if, every time her hand was taken for a waltz, it made her wince in discomfort.

At their table, Alexander Hythe-Gill, his wife, daughter and Ernest Samplestone ate according to their various personalities. Susan had tea and toast, whilst her daughter made do with tea alone. The two men, naturally, were in the process of polishing off a plate of bacon and eggs.

Randolph Harrington, in between being gallant to the three young ladies who had taken to sharing his table, kept glancing at his pocket watch, his eyes gleaming with definite excitement as he made short work of his own scrambled eggs on toast. Every now and then his gaze slid over to the Hythe-Gill table, awaiting some sort of sign from Alexander.

Today promised to be a very satisfying day, and he wanted to make sure Alexander wasn't getting cold feet.

Clarice and a bevy of Beatrice's friends were the last to arrive, and noisily descended on a table for six. They were watched, with much appreciation, by Charles Morris, who breakfasted alone at a table for two. As usual with Charles, he was reading the morning paper in between admiring the ladies nearby, when something in the written pages appeared to catch his attention.

Insouciantly, he folded the paper open at a large advertisement of some kind and smiled. 'I say, here's something rather droll,' he remarked. The tables in the Dashwood House Hotel were set close enough for several groups to hear him, but it was to the all-female entourage of Clarice and her friends that he turned his face.

'Apparently, a "fabulous blue mink" is yours simply for the asking,' he began. 'And all you have to do is convince the fur company who produces them that you are worthy of their first-class coat. And you'll never guess how you are to prove it.'

By now he had the attention not only of Clarice and the other women, but also of every lady in the room. Even Val perked up her ears. A blue mink coat? How fabulous, she mused dreamily. But when could she ever wear it? Even if such an exotic item should ever come her way, her father the vicar, would insist she sell it and give it to the poor.

'Oh, do tell,' a rather rotund friend of Beatrice's, with a mass of curly dark hair and big blue eyes, gushed. 'It sounds super.'

Charles leaned out to hand over his newspaper, which was retrieved and read avidly by the ladies. It was, typically, Clarice who spoke first. 'Oh, how absolutely squalid! They only expect people to write in with a so-called poem extolling the virtues of their wretched coat. And, presumably, whoever writes the most sycophantic opus wins.'

'I imagine it's an advertising gimmick,' Charles put in dryly. 'Either that, or those advertising johnnies who think these things up are running out of ideas. Either way, if anyone does write in with a catchy little limerick, it's all jam to the furriers. They simply publish the little jingo and the advertising writer johnnies can go sing for their supper.'

'No one of quality would stoop so low. Just think of the ridicule if they actually won! What a scream!' Clarice scoffed, secure in the knowledge that she could simply ask her daddy to buy her anything she wanted, any time she wanted it. But Beatrice, who had grown up with tales of less affluent times in her own family history, noticed uneasily that a couple of her friends were shooting Clarice rather glum and spiteful looks. Not surprisingly, since some of her chums came from land rich but cash poor families, and she dared say a new mink coat for free wasn't something that could so easily be dismissed by all.

'Well, I hope it backfires on them,' Clarice concluded, casually handing back the paper to Charles.

'It probably will,' a small blonde girl with thin lips put in wryly. 'Every shop assistant or hat-check girl in the country will try her luck, just wait and see. Not to mention all the usherettes who watch the Clara Bow or Mary Pickford pictures, and dream of owning a fur themselves. The poor things will no doubt try their best, but only end up writing in with something silly and cringe-making! That will make the furriers wish they'd never come up with the idea, having to plough through their awful poetry all day long.'

Several of the girls giggled at this mental image, but Clarice merely sniffed. 'And every word will be misspelt – and I shudder to think what rhymes they might come up with. I mean to say, what goes with mink, after all? The furriers will be inundated with letters saying such drivel as "Find yourself in the Pink, With a so-and-so's blue mink"! Ugh!'

As the women around her crowed with sycophantic laughter, over at her table, Martha eyed the little group sourly. She herself had enjoyed rather a good education at Cheltenham, and she'd always been best at English. If, as she suspected, Clarice was right and that not many ladies of discernment would bother with such a thing – and those that did couldn't come up with anything of much use – it certainly raised some interesting possibilities.

And a new mink coat was not something *she* was too proud to try for!

Talk at the girls' table gradually turned to their upcoming foray into the local town, and after the last rounds of fresh toast and coffee were handed round by the waiters and waitresses, guests began to drift away, most going back up to their rooms to collect bags or sun hats, others making their way out to the front door to get into their cars or wait for the local taxi to turn up.

Val, taking the last sip from her teacup, rose and made her way to the powder room just off the bar. Ignoring the comfortable seats in front of well-lit mirrors, she went into one of the cubicles instead and was just about to set about her business when she heard the door into the main area open and female voices flood the small room.

She recognised that of her friend Beatrice at once, and then that of Clarice.

Val didn't really like Clarice much. There was something too hard and knowing about her that made her feel uncomfortable, and she hoped the two would quickly leave. She heard a faint 'clink' as one of the girls put down their bag on the marble top surrounding the sinks and taps and extract something – probably a powder compact or a lipstick. Beatrice was very vain about maintaining the appearance of her pale, freckle-free skin, and Clarice, she'd noticed, liked to have scarlet lips at any time of the day.

'Did I see you flirting with my intended's best friend the other night?' Beatrice quipped.

'Oh, darling, honestly, I'm not guilty this time. Cross my heart and all that. *He* approached me! I thought for a moment my virtue was about to be tested, since he insisted on leading me out into the rose garden to see the moonlight.'

'Oh my! And I always thought of Randolph as being a bit of a dry old stick. He certainly doesn't have the reputation of being fast. Ernie tells me he has this huge electric train set that he plays with up in the attic of his house! Can you imagine? Hardly the material for love's young dream, is he? Mind you, someone *did* tell me that he was hung up for ages on a girl-next-door type, so he can't be as dried up as all that. But something tragic happened to her apparently. Obviously he's bucked up now though, so spill the beans, old thing, there's a dear. I'm all agog!' Beatrice said, lowering her voice in anticipation of learning something scandalous.

Unfortunately for Val, Clarice responded in kind, and through the door of the cubicle, she could only make out the odd word or phrase or two for the next few minutes or so.

She heard Clarice say, '. . . what an awful cheek!' And, after a squeak of excitement from Beatrice and a question that Val couldn't quite make out, Clarice again said scathingly, '. . . it's not that so much. I can be a sport as well as anyone else, but really! I think . . .'

Val, her business now totally forgotten, had somehow found herself with her ear pressed to the door of the cubicle, but annoyingly the two women were still talking with lowered voices. Luckily for her, Clarice was the more audible of the two, which was illuminating, as from what she could make out, Beatrice was only interested in warning her friend to be careful.

'. . . Oh, don't be so vapid, Bea darling. I wasn't *that* shocked. And had it been anyone else it might have been rather fun but, darling, really! Vamping someone like him . . . *mumble mumble* . . . even in such a good cause, it's . . . *mumble mumble*.'

Then Beatrice said something else, and Val could clearly hear Clarice heave a theatrical sigh. 'Of *course* I'll be careful, darling. Aren't I always? But a little danger can add a touch of spice to life.'

Beatrice, using her normal voice, said rather archly, 'I can't say as I particularly noticed! Anyway, Clarrie, are you really not coming into town with us today?'

'Sorry, sweetie, but like I said, I want to get some serious swimming done this morning, once the sea's warmed up a bit. Besides, I've got everything I need for your party – I brought it all with me. I know how hard it is to get anything decent in these provincial seaside places. I had my maid run up my costume – she's a whizz with the needle. You wait until you see it, it's a hoot. It has . . .'

The voices faded as the two girls passed back out through the main door. Val, frustrated and intrigued, decorously set about doing what she'd came for, then washed her hands and checked her appearance in the vanity mirror.

She was wearing a white dress patterned with small, embroidered flowers in pink and forget-me-not blue that she had done herself. It was four years old, but it still looked good on her – which was just as well. With her long blonde hair pulled back in a plait, and plain, sensible white sandals, she was ready for the day.

Whether or not Arbie liked it, he was going to do some work on his book today, and she was going to make herself so useful that he'd soon get used to relying on her. And then it would be just a matter of waiting for the right time to approach him with her proposal that she be his literary assistant in the future.

Val couldn't think of many women of her age who had careers and she felt quite proud of herself for being so brave. Even so, when she thought of telling her parents of her new plans, she felt herself quail a little. They were all for her marrying a man with land or prospects – and preferably, both.

Of course, Arbie wouldn't like the idea of her working for him either, and would no doubt try to twist and wriggle and worm his way out of it – but Val knew she was more than capable of handling Mr Arbuthnot Swift.

CHAPTER EIGHT

Charles Morris was not one of the idle rich congregating in the hall, but one of the idle rich sitting in the lounge and turning his mind to that morning's crossword puzzle in his favourite newspaper. The lounge door was wide open, and occasionally he would look up at the steady stream of people walking past as they made their way to the front door.

It was already promising to be another blazingly hot day, and the windows throughout the large building had been thrown open, allowing a pleasantly cooling breeze to circulate inside. Twirling his pencil absently in his fingers, he cast his eye over a particularly annoying cryptic clue and wondered idly if it might be an anagram.

The hotel began to quieten around him.

*

Up in her room, Clarice began to lay out her swimming things. Bathing dress, sandals, bathing cap, large beach towel – a particular favourite of hers, bought from Harrods last year. In various pastel shades, it was almost as thick as fleece and delightfully fluffy. A beach wrap for when she left the sea. A sun hat. Sunglasses. Cream for her skin. A hairbrush.

Slowly, her oversized straw bag began to fill almost to overflowing.

*

Evie Smith loved working at the new hotel. She'd not long celebrated her sixteenth birthday and had never been happy working the past two years with Mrs Stevens, helping to gut and clean the fish that came in off the boats. Her hair and clothes had always smelt of fish no matter what soap she used, and sometimes her sore red hands would bleed from all the salt the fish were packed in – and all for a mere pittance at the end of the week, which her mother took off her for her keep.

Although Mrs Penderghast was no pushover and made sure you worked hard, Evie had no complaints. She was certainly more even-tempered than Mrs Stevens and paid better too. Her mother even let her keep some of her wages for herself. What's more, the kind of work she had to do 'up at the big house' was much more to her liking. Now she only smelt of furniture polish and beeswax. And who knows – in a few years' time she might work her way up to head parlourmaid!

She'd quickly discovered that none of the older maids liked working the new-fangled electric vacuum cleaners, and still preferred dustpans and brushes, so Mrs P. had given her the responsibility of using one of the machines on the largest areas of carpets in the public rooms. It was very heavy and made her puff a bit to use it, but she felt real pride in being the queen of the noisy machine.

As she stepped out of Room 8 and onto the landing having just 'done' the beds and thoroughly dusted – she paused as she spotted a guest, and quickly ducked back into the room and out of sight. Although it wasn't like the old days, when her granny had been in service, and the servants in them Victorian mansions were expected to turn their faces to the wall whenever their lords and masters passed by, Mrs P. was always drumming it into them that, when possible, they should do their best not to 'impinge' on guests. Whatever that meant! Sally in the kitchen reckoned it meant they were supposed to become invisible, but that was just silly.

Nevertheless, Evie was determined not to lose her position in the lovely hotel by incurring the displeasure of a guest, so she kept well out of sight as the old dear toddled past her and made her way further along the corridor. Only when she was gone did Evie step out, take a quick look both ways, then leave her hiding place.

She only had three more beds to do before she was needed downstairs to help clear away the breakfast things. She didn't mind working in the kitchens, but far preferred the rooms and public areas like the reading room and lounge. Mrs P. always kept everything so pretty and nice. Fresh flowers in dainty vases, the curtains always hanging just right. How her mother's eyes would open wide if she could see all the lovely pictures hanging on the walls, and the lacy doilies on the tables, and embroidered antimacassars that hung on the backs of the chairs.

As the teenager made her way to her next room, she stopped and frowned a shade thoughtfully. Like most of the staff, she quickly came to recognise the guests who stayed for longer than just a night or two, so she knew that the old lady she'd just seen was part of the big engagement party that was being held tomorrow night. Some lady with a grand double-barrel surname, like a lot of the toffs had. Mona somebody-or-other. Sally reckoned she was a great-aunt of the bride-to-be, and so rich that everyone fussed up to her, even Mr Hythe-Gill, who was paying for it all.

But Evie, who'd been assigned to clean most of the rooms on this side of the hotel, knew that the old lady had been given one of the biggest suites in the hotel – and that it was definitely *not* the one that she'd just come out of. Was she supposed to tell Mrs P. about that sort of thing?

Then she shrugged. More than half of the engagement party had rooms on this floor, so the rich old lady had probably just been visiting another relative or party guest. Or maybe she'd just got confused and gone to the wrong room by mistake? She did sometimes go about muttering to herself, and tended to leave things scattered around the public rooms and then forget where they were. Mrs P. or other members of staff were always finding things for her and returning them. Evie wouldn't put it past the old dear to have forgotten which was the door to her room.

Forgetting all about it, Evie went on her way. Below her, she could hear the guests congregating in the hall, which meant they were about to set off for the day. Briefly, she wondered what it must be like to have the leisure and money to do anything you pleased. It must be nice, mustn't it?

*

In the kitchen, Arbie begged for some more carrots from the still-bemused cook, and artfully dodging the prowling Val (whom he darkly suspected had plans to make him do some work or something equally hideous), nipped out of the French windows in the deserted reading room and skirted around towards the side of the hotel.

He felt a bit like Bulldog Drummond avoiding an enemy agent, but that didn't stop him from keeping a wary eye over his shoulder as he made his way towards the neighbouring paddock.

By now, the donkey recognised him and his daily morning visits, and was doing a smart trot towards the fence, anticipating his tasty treat. The fat white pony looked uncertainly on. The fact that her companion was onto a good thing hadn't gone unnoticed, but on the other hand, she was too fat, and her legs too short, to want to run fast. So, with a contemptuous toss of her white mane, she bent her head to the grass once again and continued to graze.

'Hello, old son,' Arbie, leaning over the top wooden rail, cooed at his new friend, creasing the palm of one hand around a large, silky ear, and offering half of the carrot with the other. 'Try to leave me with some fingers, eh?' he admonished, though in truth, the animal took the vegetable with the merest brush of his soft lips.

*

Martha Van Dyne glanced out of her bedroom window, watching without much interest as Alexander ushered his wife and daughter into the local taxi and waved them off. As he did so, she saw Randolph Harrington briefly join her cousin, before both men walked towards a parked car – presumably Harrington's – and climbed inside.

They seemed to have a lot to talk about, and even sat in the car for a few minutes, earnestly discussing something, before the younger man finally drove them away.

Collecting her bag, she remembered just in time to lift it with her left hand, since her right wrist was still stiff and sore and objected to having too much pressure put on it. Carefully hanging it from her left arm – it felt a trifle heavier than usual, because it now held her leather-bound notepad and a pencil amongst its usual items – she walked to her door and down the corridor. At the head of the stairs, though, she paused cautiously to watch and listen. But as she suspected, at this hour, the hotel was now all but empty.

Satisfied that she wouldn't be seen, she walked down the stairs and to the table in the middle of the hall, where a collection of newspapers was laid out every morning for the use of the guests. Quickly sorting through them, she extracted the same national newspaper that Charles Morris had been reading an hour earlier at the breakfast table and retired with it to the reading room.

A quick, reassuring glance told her that she had the room to herself. The insufferable Clarice, it seemed, hadn't collected her mail and deigned to reply to her usual avalanche of invitations just yet!

As if thinking of her had somehow summoned her image, through the open French doors, Martha saw the younger woman's figure moving about in the garden. She was heading towards the far end of the flower borders, where there was a gate in the clipped evergreen hedge that led out, almost onto the beach itself. She was dressed – if it could be called that – in a bathing dress and an exotic wrap. Slung over one shoulder was a capacious straw bag, and she carried over one arm a large fluffy towel.

Perfect, Martha thought with satisfaction. With any luck, the awful, self-satisfied little cat would be swimming for hours.

Settling down at the table, Martha turned her attention to poetry – and mink coats. No mere shop girl or usherette was going to beat her to that free coat! It wouldn't be easy writing with her left hand, but she was sure she would find a way to manage.

*

As Martha racked her considerable brains for rhyming puns suitable to impress a furrier, Millie Penderghast made her way from the kitchens to the hall. She was just in time to see Charles

Morris check the 'Post In' tray and, finding two bearing his name, tuck them into his inside jacket pocket and stroll casually towards the front door, where he disappeared into the blazing sunshine.

She slipped behind the desk and automatically started tidying up. Later today was going to be busy – with the big engagement party set for tomorrow, she expected the first of the trades to begin their deliveries. Not those with perishables of course, they'd need to be sorted out on the day – but the men who were to set up the stage for the orchestra would be arriving soon. As would the decorators for the ballroom – people with balloons, swags, bunting, that sort of thing. Then the people delivering extra chairs. What else?

As her ever-active mind anticipated what else she would need to do that day, she automatically found herself tidying the top of the desk. That was odd. Now the 'in' tray seemed *fuller* than it had been before. But that wasn't likely, was it? Not with so many guests having already checked it for their mail and taking it away with them before leaving for the day.

She frowned a little, then gave a mental shrug. She had other things to occupy her mind than such trifles. She must make sure that most of the disruptive work to be done in the ballroom was completed before the evening meal. She wouldn't have guests bothered by hammering or what have you when they were dining. Especially not Mr Swift.

*

Val finally tracked Arbie down just as he was heading off to the road that led towards the village. 'Ah, Arbie, there you are,' she called out to him, and stepped out a pace.

Arbie, who'd been contemplating a pint in the pub when it opened, followed by a laze in the sand dunes somewhere, felt his spirits distinctly dip. But he'd plastered a smile onto his face before he turned to wait for her to catch him up and answered her hail.

'Hello, old thing,' he greeted her affably.

'What's the plan for today then?' Val asked, looking at him expectantly. 'Spill the beans.'

Arbie mentally waved goodbye to his lazy day and said brightly, 'I thought I would walk up to the "high road" as they call it around here and check out the spot where our ghost and his loyal steed are said to frequent. Maybe check out the light and angles for a photograph for the book,' he lied brazenly. 'There's nothing my readers like more than to see an actual photograph of the spot where the ghosts do their business. Makes 'em feel as if they're already there, so to speak.'

'Spiffing,' Val said, companionably linking her arm with his. 'I could do with stretching my legs. I'll even help you carry up the camera equipment later if you like, so you can get a photograph while the weather's so good.'

Arbie's grin didn't falter by so much as a flicker of his eyelids. When needed, the Swift menfolk could be relied upon to summon an upper lip stiff enough to compete with the best of 'em!

*

Back in the reading room, Martha, her preliminary notes somewhat illegibly made, closed her notebook with a sigh. It had been many years since her school days, and writing poetry hadn't come quite as easily as she had expected. Nevertheless, she was sure she had now the bare bones of something pretty decent. She'd have to work on it for a day or two, and check it was polished and slick enough to pass muster, but she felt certain she'd come up with a winning entry if she persevered.

Getting up off the easy chair, set in front of a convenient coffee table, she glanced towards the big writing bureau against one wall to the left of the French windows. It was a large, handsome Chippendale-inspired creation of glinting red mahogany with one long top drawer that could be opened by pulling on the two shiny brass rings set at the far left and right of it, and three half-drawers each with a single centre handle, either side of the knee-well. Above, a Welsh-dresser-like addition of alcoves and pigeon-holes stretched almost to the ceiling, containing ink wells, pens, ornaments, paperweights, spare blotters and the like.

She knew, from having used it in the days before, that a supply of the Dashwood's nice headed notepaper, made of good-quality, thick off-cream bond, and matching envelopes were kept in the top drawer.

Absently pulling out a rather heavy tapestry-seated chair with both hands, she immediately gave a small cry of pain as her injured wrist gave out an agonising protest and began to throb in warning. 'Oh, blast this stupid hand,' she muttered, instinctively cradling her afflicted wrist against her warm breast, and stood for a moment, swearing softly under her breath.

She glanced casually outside, her gaze coming to rest on the figure of Charles Morris, who was sitting on one of the benches underneath the shade of a large apple tree. He had a Panama hat on and appeared to be dozing.

Martha's lips twisted in a bitter little smile as she looked on his form. If she didn't have other things on her mind right then, she might just have gone out to join him and have a little fun. But that could wait for another day.

When she wanted something, Martha had always been prepared to do whatever it took to get it.

*

About an hour or so later, Alexander Hythe-Gill and Randolph Harrington returned to the hotel. Evie Smith heard the clattering of the car's engine motor as it was parked in a shady spot, and glancing down from one of the open windows on the upstairs landing, she saw the two men climb out and make their way towards the entrance below.

She thought they looked, even from this odd, foreshortened angle, to be in high spirits and pleased with themselves, and their voices had something of the eager schoolboy about them. Whatever they'd been doing, they'd clearly enjoyed their outing.

Not wanting to be caught dawdling, she quickly set off with her pile of fresh towels to set about restoring order to the first of the communal bathrooms in her area. Every morning it was always the same – the guests all wanted a bath and left damp towels everywhere.

*

As Evie began to scrub some bathroom tiles, Clarice, submerged in sea water, headed reluctantly for the shore. By the positioning of the sun, she reckoned it was somewhere between eleven and eleven thirty, and she was finally beginning to tire.

She trod water for a moment so that she could lift her head to check her position and searched for her chosen landmark. She'd memorised the horizon well before heading into the incoming tide and quickly spotted the large dark cedar, halfway between the hotel roof and the harbour wall, that she had selected. She headed towards it with a lazy, efficient overarm crawl and when she was close enough, felt for the sandy floor beneath her.

Wading out towards her pile of belongings on legs that felt just a little leaden, she headed across the sand, pulling off her bathing cap as she did so, running a hand luxuriantly through her short, ebony hair and giving her scalp a good scratch. It was only when she reached her large beach bag that she realised something was amiss, however.

Her lovely, expensive beach towel was gone!

For a moment, she simply stared down at the denuded contents of her belongings and then swore – softly, and using some very unlady-like words. Fortunately, the beach was deserted, and so no sensitive ears had to suffer from this shocking display.

With lips tightened in annoyance, Clarice shook herself, a bit like a spaniel did after a dip in the river and reached angrily for her wrap. Still damp as she was, she knew the sheer silk would become almost translucent and would cling uselessly to her skin, like flower petals that had been caught out in the rain. Luckily the sun was now at its hottest, so she didn't feel the chill, but she was not best pleased.

Slipping the silken wrap over her shoulders, she tied the belt tightly at her waist, picked up her bag and stalked angrily back to the hotel. For once she was pleased not to have an audience watching her.

*

Martha, who was in the hall, was the first to spot Clarice as she came storming through the lounge door, having come in from the gardens and up onto the patio, then entering via the first set of French windows.

'Why, Clarice darling, you do look rather ruffled and not your usual sanguine self,' she said delightedly. 'And rather damp too, I see,' she added archly, looking her up and down fastidiously, a sweet smile on her perfectly made-up face.

Clarice shot her a sharp look. 'Oh, do dry up, Martha, sweety, there's a dear. I've no time to cross swords with you just now, fun though it always is. Some awful little sneak thief has stolen my beach towel! Right off the beach! And it was from Harrods too,' she wailed.

Martha drew her breath in sharply at this calumny. 'No! Mind you, I'm not surprised. And I can tell you right now just who did it.'

At this rather grandiose and unlikely claim, Clarice's large eyes widened perceptibly. 'Really? Well, do tell,' she demanded.

Briefly, Martha told the tale of the three young lads she'd seen loitering on the beach the day before, and who'd stolen from the tourist children. 'Naturally, I complained to Captain Penderghast about it right away, and he promised he'd have a talk with the parents,' she concluded flatly.

'Well, it clearly did no good,' Clarice spat. 'The parents probably refused to believe it of their little angels or something and showed him the door. And let's face it, the Captain's a bit of a pussycat, isn't he? I don't suppose, as a threat, he was much use at all,' she added contemptuously. 'Well, *I* won't stand for it.' Her greenish eyes flashed spitefully, like those of a cat. 'And they won't put *me* off so easily.'

'I don't blame you,' Martha said shortly. 'If I were you, I'd write a stiff letter to the parents right now and insist that Captain Penderghast deliver it in person and at once. Threaten to make it a police matter if you don't get satisfaction. I daresay they'll sing a different tune then,' she predicted, her voice dripping with self-righteousness.

'Oh, don't you worry!' Clarice growled. 'If my towel isn't returned immediately, I'll know the reason why all right!' she added ominously, stalking towards the reading room, her damp state of dishabille all but forgotten in her growing rage.

*

As Martha followed eagerly on Clarice's heels, two people in the Dashwood House Hotel observed the women enter the reading room.

Mona Rice-Willoughby, peering over the banisters from the floor above, watched with a small smile of satisfaction flickering across her face. Martha, she all but ignored, keeping her eyes fixed instead on Clarice's stiffened back, a gleam of anticipation making her old eyes sparkle. She even gave a little chuckle to herself as she stood there, all but hugging herself with glee over the little surprise she'd arranged for the heartless dog-killer.

Wouldn't the little madam have a shock! Serve her right too. With a little bounce in her step, the old lady began to descend the stairs. It was only then that she noticed someone else was also in the process of going downstairs ahead of her, and had, in fact, almost reached the bottom step.

For a moment she didn't recognise the man from behind, but when he turned to look towards the open door of the reading room, she recognised him as that nice young man, Randolph Harrington, the best friend of Beatrice's intended, and soon-to-be best man at the wedding. In her younger days, Mona mused wickedly, she might have set her cap at one such as he!

Randolph, unaware of the old lady behind him, was frowning slightly. He was worried about Clarice, no two ways about it. He rather thought he might have made a bit of a boo-boo there.

Had Clarice confided in anyone what he'd been up to? He fervently hoped not. Because if she had, he could be on a bit of a sticky wicket, right enough.

Reviewing it all in his own mind, he thought he had put it across to the girl well enough, laying it out as being a bit of a practical joke and all that, but he was not totally sure that he had altogether succeeded.

He was not, he knew, one of nature's most gifted actors, and she might have smelt a rat.

So, as he looked at the disappearing back of the beautiful Clarice, he felt his heart thump uncomfortably. But there was nothing he could do about it now, he realised fatalistically. The die was cast.

And that was when the screaming began.

CHAPTER NINE

Arbie and Val had just returned from their exploration of Roger 'Red-Dog' Briggs's preferred haunting ground on the road above the bay and were now walking up to the front door of the hotel to retrieve Arbie's camera. As Val had threatened, she had insisted that there was no time like the present to take a photograph of the area for 'their next book', given that the weather might turn, and it was silly to waste such good, bright light.

Arbie had gulped a bit at her proprietorial term in regards to *his* next edition of *The Gentleman's Guide* and was beginning to get a very uneasy feeling that Val was cooking something up. She had that determined gleam in her eye that never boded well for him, and so was already feeling rather skittish. Which was why, when the sudden screaming from within the hotel began, his nerves were already feeling a little hard done by.

They had just turned off the short lane that led uphill and into the parking space in front of the hotel when the first rolling, horrendous high-pitched yelps of terror rent the air. Through the open front door of the Dashwood they came, making Val freeze momentarily to the spot, but sending Arbie, without being aware of having given a conscious instruction to his brain, instantly sprinting towards the entrance and the source of all that noise.

Val, her mouth slightly open in shock by the speed of his

reaction, saw that he'd almost made it through the door before she herself could gather her scattered wits and follow him. As she did so, the screaming stopped for a moment, but then very quickly continued, as if the screaming woman had needed to refill her lungs before she could continue making that awful sound.

Coming in from the bright sunlight into the darkened hall, Arbie, in the moment that it took for his eyes to adjust to the different level of light, was temporarily blinded, but he was aware of movement somewhere. Turning his head towards it, he found himself looking at the staircase.

On the stairs, he saw Mona Rice-Willoughby. She had just sat down abruptly on the second step of the stairs, a hand going up to cover her mouth. But it was not she who was making all the noise.

As Arbie, already moving further into the hall, turned his attention back to the source of the screams – which seemed to be coming either from the bar, reading room or lounge – he noticed that there was another occupant nearby. Standing frozen in place almost in the middle of the hall was the tall figure of a man. Since his eyes still hadn't had time to adjust, he wasn't quite sure for a moment who it was. The screaming stopped, but then started up again almost at once, this time sounding less horrified and more pitiful.

It chilled his blood.

Seeing the man was staring at the open door to the reading room, Arbie took a few swift strides past him and, with some trepidation, forced himself to look into the room.

At first, he was not sure what he was seeing. His eyes went first to the woman making all the noise – and recognised Martha Van Dyne. She was on her feet, but swaying ominously, and her moaning wail finally began to subside into quieter, distressed sobs. She was as white as a sheet, which made her rich red hair look even more fiery, and was staring across at the writing bureau with a look of horror in her sherry-coloured eyes.

Even as Arbie turned to look at what had her so transfixed, he half-noted that Martha's lips had a blue-ish tinge to them that he didn't like the look of one little bit.

Tentatively, he took a step towards the writing bureau. It took his puzzled mind a few seconds to make sense of what he saw. Someone in a weird, silk thing was sitting at the bureau. But sitting was perhaps not quite the right word, since Arbie could not see the back of anyone's head!

Instead, it seemed as if a headless torso had been placed there, and for a moment he wondered if someone had actually been *beheaded*, and almost added his moans of horror to those of his companion, before common sense quickly prevailed.

He moved another step closer and, peering over the rounded shoulders of the figure, caught a glimpse of raven-black hair and realised that a woman was half-sprawled, facedown, across the top of the bureau.

Another step closer, his hand instinctively going out towards her, he had a vague idea that he might shake her gently. Perhaps it was just possible she'd fallen asleep or fainted?

'Don't touch her!' A harsh voice shouted out the warning, and Arbie leapt back, like a scalded cat. He hadn't recognised the voice, and it took him a moment to realise that it was Martha who had spoken. 'There's something terribly wrong about her! You didn't see it. It was . . . hideous. If you'd seen it, you wouldn't want to be anywhere near her, I tell you. She began to dance, you see,' the redhead added, her voice wavering hysterically.

Arbie blinked a bit at this.

'Dance?' he repeated blankly. Surely not! He couldn't have heard her correctly, could he?

It was at this moment that Val appeared in the doorway, and

close behind her, Randolph Harrington, peering gingerly over her shoulder.

It had been the advent of the vicar's daughter into the hall that had finally unlocked Randolph's frozen feet and brought him to his senses. No man could allow a young woman to go, unaided, into an unpleasant situation, after all.

Quickly, his eyes assessed the scene.

Val began to walk towards Arbie, but he instinctively put his body between her and the sight of the woman at the bureau. For, although he'd tried earlier to convince himself that Clarice might just have taken ill, he knew in his bones that she was very much dead. And that her death hadn't been natural or kind.

'Val, old girl, don't look,' he said urgently, then his eyes swivelled again to Martha as she began to laugh hysterically.

'She did a sort of j-j-jitterbug, all j-j-j-jerky arms and legs,' Martha howled, peals of laughter now replacing her earlier screams, and tears of shock were running down her pale cheeks, leaving little marks in her make-up. And then, without warning, she began to sag at the knees.

'Val, catch her!' Arbie shouted and pointed, and Val ran towards the older woman and just managed to get her strong, athletic arms around her. Fortunately, an easy chair was just behind them, and hauling Martha rather unceremoniously under her armpits, Val heaved her into it.

Kneeling in front of the older woman, Val looked at her anxiously. 'Martha, do you have any pills?' she asked quickly. Like most of those who'd been present in the dining room on the evening that Martha had admitted to having a weak heart, she'd overheard the remark. And, as Arbie had done just moments before, she'd noticed – and didn't like the looks of – the blue tinge to the older woman's lips.

'Pills?' At least the hysterical laughter ceased as she became distracted.

'Yes. For your heart,' Val said gently, and reaching for her hands, which were chilly to the touch, began to massage them, trying to help her circulation flow better.

Martha only gazed back at her with blank eyes.

'Did the doctor give you anything to take if you suddenly came over all of a flutter?' she persisted patiently.

Finally, Martha understood what was being asked of her, and nodded numbly. 'Handbag,' she said succinctly.

One swift glance told Val that Martha didn't have it with her. 'Is it in your room?' she asked quietly.

Again, Martha nodded numbly.

'All right, I'll run and fetch it. Just sit quietly, and I'll be right back,' Val promised. As she rose, she saw that Randolph was still standing silently in the doorway. 'Phone for a doctor,' she told him sharply.

Randolph nodded, glad of be given something to do, and stepped back into the hall and headed for the telephone booth as Val dashed past him and diagonally across the hall. She barely registered the old woman who was sitting on one side of the stairs, wide-eyed and watchful, as she ran past her.

In the reading room, Arbie shot a nervous look at Martha, who was now staring blankly down at her feet and turned once more to the woman at the bureau.

He took a deep breath and, mindful of Martha's bizarre warning not to touch her, approached cautiously and with his hands clasped behind his back. He half-crouched and bent his head to one side so that he could look more easily into the face of the dead woman. He was not sure, exactly, what he was expecting to discover, but at first glance, there didn't appear to be anything very outlandish about the scene.

Clarice simply lay with the left side of her face pressed against the wooden desktop. Her cat-like eyes were wide open and staring in a look of horrified surprise.

He watched her closely, just in case there might still be hope, but after a while was sure that she was not breathing. As he leaned closer, however, his nose picked up an odd scent, something that he couldn't quite place.

Had something been burning recently? Then he noticed that one of her hands had fallen limply by her side and that the tips of all her fingers were black.

For a moment he could only stare at them in astonishment. That the always elegant, well-dressed, perfectly presented and impeccably fashionable Clarice Fotheringham should have been seen with dirty hands seemed to him, in that moment, to be completely unfathomable. Something else to be added to the growing list of things that made no sense – like this woman having recently been dancing a jitterbug. Why, there wasn't even a gramophone in the reading room.

Then, with a rush of horror, his brain made a leap of logic, and he understood the meaning of Martha's distraught warning not to touch her.

He took a rapid step backwards, then another, his flesh beginning to creep as he realised just how this poor woman had met her sudden end.

As Arbie did so, Randolph returned to the doorway. 'The doctor's on his way. Fainted, has she? Been taken a bit poorly? I say, shouldn't we move her?' He approached Arbie reluctantly, his eyes shying away from Clarice's exotically clad, half-dressed form. 'She's been swimming,' he said vaguely. 'We have to cover her with something – her modesty . . .'

'No, don't touch her,' Arbie said sharply as Randolph began to remove his jacket, intending to cover the lady with it.

At this, Randolph stiffened slightly, taking offence. 'If she's been taken ill, wouldn't she be better off lying on a sofa or something? And we should put something over her – she must be getting cold in here, out of the warmth of the sun.'

Arbie was sure that Clarice Fotheringham probably *was* getting cold – and would get much colder still, given time. But what he said was, 'I think she's been electrocuted.'

*

For a moment after he spoke there was total silence in the room. Even Martha had ceased her crying and made no more noise. Randolph stared at Arbie as if he'd grown another head. And into this scene, Val returned with a small box of pills that she'd found in Martha's bag, up in her room.

Val went straight to the stricken redhead and poured out a glass of lemonade from a large jug standing on a sideboard. During the hot weather, Mrs Penderghast had taken to leaving such jugs of refreshments in all the public spaces, set on a silver tray with plenty of pretty, cut-glass drinking beakers.

Val carefully inspected the writing on the box of pills, saw that the instructions said to take just one pill should the patient have palpitations and carefully shook one out. She held the pill up and Martha, like a little girl, obediently opened her mouth and let Val put it on her tongue. Her teeth chattered against the glass a bit as Val patiently held the glass of lemonade to her lips.

After seeing that she'd swallowed it, Val straightened and looked at the two silent men who were watching these proceedings with similar helpless expressions on their faces. Her eyes then went to the bureau where she recognised the exotic silk wrap at once.

'Is it Clarice?' she asked, her voice shaken and uncertain.

'Yes, old thing, I'm afraid it is,' Arbie said, swallowing hard and watching her anxiously. 'I'm afraid she's a goner, old girl,' he said softly. 'Sorry and all that, but there's nothing to be done about it. I think you should take Martha into the lounge. Let her lie down or something. The doctor will be here soon, and I'll have to phone for the police. She won't want to have any more upsets just now, so she'd be better off somewhere quiet and out of the way.'

'The police?' Randolph said sharply.

He looked as if he were about to object, but Arbie shot him a quelling look. He had the feeling that Randolph hadn't taken him seriously about the cause of death, and he didn't want the fellow getting in the way and making a nuisance of himself. 'I say, Val,' he swept on instead, 'do you need any help? I'm sure Mr Harrington here will be glad to lend you a hand. Right, old boy?'

But Val was already helping the now thoroughly quiescent Martha to her feet by the simple expedient of putting a hand under one armpit and bringing her up out of the chair – a feat that didn't seem to cause her any difficulty at all.

But then, Val hadn't been a hockey champion at her school for nothing – not to mention her success at tennis, archery and who knew what else.

'No, I've got her,' Val said, and without another word, steered her charge towards the door. Out in the hall, Arbie could hear Millie Penderghast's voice ask sharply what was wrong.

*

As the sound of the women's voices became more muted as they disappeared into the lounge next door, Randolph eyed Arbie warily.

'I say, Swift, what is all this about the police?' he said, beginning to get a stubborn look in his eye. 'Surely this can't be a case for them? I'm sure the doctor will find Miss Harrington died of natural causes. Taken suddenly ill, probably, after all that swimming she does. That's it!' He snapped his fingers. 'She probably overexerted herself or something. And then came back here and had a funny turn. Everyone knows she spent far too much time exercising in the sea. It can't be good for you.'

He seemed set to continue in this vein for some time, but it was not his voice that suddenly filled the air. 'I say, sorry about this, but the blasted electricity has gone off,' Captain Penderghast said, sailing into the room, having been attracted by their voices. 'I'll just nip down to the fuse box and see what's what. Sorry for the inconvenience – I won't be a jiffy.'

Before he could turn towards the cellars, however, Arbie abruptly stopped him. 'No, Captain, don't touch anything down there! I'm afraid it's something more serious than a blown fuse or a downed power line.' He stepped to one side so that the Captain could see behind him.

Captain Penderghast took one look at the woman slumped, unmoving over the desktop, and said blankly. 'Oh Lor'. The missus isn't going to like this.'

*

Someone else who also didn't like 'this' was Detective Inspector Julius Gormley. Somewhere in his early fifties, Arbie gauged, he was a shortish, thickset man, with dark hair and big puppy-dog brown eyes. The eyes seemed to say that he'd been kicked – and for no good reason either – by his master only a few minutes or so ago.

Arbie only had to take one look at his perpetually hangdog expression to feel instantly sorry for the man.

The local constable, who'd arrived from the village within minutes of Arbie's phone call, had taken one look at the situation and had immediately telephoned to his superior for assistance. With him, the Inspector had brought his sergeant, whom he introduced as Thomas Innes. Innes looked to be about twenty years Gormley's junior, and was nearly a foot taller and lanky. A ginger-haired Scot, he had piercing blue eyes and a pale, freckled complexion, and if the Inspector resembled a woebegone pup, he looked more like a police Alsatian ready to sink his teeth into any perpetrator in the vicinity.

Right now, those shrewd blue eyes were peering intently at the bureau drawer.

Captain Penderghast hovered unhappily in the doorway to the reading room. Randolph Harrington had promptly taken himself off to the bar – where he was probably having a stiff whisky right about now, the lucky blighter, Arbie mused enviously. He himself was standing near the open French windows and trying to make himself as invisible as possible. If he just slipped out onto the terrace and shuffled off somewhere, would anyone notice? The thought was tempting. Very tempting.

Val was still next door in the lounge, watching over the stricken Martha. The local doctor was now seeing to her, having somewhat briskly confirmed that the young lady at the bureau was deceased, and pragmatically turning his attention to a patient in need who was still breathing.

'Inspector, there's something odd with this top drawer,' the Sergeant said, peering at said article. 'There are two small holes on one side of it that look as if they've been made recently and . . .' he moved closer and squinted a bit, 'yes, further along I can see something . . . Inspector, there's some sort of gadget in here!' Innes said, his accent slightly thickening with excitement. 'I can see wires too.'

'Well, whatever you do, *don't touch it*,' the Inspector yelped. 'Who knows what's gone wrong here.' He sounded distinctly cross. Arbie, in spite of having only just met the man, suspected that Gormley usually did. 'Mr Penderghast, you're sure the electricity supply is turned off at the mains?' he added nervously.

'Yes, positive,' the Captain said unhappily. 'Cook's

complaining something awful. Says we'll all be eating cold cuts for dinner if it doesn't come back on soon.'

The Inspector ignored this broad hint and reluctantly stepped closer to the body. 'The doctor arrived at the same time as yourself, you said, Constable?' He turned to look at the uniformed man who had been first on the scene.

Constable Hubert McGraw, a rather fat and florid-faced man with friendly watery grey eyes and an abundance of sandy hair, stiffened automatically to attention. Although he was probably similar in age to the Inspector, promotion had never been a priority for him, and Hubert had been content to live all his life in the village and patrol the surrounding countryside, where his biggest problems were usually poachers and drunks turning out after closing time and causing a disturbance.

'Yes, sir, I was just pedalling up the drive when the doc passed me in his Lagonda.'

At this, Arbie's ears perked up. A Lagonda! He'd considered buying himself one of those beauties for some time. Perhaps he should just sneak out and look it over?

The Inspector also brightened a little at this nugget of information. Not that he was in any position to buy such a car himself – his Morris Oxford would have to see him through for many more years to come yet – but because it meant that the local medical man clearly wasn't short of a bob or two. Which, in the Inspector's experience, meant that he'd probably come from money and had gone to a good training hospital, and was thus the sort who knew his onions.

'Did he give you a cause of death?' he asked hopefully.

'Yerse,' the Constable said, sucking the word in through his teeth thoughtfully. 'And he reckons this young man,' he nodded briefly at Arbie, who blinked back nervously at him, 'was right when he said that she'd probably been electrocuted.'

'Is that so?' the Inspector said, fixing Arbie with a firm stare.

'Yerse, sir. The doc, he lifted up the poor young lady's hands and examined her fingers good and proper, he did,' the Constable elaborated with some relish. 'And then he said something else about blood vessels in her eyes. Bursting or something. I didn't like the sound of it. It fair turned my stomach, it did.'

At this, everyone's eyes went to Clarice Fotheringham's burnt digits and then skittered hastily away again.

'Hmph,' the Inspector said. 'We'll have to call in an expert on this sort of thing. This sort of jiggery-pokery is beyond me. I'm happy with my gas lamps.' And so saying, he turned abruptly to Arbie. 'And you are, sir?' he demanded.

Arbie, who'd resumed staring longingly out at the garden, shot the Inspector a quick glance and saw that he was indeed, addressing himself.

'Er, Swift, sir. Inspector, I mean. Arbie Swift. How d'you do.'

'How d'you do,' the policeman responded automatically. 'And are you a medical man too?'

'Who, me?' Arbie said, thoroughly taken aback. 'Good heavens, no.'

'Then how did you know the deceased had been electrocuted, Mr Swift?' the Inspector asked, with a distinct overtone of suspicion in his voice.

Arbie swallowed hard. 'Well, it was a few things, I suppose,' he admitted glumly. 'Something Mrs Van Dyne said about her dancing a jitterbug for one.'

At this, the tall, lanky Sergeant straightened up from his bent-over perusal of the crime scene and joined the Inspector and the Constable in staring at Arbie as if he'd grown another head.

In response, Arbie shifted nervously on his feet. 'Yes, I know, it struck me as damned odd too,' he said defensively.

The Inspector began to look more forlorn and put-upon than ever. Now he began to resemble a dog that had not only been unjustly kicked but had been denied any dinner as well. 'And who exactly is this Mrs Van Dyne?'

'The woman who was here when it happened. At least, I think she was,' Arbie said. 'She might have just been the first one on the scene though. I'm not actually sure of the sequence of events I'm afraid – you'll have to ask her about that yourself. I can only say that when I got here,' he indicated the room with a vague wave of his hand, 'Mr Harrington was standing out in the hall, and an elderly lady was sitting on the stairs. Oh, and Val was with me.' He paused to take a much-needed breath. 'But only Martha Van Dyne was actually in here.'

The Constable opened his notebook and wrote all these names down.

'I see. And where is this lady now?' Gormley asked patiently.

'She's in the lounge next door. She has a weak heart, I think, and the shock gave her a nasty turn. The doctor is with her now,' Arbie informed him.

'That's right, sir,' the Constable confirmed. 'I took a quick look at her myself before you came, like, and she looked proper pasty.'

'You said there were a few things that made you suspect how the lady might have come to her end,' the Inspector said, keeping his eyes fixed on Arbie.

'Yes, mainly Martha's description of how she appeared to be jerking about. She described it as dancing, but I think that's how people who have an electric current running through them react to it. My uncle told me about it once. I'm lucky I didn't touch any live wires or I might have been for it myself,' Arbie explained, breaking out in a cold sweat at the thought.

The Inspector too went a little pale. 'Well, let's skip the, er, dancing reference for now. What else made you think the deceased had received some sort of electric shock?'

'Her fingers. They looked burnt to me,' Arbie said miserably.

'Know a lot about this new-fangled electricity thing, do you then, sir?' the Inspector asked heavily.

'Me? Oh no! No. Well, my uncle's a bit of an amateur inventor. He messes about with bits of this and that – scientific stuff and so on,' Arbie confessed reluctantly. He only hoped the Inspector wouldn't feel the need to call upon his uncle any time soon. He couldn't imagine the two of them would see eye to eye at all. 'He raised me, so I know a bit about various things. But I'm no expert on electricity, I assure you.'

'Ah. Well, we'll see,' the Inspector said, somewhat ominously. 'So, I take it you're a guest at this hotel then, sir?'

'Yes. I arrived just a few days ago. And I've never met any of the people here before that, except Miss Coulton-James, of course,' he added firmly then briefly explained his history with Val.

None of the three police officers, he noted unhappily, seemed impressed by this piece of information.

'On holiday then, sir? Taking advantage of the fine late summer weather?' Somehow, the Inspector made it sound like an accusation. As if honest and decent men had no business lounging around at the seaside, taking their ease.

It therefore pleased Arbie inordinately to be able to put him right. 'As a matter of fact, no, Inspector. I'm here because of my work.' Well, he thought silently, he was now that Val was here!

The Inspector looked surprised – insultingly so, Arbie thought sourly.

For a moment, Gormley regarded him thoughtfully. The handsome, indolent youth in his Oxford bags and expensive shoes had struck him instantly as one of life's useless idlers. Yet one more 'bright young thing' with more money than sense.

His eyes narrowed in suspicion. 'What line of work are you in, sir, might I ask?'

Arbie shuffled his feet again. 'I'm writing a book.'

'Oh,' the Inspector said flatly, looking enlightened – and justified – in his scepticism. 'I see.'

Arbie felt himself flush a little. He had half a mind to tell the man that he was the author of a best-selling tome, thank you very much, and adored by half the reading public of Great Britain. Who, moreover, were eagerly awaiting the publication of his next effort. At the same time, he was unhappily aware that he could do no such thing. If there was one thing that a public-school education taught you (maybe the only thing, come to think of the state of some of his teachers) was that a chap never boasted. About anything. It simply wasn't the done thing.

It was at that moment that Val appeared in the doorway.

She took one look at Arbie's face, then turned to coolly appraise the other three men in the room. The lowly Constable felt his backbone stiffen a little. Although the young lady was a pretty sight, something about the expression in her cornflower blue eyes reminded him of his Sunday school teacher when he was a nipper. And a right tartar, she'd been!

The lanky Scot felt himself flush as the impressive tall blonde woman regarded him from head to toe, and reminded himself staunchly that he was happily married.

The Inspector gave her his usual woebegone expression that almost made Val smile. But not quite.

'These are the police, I take it?' Val said, her voice imperial and yet somehow polite. 'Splendid. Arbie, I hope you've been making yourself useful?' she demanded.

At this, all three men looked at Arbie, but this time with pity in their eyes.

Arbie shuffled his feet. 'Doin' my best, old thing. You know me.'

Val did. That was the problem. With a sigh, she walked in, closing the door behind her, and turned to the sad-faced man who was clearly the ranking officer, and held out her hand. 'Valentina Coulton-James. I'm Mr Swift's literary assistant.'

At this, Arbie's mouth fell open.

'Now, how can I help you?' she swept on. 'I expect you want to know all about what's happened to . . . Clarice?' For all her show of cool efficiency, her voice faltered a little over the name of the dead woman.

'You expect right, Miss Coulton-James,' the Inspector said resignedly. 'I've been told that the lady who, er, did all the screaming is next door in the lounge? Perhaps we should all retire there then,' he added kindly. For it hadn't escaped his notice that the young lady, formidable though she appeared on the surface, was keeping her eyes averted from the still form draped over the bureau.

Which might be an indication of nothing more than an attack of understandable nerves.

Then again, he mused thoughtfully, he didn't yet know exactly what he was dealing with here. And until he had proof that there was nothing suspicious about this fatality, he could rule nothing out.

Could it be that the young lady kept her eyes averted because she had something to feel guilty about?

CHAPTER TEN

On the way through the hall, the Inspector left them to detour to the telephone booth, where he requested that an expert in electrical gadgetry be sent to the Dashwood House Hotel, then led Val and Arbie into the next room.

Here the doctor was just closing his black leather medical bag. Small, dapper and seemingly fizzing with energetic vitality, he was also slightly cynical-looking and brusquely informed the Inspector that his patient had had a bit of a turn due to shock. This shock had, in its turn, exacerbated his patient's minor heart condition, leaving the lady in a rather weakened state.

'You can talk to her for a bit if you must, but no hard questioning for now,' he warned. 'She should really be in bed. A little nap would do her the world of good,' he added. Already on his way to the door, he doffed his hat half-heartedly to Val and was gone.

'Nice bedside manner he's got, I don't think,' the Inspector said with a sigh. He looked at Martha Van Dyne hopefully, who was lying full length on the sofa, and the sigh quickly turned into a slight smile. He'd always had a weakness for redheads. His own lady wife had been blessed with auburn hair. 'I'm Inspector Gormley, Mrs Van Dyne. I understand you've had a very nasty shock?'

As he spoke softly, he drew up a chair and sat down beside

her. Behind him, the large Constable, who had trailed after them into the lounge, drew out his notebook and awaited developments. Arbie gave a discreet nod of his head, first towards Val and then to two neighbouring armchairs, and they made themselves comfortable.

'It was awful,' Martha said, her voice calm now, if a little faint.

'Can you just tell me, if you can, what happened? Try not to upset yourself though,' the Inspector added hastily. He didn't relish being hauled over the carpet by his superiors if his most important witness had another turn and had to be admitted to the local hospital.

Martha sighed. 'Well, poor Clarice came inside all dripping wet from her morning swim. She told me she'd had her towel stolen . . .' Carefully, Martha told her tale about seeing the local children stealing things before, and how she'd told Clarice this, her voice only faltering when she began to get to the part where Clarice had sat down at the bureau to write her letter of complaint.

'Then I don't really understand what happened next,' Martha said plaintively. 'I saw her reach out to pull the long top drawer out – that's where the hotel keeps its writing paper and envelopes and so on. And then suddenly she began to, well . . . I don't know quite how to describe it. She sort of jerked and jiggered about, like she was doing one of these awful modern dances you see the younger set doing nowadays in the nightclubs – only she was still sitting down.'

'Did she say anything? Cry out perhaps?'

'No. No, I don't think so,' Martha said, frowning as she tried to picture the scene. 'No, I'm sure she didn't. I think I called out to her, to ask what on earth she was doing or something, and then there was a sort of fizzing sound and a dull pop and then she just went all limp and collapsed facedown onto the desk.'

That must have been when the electricity short-circuited, Arbie thought.

From the facts he'd been able to glean so far, it was becoming clear that someone must have set up a deadly booby trap inside the bureau and connected it to the electric current. And common sense told him that that someone almost certainly had to be connected in some way, to the hotel. It was practically inconceivable to him that a total stranger had just wandered into a random building to just as randomly set up a diabolical killing device in a bureau drawer.

Which meant, he mused glumly, that there was a killer amongst them.

And since a very large portion of the hotel's guest list was taken up with the engagement party, it had to be odds on, he supposed unhappily, that the killer was someone in the Hythe-Gill contingent. He could hardly countenance that any of the unaffiliated guests, like that nice old couple the Babbacombes for instance, were homicidal maniacs who just happened to have a penchant for killing any old stranger.

No, someone at the Dashwood must have a reason for wanting Clarice dead. And what were the usual motives for that? Revenge, money, love or fear. And for the victim to have had a chance to implant any of those emotions in someone, you surely had to look at those closest to her – and who were on the spot. And that meant, as far as Arbie could see, a friend or a relative of Val's best friend, Beatrice.

Which was going to upset Val considerably.

What's more, Arbie didn't think it would take the Inspector long to come to the same conclusions. Which would mean serious and intrusive questioning lay ahead for all concerned. And once those closest to the dead girl realised they were all suspects, how long then, before suspicion and paranoia followed? Soon, people would be scared to be alone with those they'd known, liked and trusted for years.

As Martha continued giving her story to the Inspector, Arbie's thoughts ranged far and wide – and none of them were happy ones. Surely nobody would suspect Beatrice herself? The poor girl's engagement party was already ruined, and her happiness blighted. Right now, she and all the others were in town, shopping and being light-hearted, happily ignorant of the tragedy awaiting them back at the hotel. But Clarice was one of Beatrice's best friends. Beatrice wouldn't have any reason for wanting to see her dead, would she?

But somebody must have done. He knew that Clarice wasn't exactly the most popular person in the tight-knit group. She'd had an unfortunate way of making it clear that she felt herself a cut above the others. And was perhaps rather careless about her off-hand remarks, which had sometimes caused annoyance or offence. But that was no reason to *kill* her, was it?

Arbie sighed and turned his thoughts to Randolph Harrington. Apart from the fact that he'd been in the hall nearby when Martha had started to scream, was that any reason to suspect him more than any of the others? Arbie couldn't for the life of him think why it should. He didn't think that Randolph and Clarice had something going on between them, but he made a mental note to pass this by Val. *She* was bound to know.

Could the motive be financial? He had the feeling that the dead girl had come from a well-to-do-family. Had she any money of her own to leave? And if so, had she made a will? Did anybody here inherit? It seemed unlikely.

What else . . . His thoughts came to a halt as the people around him began to stir, and he forced himself to pay attention as Val rose and went across to help Martha stand.

'Well, that's all for now, Mrs Van Dyne,' the Inspector was saying. 'You go up to your room and have a lie-down. And thank you for all your help. I'm sure I wish most witnesses were as cooperative as yourself.'

'Thank you,' Martha said, with something of her grand manner returning.

'Do you want me to come up with you?' Val asked gently. 'See you settled? Bring you some tea?' But Martha shook her head. 'No, no, thank you. I'm feeling much better now. The doctor left me with a mild sedative – I think I'll take it and have a little sleep. I just feel a little weak about the knees, that's all.'

'Constable, escort Mrs Van Dyne to her room,' the Inspector commanded crisply, and the big, sandy-haired man snapped to attention. Self-consciously offering her his arm, he walked her slowly out, as if fearing she might shatter at any moment. The others watched silently.

Val returned to her chair. The Inspector, who had risen with the lady, sat down again as he turned to the two younger members of the party.

'Now then, I'll just have your details. Miss Coulton-James, we'll start with you. Your address please.'

When Val cited the vicarage at Maybury-in-the-Marsh as her residence, and confirmed that her father was the vicar, Arbie was silently amused to see Gormley sit up a little straighter and regard her with a kinder eye. Having now got his measure, when the Inspector turned to him, Arbie let it slip that Val's father was the younger son of titled gentry, and that he himself had lived next door to her all his life.

He firmly ignored Val's admonishing look at this bit of social snobbery. If she couldn't see the writing on the wall, he certainly could.

'So, what can you tell me about Miss Fotheringham?' the Inspector asked Val. 'And how she came to be staying here at the hotel?'

Val obligingly explained about Beatrice's party tomorrow night, and how, as future bridesmaids, she and Clarice had been invited to attend the fancy-dress engagement celebrations. She had to admit she didn't know Clarice that well but had known Beatrice and her parents for many years.

The Inspector listened, nodding now and then. Then he turned to Arbie.

'And are you also a member of the Hythe-Gill party?'

'No, Inspector. I arrived some days before in order to research my book. As I said.'

'Ah yes, so you did. And, er, what research would this be?'

'I write a travel guide,' Arbie said modestly. 'You know, where to stay for a perfect holiday, and all that.'

'With ghosts,' Val put in.

This, not surprisingly, made the Inspector's eyes boggle a bit. 'I beg your pardon?' he said.

'Ghosts. Arbie here wrote *The Gentleman's Guide to Ghost-Hunting* and has been commissioned to write a second volume,' Val elaborated.

'I've read that!' The voice belonged to the big PC, who had returned from upstairs. 'My missus bought it, because her book club was doing it. Very took with it, they all was. Me too. I don't often read books, but I enjoyed that one.'

Arbie shot him a beaming smile. The Inspector looked at his underling and sighed heavily.

'Very funny it was too, sir,' the PC said, turning to the Inspector. 'Some of them stories this gentleman told about his attempts to find and see ghosts and whatnot made me laugh out loud,' the PC swept on, oblivious to his superior's unimpressed visage. 'Many a night I chortled over a chapter or two. Not that we could afford to stay at any of them places you mentioned, Mr Swift. Me and the missus always goes to this guest house in Bog—'

'Perhaps we can get on with the matter in hand?' the Inspector interrupted firmly, and the PC retired, abashed. 'So, I'm a little confused. You say, Miss Coulton-James, that you came as a part of the Hythe-Gill party. And Mr Swift says he came to work and hadn't met any of the other guests before. And yet, you say you're Mr Swift's literary assistant. So, are you here to celebrate Miss Beatrice Hythe-Gill's party, or work for Mr Swift?'

'Both,' Val said simply.

The Inspector gave a mental shrug and gave them up as a bad job. 'Well, thank you for your help.' He said the last word uncertainly, and waved a hand vaguely at the door. 'You may go for now, but I may want to ask you some more questions later.'

Arbie needed no second bidding and was out of his seat in an instant. Val followed on more slowly and with some reluctance – a fact that was not lost on Arbie.

He really hoped Val wasn't going to do anything he might regret.

The Inspector watched them go with his usual woebegone expression, then rose ponderously to his feet.

'Right, Constable, go next door and stand guard over the deceased. I want no one entering the crime scene until the expert I've called in arrives. Tell Sergeant Innes I want him to meet me in the victim's room to help me search it. I'll get a key from the proprietors here. I want a word with them too.'

The Constable left smartly to do his bidding.

*

He found the owner behind the desk. She looked pale and unhappy, as well she might. Having a guest die on the premises must be a hotelier's worst nightmare.

The moment he introduced himself, she launched into a speech. 'I'm sure it can't have been our fault,' she said, her voice anguished. 'The people we had come to fit the electrics were top in their field. We only used the best. I can't understand it. I was assured electricity was all perfectly safe, and we've had no trouble with it at all until now,' she all but wailed.

A handsome woman, she was wringing her hands and her eyes were bright with suppressed tears. 'Do you think the newspapers will get a hold of this?' she asked, her voice fraught.

The Inspector couldn't help but feel sorry for her. A nice little woman, this, and cut from good cloth, if he was any judge. 'I can't say, Mrs, er . . . ?'

'Penderghast. My husband, the Captain, and I are horrified – *horrified* that such a thing should happen here at the Dashwood. Oh, Inspector, do say that you can keep this ghastly business from the press.'

'I can assure you, madam, that neither myself nor any of my underlings will be speaking to any reporters,' he promised. But silently added to himself that once an inquest was held, she would be very lucky indeed if some journalist or other didn't pick up on it. Even in this out-of-the-way little seaside village.

'Can I have the key to Miss Fotheringham's room, please, madam? Have the maids cleaned it yet, do you know?' he inquired.

'Oh, yes, they will have done,' Mrs Penderghast said absently, reaching behind her to extract the appropriate key. The Inspector sighed at this bad news, but he'd been half-expecting it. 'Here it is, but you probably won't need it,' the unhappy woman said, proffering the brass key. 'Most of our guests leave their doors unlocked. They keep their valuables in the safe, you see.'

The Inspector nodded, took the key and thanked her, informing her that he'd want to interview her later. And added that he'd have to talk to all the guests at some point in the next few hours.

This warning set Millie's hand-wringing gestures into new convolutions, and she watched him miserably as he climbed the stairs out of sight. She foresaw a mass exodus of guests from her hotel the moment the news got out.

Her only consolation was that it was late in the season anyway.

Clarice had been given one of the hotel's best rooms, and from what Martha Van Dyne had told the Inspector of the dead woman's personality, he assumed that she would have insisted on nothing less.

As he opened the door and walked in, Innes faithfully following behind him, he paused to take in the attractive room.

'How the other 'alf live, eh, Sergeant?' he murmured, looking at the satin sheets, the fresh flowers on the dressing table, the fine wallpaper and lush carpeting. The place looked neat, tidy and immaculately turned out, all except for one little oddity.

The Inspector spotted it at once. In the middle of the crease-free floral bedspread was a sheet of folded paper.

He walked to it curiously and, leaning over the mattress, picked it up.

As he unfolded it, he was vaguely expecting to see an overlooked piece of the victim's mail, perhaps. Or a keepsake from a theatre programme from some play she had attended in town and then discarded. Or maybe some advertisement for a local attraction she intended to visit.

He certainly wasn't expecting it to be a death threat.

CHAPTER ELEVEN

As the Inspector read it, he drew his breath in sharply through his teeth, and the near-silent whistle brought the keen-eared Sergeant to his side.

The Inspector read it through twice, then silently handed it over to his underling, who read it out loud, his Scottish sibilants lending the missive unneeded extra drama.

> **Hussies like you always get what's coming to them. Sooner or later.**

'My, my,' the lanky Sergeant said, shaking his head. 'The lassie certainly had enemies, didn't she? And carefully printed, so no help from a handwriting expert to be had there. And it looks like standard fountain pen ink, Inspector. And on the hotel's own headed notepaper, so anyone could have just helped themselves to it.' He tut-tutted over it for a while. 'This must have put the wind up her a bit. It's a wonder to me that she went off swimming this morning as if she hadn't a care in the world. I know our witnesses all agree that she swam like a fish and loved the water, but you'd have thought that going out alone to the beach and then going unprotected into the sea after receiving *this*,' he rattled the piece of paper significantly, 'would be the last thing on her mind. Unless she knew who wrote it, and didn't take it seriously?'

The Inspector shrugged. 'Either that, or she simply never had the chance to find it and read it. Most people, after receiving nasty poison pen letters like this, either bunch them up and chuck them in the bin, or else they put them away somewhere private to brood over later. I doubt many of them simply leave them lying about on the bed, willy-nilly.' He walked to the door, opened it and stood looking thoughtfully up and down the deserted landing outside. Then he returned and – somewhat belatedly thinking about fingerprints – carefully folded the paper back in half and put it in his pocket for safekeeping. 'Innes, go and find the maid who did the room this morning. Ask her what time she'd finished in here and if she noticed anything out of the ordinary.'

The Sergeant nodded and left, allowing the Inspector to begin a neat, methodical search of the dead woman's domain. He found a small pile of invitations to dine locally in the drawer of the vanity unit, along with the usual woman's accessories. A book – a rather scandalous tome that was currently in favour with those who didn't possess a nervous disposition – rested on the bedside table, along with a black satin sleeping mask and a fine hairnet. Feathery mule-type slippers had been pushed back further along the wall. No doubt, Clarice Fotheringham had expected to slip back into them tonight – but now they had an abandoned, sad look. As if they knew their owner would never use them again.

Her clothes were neatly assembled in various dresser drawers and the heavy burr-walnut wardrobe, and apart from noting their quality and quantity, he found nothing much of interest in any of them. Her purse – a reticule that had been beaded in an intricate art deco design – had more money in it than he thought wise, but other than that, there was nothing remarkable to be found in the dead woman's room at all.

Innes came back. 'The girl says she did her usual rounds,

sir. Apparently, all the maids wait until the guests have gone down to breakfast, then nip in and do the necessary. She can't say for sure, but she's confident she was finished in here at least ten minutes before she saw the young lady return to her room. I asked her if she'd seen her leave again, and she says no, but another maid *did* see her from the window when she was crossing the garden lawns with all her swimming bits and bobs at around a quarter to ten or so. Of course, at this distance, she couldn't tell if the lady seemed upset or was her usual self.'

'Hmmm,' the Inspector said, staring vaguely out of the window.

'You're thinking whoever left the poison pen letter here did so after she left for the beach, sir?'

'I think it more than likely,' Gormley agreed. 'Do some more general asking around of the maids and see if any of them remember seeing someone either going into or lurking around Miss Fotheringham's door at any time this morning.'

'Yes, sir. Anything else?'

'Not up here, at any rate. I think we'd better get on and start questioning the guests who are in the hotel now. According to what Mrs Van Dyne said, most of them are scattered about in various nearby towns, amusing themselves buying who knows what and enjoying themselves. Join me in the lounge when you've finished with the staff.'

'Sir.'

*

Charles Morris entered the lounge ten minutes later, looking intrigued. 'Hello. Mrs Penderghast tells me you wanted to speak to me? I gather there's been some sort of tragedy?' he began amiably.

The Inspector merely nodded at a chair and watched as the other man sat down in it. He saw a well set up chap in his middle years, dressed in that comfortable style that instantly told you he was worth a bob or two.

Gormley already knew, after coming down and having a brief chat with Captain Penderghast about his current guests, that this man was 'something in antiques' and had no connection with the engagement party whatsoever. The Captain thought he enjoyed a spot of fishing and played the odd round of golf at the local course now and then, but other than that, wasn't sure how he spent the rest of his days. 'I think he's just here to have a general breather, Inspector,' had been his verdict.

With that in mind, the Inspector began to probe delicately. 'Mr Morris, isn't it?'

'Yes, that's me,' the fair-haired man said with a brief smile. 'And you are?'

'Inspector Gormley, sir.'

'Inspector, eh?' Charles repeated thoughtfully. 'Sounds serious. I saw what I thought was a doctor chappie come and go. Has one of our number taken ill?'

Gormley inclined his head but wasn't to be drawn. 'Can you tell me when you arrived at the Dashwood, Mr Morris?'

If the other man was put out at not having his curiosity satisfied, he showed no sign of it. Instead he crossed his legs at the ankle to make himself more comfortable, and seemed to do a quick mental calculation. 'Last Sunday, it would have been. I had a leisurely motor down in the old jalopy and arrived in time for dinner. Jolly good dinner, it was too.'

'Any reason for choosing this particular spot, sir?'

'No, not really.' Charles frowned a little. 'I just happened to read in some magazine or other that Galton-next-the-Sea was a charming, unspoilt place that was tipped to be the up-and-coming thing and that a new and rather splendid hotel had just opened its doors there. And since I haven't been down to this part of the coast in donkey's years, and the weather had turned so warm, I just fancied a little holiday. A sort of spur-of-the-moment thing. You know how it is.'

The Inspector, who had to book and arrange his holidays well in advance, with both his superiors, his lady wife and their usual seaside landlady, most definitely did *not* know how it was. However, he felt no real envy of this man. Each to his own, as his old dad used to say.

'Do you know the proprietors, sir?' he tried next.

'The Penderghasts? No, no, nothing like that. A nice pair though – both of 'em. The Captain's a bit of a raconteur, you know, runs a jolly bar and all that. And the little woman keeps a very fine establishment. Recommend it to anyone. Not at all surprised that that writer johnny has come down here to do a write-up on it for that book of his.'

'Mr Swift. Yes,' the Inspector said, tonelessly. 'I understand he arrived the day after you?'

'Did he? Yes, yes, that sounds about right.'

'And then you started to be joined a day or two later by this large engagement party contingent, I understand?'

Charles nodded. 'Yes. And between you and me, Inspector, I have to say I was happy about it. Although I do enjoy a bit of peace and quiet when I'm on holiday, it's always nice to have the ladies around and see a bit of life about the place and so on. I think ladies really do add a delightful spice to life, don't you, Inspector? I've certainly found their company very appealing.' He grinned, a touch too wolfishly for the policeman's liking. 'Still . . .' He shrugged elegantly.

The Inspector, whose experience had made him a fair judge of humanity, made a neat little notation in his notebook. *'Charles Morris – fancies himself a ladies' man.'* 'Were you acquainted with any of these people, sir?' he asked next.

'Me? Oh no. Never met any of them before in my life.'

'What was your impression of Miss Fotheringham, sir?'

Charles sat up a little straighter in his chair and uncrossed his legs again. 'Miss Fotheringham? You mean the rather striking girl with the black hair? Is it she who, er . . . has been taken ill then?' he asked delicately.

'I'm afraid it's rather more serious than that, sir. The young lady is dead.'

Charles swallowed hard. 'Oh dear,' he said inadequately. And then shot the Inspector a quick glance. 'I never met Miss Fotheringham before making her acquaintance here,' he said firmly.

'I've no reason to suppose that you have, sir,' the Inspector said placidly. But naturally, he'd make it his business that all the hotel guests' backgrounds were checked out thoroughly. 'You were about to tell me your impressions of her, sir,' he prompted.

'Was I? I'm not so sure that I was, Inspector, you know,' Charles said quietly. 'Especially now that I know the young lady is no longer with us.'

Gormley sighed heavily and looked even more woebegone than ever. 'I'm sure it's all very well not wanting to say anything critical of the dead, sir. But we have reason to suspect foul play.'

At this, Charles Morris went rather pale.

'And it's our duty to investigate, of course,' the Inspector swept on. 'And for this, we need the help of the public, and it's their duty to aid us in any way they can.'

'Oh yes, yes, I quite see that,' Charles muttered unhappily.

'And any inquiry of this nature always starts with the victim,' Gormley swept on as if the other man had not spoken. 'So I'm sure you can understand why we need to find out all we can about Miss Fotherington, sir. What she was like, had she argued with anyone recently? Was she a gossip or a snoop or maybe had a gambling habit? That sort of thing.'

'Good gracious, what a sordid world you must live in, Inspector,' the businessman said faintly. 'And I'm afraid I can't really help you at all. Like I said, I never met the young lady until now.'

'But you must have formed some impression of her, sir? You strike me as a man of the world. You've knocked about a fair bit, I dare say, and in your business, you must have met all sorts. I'm sure you notice things. Married, are you, sir?' he suddenly shot at him, out of the blue.

'I'm a widower,' Charles returned flatly.

'Sorry to hear that, sir,' the Inspector said, a shade perfunctorily. 'Would you say Miss Fotheringham was popular? With her set, I mean?'

Charles visibly hesitated, then sighed. 'Well, I don't know about *that*, Inspector. I may be wrong, but it seemed to me that she had a rather unfortunate way about her. A sort of air of superiority that . . . well, once or twice, I saw some of the other women in the party exchange glances with one another at some of the things she said. You know how women are. As if she was getting on their nerves a bit.'

The Inspector nodded. 'Who was her closest confidante, would you say?'

'Oh, the bride-to-be, Inspector,' Charles said without hesitation.

The Inspector duly made a note. 'Now, this morning. You came down to breakfast at the usual time?' For ten minutes or so, Charles informed him about the various conversations he could remember occurring over the bacon and eggs and was just finishing this account when Sergeant Innes joined them.

'And this is when most of the guests started to disperse to go off on their various jaunts?' the Inspector was saying.

'Yes.'

'But you didn't leave the premises?'

'No. I've already explored the local towns and didn't particularly feel like doing it again. Instead, I was going to saunter down to the village later, have a pint, watch the boats come in, that sort of thing. But for an hour or so before doing that I was content to just sit in the garden with the papers.'

'You saw Miss Fotheringham leave to go to the beach?' the Inspector asked, watching him closely.

Charles didn't seem to realise that this might be construed as a loaded question, for he merely shrugged. 'Yes, I think so. That is, I vaguely remember seeing a female figure carrying a large straw bag and a towel and whatnot, passing by on the other side of the flower beds. I assume that would have been Miss Fotheringham. But I was doing the crossword, and didn't really take much notice, so it might have been someone else.'

'And did you notice her come back?' Unfortunately, Martha Van Dyne hadn't been able to be accurate about the time, but it hadn't been hard to get a rough estimate of the time of death from the testimony of Mr Swift and the vicar's daughter, who'd come running at the first sound of screaming. 'This would have been some time around noon, sir,' he prompted.

Charles frowned. 'Not sure that I did, Inspector, now that you mention it. I may have had my hat over my eyes, keeping out the glare of the sun, you know.'

The Inspector nodded and made another neat note in his book. *'Mr Morris probably having forty winks. Too vain to admit it.'*

'So you were still in the garden then? Did you not hear the screaming, sir?'

Charles shifted a little on his seat. 'Oh – yes! Now *that* I remember. I was over by the tennis courts, I think, so I wouldn't have seen anyone coming back from the beach. The courts are surrounded by tall pines, you see. I did hear some odd sounds, but wasn't quite sure what it was. The seagulls can make an awful racket, can't they? Honestly, they can sound otherworldly sometimes. The cries they make, I mean . . .' he trailed off uncomfortably.

The Sergeant's lips twitched at this, but he wisely remained silent. It didn't stop him from thinking though – and what he was thinking was that this witness hadn't been in any hurry to get back and be mixed up in anything unpleasant.

'Do you usually find tennis courts so fascinating, sir?' the Inspector asked dryly.

'Oh, I just thought I might see if I could get up a doubles match some time and wanted to check out the clay.' Charles met the Inspector's gaze with a bland one of his own.

The Inspector knew fallow ground when he came across it and changed course abruptly. 'Do you know if Miss Fotheringham argued with anyone whilst she was here, sir?'

'Not as far as I'm aware.'

'Did you get the impression that she was fond of any particular person here, then? Mr Harrington, for instance?' The Inspector wasn't about to lose sight of the fact that Randolph Harrington had been right on the spot, at the appropriate time.

'No, I don't think so,' Charles said. 'I got the feeling he just wasn't interested. Or maybe it was the other way round, and he wasn't her type.' He gave a helpless shrug.

'Was Captain Penderghast her type, do you think?'

'Mine host?' Charles Morris said, this time with a genuine grin. 'I doubt it. Besides, if he was, his lady wife would nip it in the bud fairly smartish, let me tell you. I shouldn't underestimate Millie Penderghast if I was you, Inspector. She's the real brains and force behind this place, you mark my words,' he said, indicating their surroundings.

'And did *you* find Miss Fotheringham attractive, sir?' the Inspector asked mildly. But if he expected to disconcert his witness into revealing anything of interest, he was quickly disappointed.

Charles merely grinned again and said, 'Oh my, yes. I should think most red-blooded men would. But I was wise enough to leave well alone. Miss Fotheringham struck me as the kind of young woman who could look after herself well enough, and not the sort to be particularly kind to any of her suitors.'

'And did she have many suitors, sir?' Gormley asked, now very interested indeed. When an attractive young lady was murdered – if indeed she *had* been murdered – then you had to look long and hard at any available and jealous young men.

'Oh, I'm sure she did,' Charles said laconically. 'But you'd have to ask her closest friends for details of that nature!'

*

When Charles was finally dismissed, the Sergeant was sent out and returned with Randolph Harrington.

Unlike his self-possessed predecessor, this man looked clearly ill at ease, and when asked to sit down, perched nervously on the edge of the seat.

'Mr Harrington,' Gormley began amiably. 'Can you tell me what you were doing in the hall around noon today, and exactly what it was that you saw and heard?'

Randolph nodded and cleared his throat. 'Yes, of course. I'd just come down from my room . . .'

Not wanting him to get into his stride too quickly, the Inspector decided to interrupt him. Sometimes, when a witness was jittery, there could be more reason for it than merely the usual, standard wariness around the police. And if this man was about to start telling fibs, it was easier to pick them out if he wasn't allowed to get his story out pat. If, indeed, that was what he was trying to do.

'Sorry, I should have asked before. Can you tell me what time you came down to breakfast this morning?' he said with a smile. 'My sergeant needs to take a full statement from everyone at the hotel about their activities today.'

Instantly, Randolph looked at the tall redheaded man who was poised with a pencil hovering over his notebook. 'Really, is that necessary, Inspector?' he complained pettishly. 'I can't see how anything I did could be relevant. I know nothing about this business.'

Gormley shrugged, but his eyes had sharpened. Now why should the witness be reluctant to go into details? 'If you wouldn't mind, sir. It's purely routine, we'll be asking everyone the same, not just you,' he cajoled. 'Now, you came down when . . . ?'

Randolph sighed. 'Around eight, I think. Maybe a little earlier. I didn't look at my watch.'

'No, sir, no reason why you should,' the Inspector agreed comfortably. 'Did you breakfast alone?'

'Yes, that is, I sat at one of the tables for two, and nobody joined me. Other tables were set for four or six, and those, naturally were used by family members of the Hythe-Gills.'

'Nice to catch up with relatives, I'm sure,' Gormley murmured. 'And after you ate?'

'I went upstairs to, er, use the facilities and so on.'

'And then?' the Inspector persisted.

'Then I went off on a bit of a jaunt. You know, as you do, when you come away to somewhere new.' The younger man was beginning to sound more and more exasperated, but the Inspector would have bet a week's wages that he trying to use impatience as a cover for something else.

Gormley merely nodded, his face giving nothing away. 'Where did you go?'

'Go? Oh, nowhere special. Just took a ride, found a nice view, went for a bit of a walk. Just passing the time, you know.' He shrugged, somewhat elaborately.

'And you were alone, Mr Harrington?' he asked. For now,

the Inspector thought that he might just have found the root of the man's reluctance to fully cooperate, and it made him smile inwardly. For Randolph Harrington wouldn't be the first young man reluctant to admit that he'd been escorting a young lady to a private spot, far away from inquisitive eyes.

Perhaps something about his tone of voice sounded suggestive, or maybe he'd touched some other nerve, but a slight flush stained Harrington's high cheekbones and he looked, for the first time, more annoyed than nervous. 'No, Inspector. I was with Alexander, as it happens,' he said, a definite note of defiance in his voice now.

'Alexander?' the Inspector repeated, a touch surprised to discover his deductions had been way off course.

'Mr Hythe-Gill. His daughter is going to marry my best friend, Ernie,' Randolph clarified stiffly.

'Oh yes, Mr Samplestone. He was out this morning, no doubt with his fiancée?'

Randolph made something of a show of shrugging. 'So I believe. Most of the engagement party went off to the local towns. To do a bit of shopping and have some lunch, maybe take a boat trip or what have you.'

'Sounds very jolly.' The Inspector nodded, then added keenly, 'But you didn't fancy joining them, sir?'

'No. Not really my thing. Not that I want to sound like an old fuddy-duddy or anything, but a chap can have too much of youthful high jinks, you know.'

'I understand, sir. So you decided on something more quiet. Had you arranged with Mr Hythe-Gill to go out together this morning beforehand or was it a spur-of-the-moment decision?'

For a moment, the Inspector was sure that he saw a flicker of real alarm cross the other man's face. Although why such a seemingly innocuous question should cause such a reaction was hard to fathom. Unless, the Inspector mused craftily, for some reason this rather self-contained young man was worried that any answer he might be forced to give wouldn't tally with that of Mr Hythe-Gill, when he was asked the same question.

'Er, we arranged it all yesterday, as a matter of fact. As a father of the bride-to-be so to speak, Alexander was glad of a few moments' peace and quiet, I think. Although it was his wife and daughter who were responsible for arranging the party, poor old Alex has come in for his fair share of it. I think all this endless talk of costumes and music and food and so on was wearing a bit thin for him. A chap can get fed up with too much fuss, don't you agree?'

The Inspector nodded in agreement, but he was thinking that that was a lot of explanation for something that could have been summed up in just a few words. In his experience, people who talked too much were trying to distract your attention from something else.

He made a mental note to have someone check out both Harrington and Hythe-Gill most thoroughly.

'So, you left on this morning's expedition at what time?' he pressed on.

Again, the other man shrugged unhelpfully. 'Couldn't say for sure. Somewhere around half past nine or quarter to ten at a guess.'

'And you came back?'

'Half past eleven maybe?' he tossed out uncertainly.

'And presumably you separated once you got the hotel?'

'Yes. I went up to my room. Alexander only dropped me off here and then carried on to meet up with his wife and daughter for lunch somewhere.'

'So he never came back into the hotel at all?'

'No,' Randolph said firmly.

'I see, sir, thank you. That's very helpful. So – you went up to your room, and came down a little while later? Is that the ticket?'

Randolph nodded, casting a nervous glance towards the Sergeant who was busy scribbling down his replies.

'And what happened then, sir?'

'Well, I'd just got to the bottom of the stairs and was crossing towards the hall table to pick up a paper, when I heard this awful screaming. I just . . . Well . . . for a moment, I just froze to the spot. It was so unexpected, you see.'

'Indeed.'

Again, perhaps sensing criticism or scepticism, a faint red stain came over Randolph Harrington's cheekbones. 'I can assure you, Inspector, the Dashwood isn't the kind of place where you expect . . . well . . . goings-on. Of any kind. And a loud scream here is as out of place as . . . as . . .' But here the young man seemed unable to find a suitable example.

'And then what happened, sir?' Gormley said encouragingly.

'Well, that writer fellow came sprinting in through the door and dashed past me, followed by that charming blonde girl he seems to be going around with. They both disappeared into the reading room, and that's when I went in as well, to see if they needed assistance, and saw . . .'

For a moment, the young man could only swallow hard. Then he seemed to get himself in hand, and his chin came up. 'I saw a young lady collapsed at the writing bureau, and Mrs Van Dyne being comforted by . . . Miss Coulton-James! I remember her name now.'

He swallowed hard again, and then spread his hands helplessly. 'At some point the Captain came in to say that the electricity had gone off, and the writer fellow . . . No, can't recall his name at the moment . . . Anyway, he asked me to telephone for the doctor. And so I did. And then you arrived at some point and . . . well, that's it, I'm afraid. I'm not much use as a witness. Sorry. But it's all been a bit of a shock. I mean, the war was . . . well, that was one thing, but pretty young girls dying at a top-notch hotel like this . . . Well, it sort of makes a chap all flummoxed.'

As if running out of air and words simultaneously, Randolph slumped back in his chair. 'Is that all?' he asked hopefully.

'Not quite, sir. Did you see anyone coming into or out of the hotel at this time? Either in the hall, leaving or entering by the open front door, or going into or out of the reading room?'

'No. I'm sure I didn't,' Randolph said firmly.

'You didn't see either Mrs Van Dyne or the deceased talking in the hall or going into the reading room?'

'No,' Randolph Harrington said flatly.

'Thank you, sir,' Gormley said mildly. 'And just how well did you know the deceased?'

'Clarice? Hardly at all. I'm Ernie's friend, you see, and until he met and got fond of Beatrice, I didn't know any of that particular set. I think I must have met Clarice four or five times all told, at parties or clubs, that sort of thing.'

'I see. And did you find the lady attractive, sir?'

At this, Randolph glared at the Inspector with unquestionable disdain. 'Can't say I did, Inspector. No. Too flash for me. Too hard-bitten. I prefer ladies who are rather, er, more demure in nature. Now, if that's all, I really must be getting along. In point of fact, I could do with a stiff drink, if that's all the same to you?' he added in definite challenge.

But the Inspector merely waved a hand airily. 'Of course, sir. If I weren't on duty, I wouldn't mind one myself,' he said equitably.

After shooting the policeman a suspicious last glance to check that he wasn't having his leg pulled – Randolph nodded curtly and left.

Both policemen watched him go in silence.

'There's something he's not happy about, sir,' the Sergeant said flatly. 'And I don't mean about having to look at a dead girl.'

'I know what you mean, Innes,' the Inspector agreed. Then sighed. 'But getting it out of him isn't going to be easy.'

Just then, they heard a loud engine arriving outside, and went through the hall to the front door, where they watched a young man pull up in front of them. He turned off the noisy engine before climbing off the two-stroke Enfield motorbike. He ran a hand through his windswept hair, and retrieved an intriguing-looking leather bag out of a side pannier before approaching them jauntily.

'Inspector Gormley?' he asked, going instinctively towards the hangdog older man. 'Theo Jennings, sir. I'm an electrical engineer. Your boss called my boss and said you might be needing someone to look at something odd that's been going on over here? Something concerning the electricity supply?'

The Inspector nodded curtly. 'Yes, follow me,' he said heavily. 'Someone's been killed, and I want to know how. I suspect that electricity might well be at the root of it – which is where you come in. If there's been any monkey business going on here, I want you to find it out and explain it to us.'

CHAPTER TWELVE

As the now distinctly unnerved electrical engineer was shown into the writing room containing a beautiful dead young woman, Arbie and Val were outside in the garden, having an argument. This was not particularly unusual, it had to be said.

Since the age of five or six, Arbie had not won an argument with the vicar's daughter, and for the life of him he couldn't understand how his flawless logic and calm reason never seemed to win the day. That, however, never stopped him from constantly trying to use them on his recalcitrant friend.

'Now look, Val, please be reasonable about this,' Arbie pleaded, for about the fifth time. 'Just because I . . . er . . . I mean *we* helped solve a murder case last year, it doesn't mean that that's any reason for us to get mixed up in another one!'

Val, arms akimbo, watched him broodingly. 'You don't need to be so magnanimous about it. Everyone knows that you were the brains behind catching the killer last time. But that's only because you deliberately kept me in the dark so much about what it was that you were thinking.'

'I never did!' Arbie squeaked, outraged at the very truthful – if somewhat Machiavellian – accusation.

'Yes, you did, don't fib,' Val contradicted him flatly. 'All the time you were busy figuring it out, and you never once took me into your confidence! And don't bother trying to come up with any tommyrot about needing to protect me or guard my reputation or anything of that sort. You were just plain scared of what Daddy would say if he thought you'd got me mixed up in a scandal.'

Arbie opened his mouth to hotly deny this, then realised there was no point. For although he was perfectly *capable* of denying it and lying to her face, he knew from vast and unhappy experience that Val would never let him get away with it. Women, Arbie had often thought sadly, could be very unreasonable about not believing a chap's lies.

'That's beside the point,' he mumbled now instead, whilst desperately trying to think of some other ways to steer her away from getting involved in yet more trouble. And, worse still, getting *him* involved in it. 'Besides, we don't know for sure it wasn't some sort of accident,' he proffered hopefully.

'Oh. She just accidentally electrocuted herself, did she?' Val asked sceptically.

'It's possible,' Arbie insisted stubbornly. 'But even if it was deliberately done, that isn't any reason for us to get mixed up in it.'

'We did before,' Val put in sweetly.

Arbie shook his head helplessly. 'Val, it simply isn't the same! The last time it happened it was in our own village, and it happened to someone we'd known all our lives. What's more,' he carried on quickly as Val opened her mouth to try to insert some pithy comment or other, 'the victim of the crime had *asked* for our help beforehand. So, in a way, we were obligated to help.'

'You just don't want to have to exert yourself,' Val accused accurately. 'You just want to laze about, enjoying yourself on your publisher's expense account, and do the least amount of work possible. Doesn't it worry you at all that someone has died?'

Arbie winced at her palpable hit. 'Naturally it does. But look here, Val, you don't seem to understand the trouble we could be in if we're caught snooping! You must realise we're far from home here. It's not as if the Inspector is the local bobby, and we can call on our nearest and dearest to vouch for us! We could make ourselves serious suspects, and then we'd really be in the soup.'

'Cowardy-cowardy-custard!' Val sang the old school-ground chant that she knew was a sure way to rile him.

Arbie, however, manfully ignored the slur on his character, but not without an inner qualm. 'And it's not as if either of us really knew Clarice, did we? Which means that whoever killed her, or how or why, is strictly none of our business,' he added, with admirable firmness.

Unfortunately for Arbie, putting his foot down meant absolutely nothing to Val.

'How can you say that? *Beatrice* is my friend – and Clarice was *her* friend.'

'Yes, and when she gets back here and learns what's happened she's going to be very upset and will need a shoulder to cry on and all that,' Arbie said, more gently now. 'And that's how your father would expect you to help her – by offering sympathy and understanding,' he added, knowing even as he said it that it was a low blow.

But appealing to Val's nurturing instincts was one of the few things he knew of that could divert Val, once she'd made up her mind about something. 'Do you really think that coming all over like some female version of Sherlock Holmes, and going about asking questions and stirring things up, reminding her over and over again of what's happened to her friend, is going to help her any?'

Val shot him a helpless look. 'No, I suppose not,' she muttered reluctantly. Then instantly perked up. 'But I still think I should tell the Inspector about what happened last night.'

'Eh?'

'You know – about me hearing and seeing someone creeping about in the early hours. We *do* have a duty to help the police by telling them all that we know, don't we?' she asked sweetly. 'And it might be important.'

Arbie, deciding that discretion would just have to be the better part of valour after all, nodded wearily. 'All right, I suppose that won't hurt,' he conceded. 'But that's all we do,' he added swiftly. 'We'll tell the police what we know – which, let's face it, isn't much – and then leave it to the experts and professionals. Yes?' He gave her his best attempt at a gimlet-eyed gaze.

'Agreed,' Val said, not at all meaning it. Then added, very casually, 'but there's nothing to say that we shouldn't keep our eyes peeled and our ears wagging, is there? Just in case we see or hear anything that the Inspector would want to know about?'

Arbie closed his eyes for a few moments of long-suffering silence, then opened them again.

To find that Val had taken the opportunity to vanish.

A quick glance around, though, showed that she was just mounting the low steps that led from the garden onto the terrace fronting the lounge, dining room and writing room. And that her gaze seemed to be fixed firmly on the open French doors.

With a little 'yip' of alarm, Arbie shot off after her, just managing to catch her by the elbow before she could reach the entrance to the room beyond.

'What are you doing?' he half-hissed, half-whispered in her ear.

'I'm going to tell the Inspector about the prowler in the night,' she half-hissed, half-whispered back. 'You said we should tell the police all we know.'

'I didn't mean right now!' Arbie half-hissed and half-whispered exasperatedly. 'I'm sure he's busy with other things anyway.'

*

Just a few feet away, inside the writing room and observing the electrical engineer as he gingerly and carefully inspected the crime scene, the Inspector and his sergeant were indeed busy with other things. They were also blissfully unaware that two young people were out on the patio and able to hear everything that was going on at the crime scene.

'Hello – this is interesting,' Theo Jennings said thoughtfully.

After taking one look at the dead woman with her burnt fingers, he'd promptly left the room for just a minute or two, in order to see for himself that the electricity supply was indeed safely turned off before he started fiddling about with switches and plugs. The blown fuses still inside the box had told their own story, leaving him in no doubt whatsoever that the overload that had occurred must have been a serious one.

And now, after getting his first proper look at the wires and the diabolical device that had been installed inside the bureau drawer, he was glad that he had been so cautious.

A cold feeling crept up his spine and made its way to the back of his neck, where it fastened in place like a limpet.

When he'd first ascertained that someone really had died because of some trouble with the electric current, his only thought had been that it must be an accident of some kind. And, naturally, his mind had gone to all the usual culprits: frayed or mouse-bitten wire, water accidentally spilled onto the exposed elements, or maybe a wrongly earthed fuse of some kind.

But now, looking at the device in the drawer, he realised that it was something much more sinister.

He glanced at the lamp sitting on one side of the desk – used, presumably at night-time, when the overhead ceiling light might not have been quite strong enough to read or write by – and with his eye, traced the lamp flex cord back to the discreet light socket positioned behind the bureau and set just above the skirting board.

He went down on his knees to get closer and peered at it for some time, not at all surprised to find it significantly blackened. Satisfied by what he'd seen, he nodded to himself then got back up to his feet, still being very careful not to touch anything. Even though he knew that the electric current that had killed the poor woman was now harmless and utterly incapable of hurting him, it was hard for him to override his instinctive reluctance to touch the evidence.

He just had an atavistic feeling that he shouldn't chance fate by acting too cocky.

'What?' Inspector Gormley interrupted his thoughts impatiently, dragging his mind back from the macabre and making him focus firmly on reality.

'Sorry, Inspector,' he apologised, seeming to give himself a little shake. 'It's just, well, this business is the very devil, that's all.'

Slowly, warily, as if the younger man's superstitious sensitivities were somehow contagious, the Inspector approached the bureau, coming to a stop a good half-a-foot away, and then having to crane his neck to peek inside the now fully open drawer. It made him look like a cautious bird, contemplating an unappetising worm in the grass, and the engineer had to hide a grin. 'What am I looking at, exactly?' the policeman asked nervously.

The engineer opened his mouth to give a full explanation of what the set-up was, then caught the Inspector's nervous eye just in time. He coughed gently. 'Do you want me to give you all the technical details now, Inspector, or save them for my written report?' he asked tactfully.

'Save them,' Gormley said quickly. He didn't have electricity in his own house, and he had the feeling that before this case was over, he wouldn't be in any great hurry to be connected to it either. 'I'm no expert,' he added, unnecessarily, 'so just give me an idea of what's happened, in layman's terms that anyone can understand, please.'

Beside him, he heard Innes let out a sigh of relief, and guessed that his sergeant was just as happy not to have to take down a complicated report, filled with unfamiliar phrases. Also, he was not the best speller in the world.

'All right. Well, basically, someone has set up a booby trap, Inspector,' Jennings began. 'I take it you know very little about how electricity works?' he carried on rhetorically. And not even waiting for the two men to nod, he swept on, 'So the easiest way I can explain it is like this. See this little wire here?'

With a finger he pointed at one wire which had been attached, on the inside of the drawer, to one of the nuts keeping in place the metal handles on either end of the long drawer. 'That's almost certainly hooked up to what we call the neutral side of the electricity supply. And this wire here,' he pointed to a wire that ran almost along the entire inside length of the drawer in the opposite direction and was similarly attached to the metal handle on the other side, 'is attached to what we call the live side of the supply. With me so far?'

'I think so,' Gormley lied smoothly.

Jennings nodded. 'Just so. Er . . . you don't want me to go into how it's necessary to earth things properly, and . . .' he trailed off at the baffled look he was being given. 'No, no, well that doesn't matter,' he said kindly. 'All right – simply put, this is how it was done. Someone with a bit of knowledge about these things has rigged this drawer so that when someone pulls on the two metal handles to open the drawer, a connection is made that should never, by rights, ever *be* made. Resulting in the person holding on to the two metal handles – which have now been turned into two near-perfect conduits – receiving an electric shock. In this case, a significant one large enough to cause death and blow the fuses, thus shorting out the electricity supply to the whole building.'

'Hmmm. And there's no way this could have been the result of a mistake in the wiring or anything? When it was first installed, I mean?' the Inspector asked hopefully, but one look at the sheer disbelief on the engineer's face quickly had him shaking his head. 'No, of course not. So . . .' Gormley took a deep breath and glanced significantly at his sergeant, who appeared equally as grim.

'Tell me, how much knowledge would have been needed for someone to fix up this booby trap of yours?' the senior policeman asked.

'It's not mine,' Theo Jennings said at once, not wanting to be associated with it in any way. 'Whoever set this up intended to kill – or at the very least, cause someone considerable pain. And as for the level of skill needed . . . well . . . it's difficult to say. They'd have needed a *basic* level of understanding of how electricity works. For instance, if this poor young woman had been able to pull the drawer out using just one hand, she'd have been spared, because the circuit wouldn't have been closed. But whoever did this used this method because they knew that such a long and heavy drawer would require the use of both hands to open it. Mind you, things like that aren't difficult to work out, not once you understand the principles. They wouldn't need a degree in electrical engineering like me, for instance.'

'But there can't be *that* many people who'd know about this stuff, surely?' the Inspector objected.

But here, the engineer didn't look nearly as convinced, and merely shrugged. 'I don't know about that, Inspector. Nowadays, there might be a few chaps knocking about with a grasp of the basics. Who can say? Men in particular like to tinker with things, don't we? Some motor mechanics might have been curious. People who previously operated stationary engines and needed to learn the new technology perhaps. Aviators, photographers . . . There's plenty of books on the subject in print nowadays so anybody could look it up and study it for a day or two. Any hobbyist with the right kind of brain and deft fingers would be able to set this up. It's not complicated – not really.'

As he spoke, however, he was staring thoughtfully down into the drawer again; but this time, not at the fatal contraption that had recently ended someone's life, but rather at something further down at the other end of the drawer, which had just caught his eye.

Smoothly, he knelt once more and peered inside for a closer look. After a few seconds, and somewhat reluctantly, he leaned closer still and eventually put his hand inside the drawer, running his fingertips over the wood inside.

'What's that you're doing? Are you sure it's safe?' the Inspector yelped nervously. 'I've already got one corpse on my hands, and I don't want another one.'

'No more do I!' Jennings assured him with a grin. 'No – this is just plain old wood I'm looking at. But it seems suspicious to me. Look here, do you see these scratches? They look new to me. And I'm sure there's a couple of small holes that have been made in here too. Do you see?'

He shuffled out of the way so that first Gormley and then Innes could see where he was pointing to, at the spot at the opposite end from the deadly booby trap. Inside the drawer here, which was half-filled with various bits of stationery and related items, a space had been cleared, and on the flat surface that was at the back of the drawer front, there were indeed signs that something had been done to the wood.

'I can't quite make it out,' the Inspector said, peering closely. 'It's almost as if someone's taken a screwdriver to it for some reason, and then their hand has slipped a couple of times and made a scoring mark in the wood,' Gormley mused. 'Do you think it's possible that the killer tried to set the booby trap up at this end of the drawer first, and then couldn't manage it, or changed his mind for some reason, and went and set it up at the other end instead?'

'Could be, sir,' Innes agreed.

'I don't see why though,' Jennings felt obliged to put in. 'The wires are long enough to connect to the lamp no matter which end of the drawer was used.'

'Perhaps the killer tried setting it up this end first and botched it in some way, sir?' the Sergeant hazarded a guess. 'And so he had to try again down the end, and this time succeeded?'

Gormley grunted. 'Possible I suppose. The thing we need to concentrate on now though, is finding out who among the guests and staff here might have had the know-how to set this all up.'

He drew himself up sharply. 'All right, Sergeant. Phone through for the mortuary van. We can't leave this poor woman like this all day. It's not decent. And whilst you're at it, phone through to the station and tell them we're going to need more people on this. It's now officially a murder investigation.'

CHAPTER THIRTEEN

Out on the patio, Val gripped Arbie's arm painfully, and by unspoken consent, the pair of them moved quietly away and back into the garden.

The sun shone hotly down on them, but they were both shivering. Bees and butterflies flitted about amongst Millie Penderghast's lovely gardens, but the couple were blind to the delights of the colourful asters and other assorted blooms.

'Oh, Arbie, how awful,' Val said simply.

Even as she spoke, they heard a car pull up at the front of the hotel, and happy voices rang out. Arbie sighed heavily. So, the first of the engagement party contingent had returned to the hotel from their jaunt. And with a heavy heart, he could all too easily imagine how their innocent pleasure in the day was about to be ruined by the news that awaited them within.

Arbie and Val mooched around the garden for a while, each of them feeling glum, worried and unsure what to do with themselves. The news that someone had so carefully planned and executed a murder had left them both reeling, and it was a good half an hour before they eventually returned to the hotel.

By unspoken consent, they avoided entering the Dashwood through the second set of French doors leading into the lounge, not wanting to be so close to the crime scene, and instead took the trouble to walk around to the front and enter through the main doors.

As they did so, the first thing they saw was the Inspector's back. He was half-leaning on the reception desk and talking quietly to Millie Penderghast.

'I suppose I'd better go and tell him my tale about the restless chap in the night,' Val said quietly and a little forlornly. Arbie couldn't offer her much in the way of comfort other than a helpless shrug. He didn't desert her, however, but hung around in the hall as she approached the policeman.

'And did your husband talk to the children, Mrs Penderghast?' the Inspector was saying, his voice just audible in the hall's echoing acoustics.

'Yes, Inspector – that is, he went into the village to have a quiet word with the parents. To be honest, he wasn't that happy about it, as the Captain doesn't like to make waves, but Mrs Van Dyne was so insistent on it,' Millie was saying. 'And it was only one of those awful cheap bucket-and-spade sets that children seem to like so much – it must have cost just pennies. It's not as if the naughty village tykes were doing any real harm. Still, I suppose she had a point – theft of small things can lead to much worse, if not checked.'

'As a policeman I can certainly testify to that,' the Inspector concurred gruffly. 'I'll send one of the constables down to take a statement from them anyway. This is a Mr and Mrs Sullivan, yes?'

'Yes, and there was another boy with the brothers, apparently. I don't think the Captain got his name off the lads though. They insisted it was just the two of them, though Mrs Van Dyne was sure there were three. Which was admirable in a way, I suppose,' she said listlessly. 'Them being so loyal, I mean.'

Val, not wanting to interrupt, didn't approach them right

away but pretended an interest in the newspapers on the table instead.

'Mind you, if they later stole Miss Fotheringham's beach towel, that's another matter,' Millie said bracingly. 'It was a very nice towel, very fluffy and pretty, and very expensive too, if I'm not mistaken. It looked very much to me as if it was from Harrods, so it wouldn't have been cheap.'

Millie sighed a little, then looked morosely past the Inspector and spotted Arbie casually studying one of the paintings on the wall. 'Oh, Mr Swift,' she called hopefully. 'I just wanted to take a moment to say how awfully sorry I am about all this. You're not going to check out, are you?' she added fearfully.

Arbie half-waved a hand. 'Certainly not. Wouldn't think of it, Mrs Penderghast,' he said briskly. 'And don't you worry about my write-up of the Dashwood, either. I won't even mention the . . . er . . . tragedy.'

'Oh, hello, Mr Morris,' Mrs Penderghast said, forcing a smile onto her face as Charles sauntered out of the bar. 'I must apologise for all this upheaval. I do hope you're staying with us until next Tuesday, as planned?' she fished shamelessly.

'Yes, yes, I expect so,' Charles said vaguely. 'Unless business calls and I have to make another trip up to town,' he added.

Millie, knowing a prevarication when she heard one, tried not to let her smile slip. But it was clear that she was half-expecting him to make an excuse to leave early.

The Inspector came to her rescue, in a roundabout way, by nodding approvingly. 'That's the ticket. I'll be asking everyone with reservations to stay on for the next few days anyway,' he said. And although he spoke amiably enough there was sufficient iron inside the velvet glove to make Charles Morris stiffen slightly in alarm, and catching Arbie's eye, they exchanged tacit looks of understanding.

So that's the way it is, is it? Arbie mused silently. The Inspector wanted to keep all his suspects in one place and right under his nose for as long as he could. Like himself, Gormley must realise that the setting of the deadly trap in the bureau indicated someone with a good knowledge of the Dashwood House Hotel and its inner workings, and he'd be in no hurry to see his suspect pool scatter to the four winds.

'Well, I'd better get on then, I suppose,' Millie said miserably, and headed off towards the bar – either to pour herself a stiff drink, or perhaps to seek succour from her spouse. Or both.

Charles headed for the stairs to escape to the peace and quiet of his room, leaving Val to take the opportunity to talk to the Inspector.

Arbie noticed that he listened to her tale of nocturnal wanderings the night before with every appearance of interest and made a careful note of it in his notebook, and could only admire the Inspector's sangfroid.

Given the latest developments, he had been forced to reconsider his earlier belief that Val had merely stumbled upon an amorous guest caught out seeking an illicit rendezvous, and now had to admit it was possible that she had indeed heard the killer setting about his deadly work and making ready the booby trap in the reading/writing room.

But after thanking her for her diligence, the Inspector, his face as hangdog and unimpressed as ever, left them in the hall and set off about his business of setting up interviews for the returning members of Beatrice Hythe-Gill's party.

For one thing was now obvious to both Arbie and the police alike – the fact that nearly everyone who knew her best had been absent when Clarice Fotheringham was killed was no alibi for them at all. The killer didn't even need to be within miles of the place when the murder itself actually took place. Arbie didn't envy the Inspector the task of trying to find out who might have had reason to want Clarice dead amongst such a large group of people. A jealous lover – or a jealous rival? Someone she'd crossed one too many times? Or was there something more ambiguous behind it all? Something that wouldn't be so easily exposed.

*

Mrs Sullivan was indignant. The local PC, having called on the lady whilst she was in the middle of hanging out her weekly washing, sighed heavily as he was forced to listen to her continuous harangue.

'And don't you go throwing any more aspersions on my Bill or Bob neither, Hubert McGraw, or you'll not hear the end of it,' she threatened through a mouthful of clothes pegs, which she held with expert precision between her set of false teeth.

She snapped out a tea towel with a vicious 'thwack' to get rid of most of the wrinkles before extracting a couple of pegs from her mouth and hanging it up next to her husband's smalls. 'You remember, I knew your mother, bless her, and she wouldn't half have something to say about you telling lies about my boys.'

The PC sighed. 'They were seen stealing toys from the holidaymaker's children, and . . .'

'Tweren't them, then, so there,' the boy's mother defended her cubs vigorously. 'It was that Ben Sherwood, I'll be bound. Proper rascal his is. I keep telling my Bill and Bob not to go around with him, but there, boys won't listen to their mothers, will they? And me always doing my best for 'em. Why, I even called 'em by good names, so that they can be Bill and Bob when they're just young tykes, but when they grow up, like, can be William and Robert, which is more fitting and sober like. Now then, how many mothers do you know of can think on things like that, eh? You tell me? Eh?'

Constable McGraw sighed heavily. 'Mrs Sullivan, about this beach towel . . .'

'What beach towel?' Mrs Sullivan, having now used up her mouthful of pegs on her laundry, reached for the clothes prop and looked set to brandish it in sheer temper about the policeman's head. 'I keep telling you, there is no beach towel!' she shrieked. 'Do you think if they came back with something as fancy as all that, I wouldn't notice?' she demanded.

To the Constable's relief, she put the hook of the prop under the clothesline and triumphantly hoisted the line aloft. A pair of jackdaws, startled by the upheaval, took noisy flight from a nearby hedge.

'And don't you go saying nothing different about it in the village neither.' She turned to wag a finger at him. 'Why you can't use whatever sense the good Lord gave you, Hubert McGraw, I just don't know,' she said, scowling. 'Why would young lads be wanting to steal a beach towel anyway, you thought on that?' she all but shouted, arms akimbo and glaring at him. 'You've had young lads yourself – it's hard enough getting 'em to wash as it is! You'd think they were allergic to soap and water the way they take on so at bath nights! So what kiddie do you know of would care tuppence for a towel of all things?

'You ask me,' she continued, barely pausing for breath, 'them there rich folks up at the big house are all barmy!' she fumed. 'And now they be saying that one of 'em's done the other in. Just goes to show, you ask me!'

And with that triumphant piece of logic, she stormed through her kitchen door and slammed it in the Constable's face.

*

That night the bar was full but subdued. Everyone, it seemed, felt the need to drown their sorrows and seek each other's company for comfort, but, perversely, nobody seemed to want to indulge in conversation for fear of venturing onto dangerous territory.

Captain Penderghast, behind the bar, was watching his guests with a nervy eye, unhappy with the atmosphere of everyone talking in hushed whispers and not quite meeting each other's eyes when they did.

He caught his wife's worried look as she passed by with a tray of glasses filled with sherry, destined for a table of ladies who fell silent as she approached. As she moved away, Millie heard their conversation start up again behind her, and was somewhat relieved to discover that they were only discussing the party tomorrow night – and whether the Hythe-Gills would cancel it.

As they debated the question, one unspoken acknowledgement seemed to hover over the whole proceeding – that Clarice's absence wouldn't be terrifically lamented.

One of the group, a rather limp young girl who never appeared to have any spark about her at the best of times, seemed to think that it was inevitable, but another girl with much more spunk maintained that it would be a shame if the party was cancelled. Everyone had to remain, after all, and it would be a waste of the food and drink already ordered not to go ahead with it, she argued. And wouldn't it be just what everyone needed to dispel the awful gloom?

And there, Millicent thought with a leaden heart, lay the crux of the whole matter. None of her guests now actually wanted to stay at her hotel but had no choice but to remain and make the best of it. And how was she, as the hostess, supposed to deal with that? And, more practically now that she thought about it, exactly what *was* she supposed to do with all the party provisions if the Hythe-Gills *did* cancel tomorrow night's celebrations?

Oh, why did that wretched girl have to go and get herself murdered anyway!

*

Beatrice came down to dinner that evening in her least colourful dress, without even some strings of beads to brighten it up. She had the truly distressing feeling that she was living in a nightmare, from which it must be possible to wake up, if she could only work out how.

As she hesitated in the doorway to the dining room, she saw that her fiancé had yet to come down, and that likewise none of the usual gang had changed for dinner yet either. Not wanting to go and sit with her parents – who would be bound to try to jolly her up or fuss over her and make her feel ten times worse – she spotted Val and her companion with a sigh of relief and began to weave her way to their table.

Arbie saw her first and rose politely from his chair.

In spite of herself and the way she was feeling, Beatrice couldn't help but admire the cut of the famous author's jib in evening clothes and speculate that it surely wasn't possible that these two were just friends, as Val insisted. Oh, she knew they'd grown up in the same village and all that, and had played as tots in the same sandpit, which probably wasn't the most romantic of starts, but even so. Val must be positively blind not to appreciate what was right under her nose.

'Oh, Val, bless you for being here,' Beatrice said, taking one of the two empty seats available at their table for four and collapsing impressively into it. 'I was dreading having to face this alone. Mother has decided we're going to have to go ahead with the party tomorrow, but not in its original form, naturally. The costumes are *off*, of course, which goes without saying. I mean, who wants to be swanning around as Marie Antoinette or Little Bo Peep or whoever, when poor Clarice . . .' Beatrice gave a shudder, and couldn't finish the sentence. 'And the balloons and streamers and things like that are going to go too. Far too festive for words. But we think the flowers should stay – after all, they can be for a wake as well as for a celebration, can't they? And we'll have the food and drink, but probably not much dancing. Which is fine, as I don't think anyone will really want to . . . Oh, Val, what am I doing wittering on about all of this?'

Beatrice put a hand over her forehead and stared down at her place setting for a few moments, breathing hard. 'I think sometimes, I could just start screaming!'

Arbie, who like all men felt utterly inadequate when presented with any show of strong emotion, cast a pleading glance at Val, who was ignoring him and concentrating on her friend.

Leaning over the table, Val put her hand over Beatrice's and gave it a gentle squeeze. 'It's all right, Bea, old thing. We understand. Don't we, Arbie?'

'Oh, er, yes, absolutely.'

'And you can rely on us. Can't she, Arbie?'

'Oh, yes, without a doubt.'

'So, buck up, old thing. I know it's ghastly, and right now you just want to go and hide somewhere, but you'll get through it somehow. Won't she, Arbie?'

'Of course she will,' Arbie averred stoutly. And wondered, if he looked at his watch and suddenly remembered . . . well . . . something urgent, he'd be able to sneak off and . . .

Beatrice took a deep breath, raised her head and smiled tremulously at her friend. 'You're a pal, Val. I've always said as much. I know I can always rely on you when things get tough. Which is why I was hoping,' she took a deep breath, and plunged in, 'would you and Mr Swift please find out what's been going on here today? Everyone says you had a lot to do with solving that ghastly murder in your own village last year, so can't you do the same thing again here for us? And let me know?'

Arbie stared at the pretty young girl opposite him as if she'd grown a second head. Val, however, gave Beatrice's hand another squeeze. 'Oh, Bea, of course we will. Won't we, Arbie?'

'Er . . .'

'I'm sure we can find out lots of things if we put our mind to it,' Val enthused confidently.

'I'm not sure that the Inspector will be . . .' Arbie tried to interject, but Beatrice and Val seemed unaware of his presence and talked right over him.

'Oh, Val, could you?' Beatrice gushed. 'I've had time to go over things in my mind now, and it seems to me, things look awfully bleak. At first, I was simply too shocked to realise what it all meant. For all of *us*, I mean. But, tell me first, is it true that Clarice was killed by some sort of mechanical design? I keep hearing that there was something wrong with the electricity, which made me think it must surely be an accident, but everyone's been questioned by the police now, and some of the men who know a bit more about these things than the rest of us seem to think it had to be deliberate. That can't really be true, can it?'

Val nodded. 'I'm afraid it is, darling,' she said gently. 'Somebody set up some kind of booby trap in the writing bureau. And everyone knows that Clarice used it more than anyone else – every day, in fact, to write to all her friends and accept invitations to parties and things.'

'So it could have been anyone then?' Beatrice asked fearfully.

'Well, no, not anyone,' Arbie felt obliged to put in, and then looked uncomfortable as two sets of feminine eyes bore into him. 'I mean, it had to have been someone who had the tools to make the thing, and the know-how to set it all up. And knew Clarice's habits, and the timing of it all. Waiting until the hotel was nearly empty and all that, thus reducing the risk of someone else setting off the mechanism.'

'So it can't have been . . .' Beatrice said quickly, then hastily bit off the words. Then, seeing Val look at her closely, added lamely, 'a stranger then?'

Val shook her head. And tried to ignore the suspicion that her friend had been about to say something else entirely.

'Or someone like Mother, say, or dreadful Great-Aunt Mona!' Beatrice swept on, giving an unconvincing little laugh.

'No, I can't see a harmless little old lady being able to set up a lethal contraption like that,' Arbie agreed.

'Bea, do *you* have some idea who could have done it?' Val demanded bluntly.

Beatrice flushed painfully. 'Oh no. Of course not. How could I?' she appealed.

Val didn't seem totally convinced by this and Beatrice sat back a little in her chair and began to look mulish. 'Besides, if I knew who did it, I'd hardly have to ask you and Mr Swift to help with the investigation, would I?' she asked, overdoing the exasperated tone just a little. 'Oh, Val, don't be like this! Can't you see I'm out of my head with worry?' she appealed. 'What if the police get it wrong? What if they get it in their head that my Ernie did it, say, or poor old Randolph? Or some other man that Clarice might have got her hooks into? Can't you see how ghastly it's all going to be? Already I can hear people whispering behind my back, wondering if I was jealous of Clarice for some reason, or if Mrs Van Dyne did it, just because she was there when it happened. Who knows what rumours will start to go around. Soon, we'll all be afraid to be alone with anybody for fear of . . . well . . . And Daddy's worried, I can tell . . .' She petered off as if this last sentence said it all.

'I'm sure the police will get to the bottom of it quickly,' Arbie tried to reassure her.

'But you will look into it too, won't you, Mr Swift?'

'Oh, call me Arbie, please.'

'Arbie then. You're such a clever man after all. And it's not as if you haven't done it before. Solved a murder, I mean. Oh, Arbie, do say you'll do your best.'

Val watched, a rather cynical smile on her lips, as Beatrice batted her long eyelashes at Arbie and gave him her best pleading puppy-dog eyes.

Arbie swallowed hard. 'Oh, I say, you don't—'

'Of course we'll help,' Val cut in calmly. 'We'll start by searching the grounds tomorrow,' she added.

Arbie turned his head to blink at her in genuine astonishment. 'Why on earth are we going to do that?'

'Because that's the first thing everyone does, in books and in films and things, isn't it?' Val shot back, wishing she felt as confident as she was trying to sound. In truth, she had said the first thing that came into her head just to stop her friend looking so sickeningly cow-eyed at Arbie. She knew Beatrice well, and though her friend was safely engaged to Ernest Samplestone, it didn't mean it would be beyond the little madam to vamp another man, if it meant she got what she wanted.

'It's a well-known fact that all detectives need to check out the surrounds of a murder scene. After all, who knows what clues the killer might have left behind,' she continued brazenly, not averse to the look of admiration Beatrice sent her way.

'See, you *do* know all about this sort of thing. So that's settled then? I can rely on you to get to the bottom of all this?'

Val nodded, her face lighting up as she contemplated the challenge.

Arbie watched her and felt a familiar sense of resignation steal over him. Once Val was in this mood, he knew, there'd be no stopping her. Which meant he might just as well accept his fate with good grace and try to make the most of it. And, naturally, make sure Val didn't get herself into any real scrapes.

After all, what did it really matter if they *did* do a search of the exterior? Any evidence to be had was surely to be found only in the writing room, and the police would have sealed that off already. No, he was fairly confident the only thing a search of the hotel's grounds would net them would be some scratches from rose thorns, and the discovery of the odd ant nest or two. Both of which should put Val off the idea nicely.

And as a bonus, he couldn't see the Inspector getting his nose put out of joint if he caught them at it, either. In fact, it would probably entertain the lugubrious policeman hugely.

No, for once, he felt almost serene about the prospect of letting Val have her head.

CHAPTER FOURTEEN

Saturday morning dawned bright and hot once more, but the Inspector, arriving at the hotel early, glanced up at the sky without pleasure. He was already feeling uncomfortably warm, and he had a long and full day ahead of him.

His first port of call was to his principal witness.

Martha, however, had not yet risen. The Inspector sought out a maid to go and ask if she was available for questioning. She went to relay the request and reported back that the lady in question begged for fifteen minutes to make herself 'presentable'.

When the time was up, the Inspector knocked – not without some trepidation – on her bedroom door and was bidden to enter. Not used to entering the boudoir of a fetching redhead without even his dour Scottish Sergeant to protect him, he tried not to think of what his wife would say. It was with some relief then, that he found her, not reclining helplessly in bed, but sitting upright in a chair by the window and smartly dressed in an encompassing emerald green housecoat and matching emerald slippers. True, her lovely red hair had been artfully left down, and she had brushed it vigorously, giving her the appearance of someone much younger than her forty-five years. She'd also been sparing but clever with her cosmetics, and the tremulous but brave smile she sent his way made his lugubrious expression lighten a little.

Even seated, she looked petite and fragile, and as he took a chair and brought it closer to her, he hoped she wouldn't have another fit of the vapours.

'Hello, Mrs Van Dyne. I hope you're feeling better?' He set out his opening offering.

'I'm still feeling very shocked, of course,' Martha demurred, 'but I'm determined to do my best to help if I can. I can't say that I was particularly *fond* of Clarice,' she added artfully, knowing full well there would doubtless be plenty of other people ready and willing to tell him as much themselves, 'but she was so young! All her life ahead of her. It's dreadful. Really it is.'

She reached for a handkerchief that had been strategically placed on the windowsill, automatically using her right hand, and winced a little. Absently rubbing her still rather tender wrist with her left hand, she dabbed the delicate lace square to her eyes.

'Indeed. I won't keep you long,' the Inspector promised bracingly, wondering just when and how the lady had hurt her hand. Struggling with a bureau drawer perhaps? Wielding a screwdriver? But the image of this lady knowing anything about electricity was patently absurd and he banished it with a weary inner sigh. 'So, if you'll just bear with me. Do you know anything at all about electricity, Mrs Van Dyne?'

Martha shook her head. 'I'm afraid not, Inspector. I'm more of a creative sort of person, you know. I never was much good at maths, and practical things. Never have been – my late husband used to see to anything like that.' She never admitted to being divorced – and being a widow gave a woman a certain cachet that could come in very useful at times. 'Why, is that what killed her? Something to do with electricity? I *have* been hearing the maids whispering . . .' She shrugged. 'One can't help but pick these things up, can one? But I really had no idea it was so easy to be killed by it, Inspector. I thought it was supposed to be safe.'

So did the Inspector! But then, as his wife was fond of telling him, you lived and learned. 'Had you known the deceased long?' he tried next.

'Clarice? Oh well, vaguely, I suppose.' Martha waved a hand in the air. 'We sometimes met at social functions – this party of Beatrice's being a case in point. But we were not *friends* friends, if you see what I mean.'

'Yes, I understand. So you can't tell me if she had any enemies in particular?'

Martha sighed. 'I'm afraid not. You'd have to ask her little coterie about that. Mind you . . . No, I shouldn't say it. The poor girl's dead, after all.'

'Yes? No need to be shy, Mrs Van Dyne. Nothing you say can hurt her now,' Gormley encouraged.

Martha heaved another sigh. 'No. I suppose not. Well, I was just going to say that Clarice had a bit of a reputation for being rather "fast". That is, it wasn't beyond her to keep men on a string – and sometimes more than one at a time. And then not letting them down lightly when she threw them over. I wouldn't normally gossip about such things, except that it's caused such hard feelings, you see, and one gets to hear these sorts of things, whether one wants to or not. And since the poor girl's been killed . . .' she trailed off delicately.

The Inspector nodded. In fact, the petite redhead wasn't the only one to have mentioned the dead woman's colourful reputation. He'd spent yesterday talking to most of the engagement party contingent – if only in short and preliminary interviews – and many of them had hinted as much. Which meant that it wouldn't be easy to narrow down who might have wanted the girl dead.

'I see.' He nodded, and turned his mind to the more specific aspects of the case. 'I understand from her friends that Clarice often used the writing room? Whereas hardly any of them bothered?'

'Oh yes,' Martha agreed at once. 'Of course, she had a lot of invitations and correspondence. There's no question that she was a very popular social butterfly and much sought after.'

The Inspector thought that there was a certain bite in the lady's tone that might just have something to do with the green-eyed monster, but he was far too diplomatic to say as much.

'And you yourself have used the room from time to time also?' he said mildly.

'Oh, yes,' Martha admitted freely. 'Not as much as Clarice, mind. But I too have my admirers,' she said, with a little coy smile. 'And I have been keeping up a correspondence with a certain rather eligible gentleman who has been paying me court. It doesn't pay for a woman to neglect her beau when she's far away from him, you know, and I make sure that he doesn't feel neglected.'

The Inspector didn't doubt it. He cleared his throat. 'Yesterday morning, I understand you went into the writing room not long after breakfast?'

Martha went slightly pale. 'Yes. Yes, I did. Do you think . . .' She swallowed hard. 'Do you think if I'd been the one to touch the bureau first . . . ?'

'Oh, we have no idea when the device was planted,' the Inspector rushed to reassure her. Although, if Valentina Coulton-James's evidence of a disturbance in the night was anything to go by, it was just possible that they did, but he was not about to tell his nervy witness this! The last thing he needed was for her to get a fit of the horrors, thinking of what might have been. 'Did you stay in the writing room all morning?'

'Oh, no. Of course not. I just, er, read a little, then left. It's called the writing room, but it also serves as a sort of library too, you'll have noticed, and people like to read in there sometimes. There was a book of poems that I saw on the shelf that I hadn't read since I was a girl, and I'm afraid nostalgia got the better of me. I was only reading for half an hour or so though, before I left again.'

'Ah. In which case, it's perfectly feasible that whoever did this waited until you left then set about his nasty work,' Gormley said. 'The hotel was all but empty by then, the maids upstairs cleaning rooms, and Captain and Mrs Penderghast, they tell me, were mostly occupied in the kitchen. So, tell me, did you notice anyone lingering around the area in the hall – either before or after you left the writing room?'

'Oh, no. I think Mrs Penderghast was back at the desk by then though – maybe sorting out the mail? And I saw some of the staff when I went upstairs to my room. But no one you would call *suspicious*!' Martha asserted. 'I'd have noticed a stranger at once.'

'Thank you. Now, l know this is going to be a bit of an ordeal, but can we just go over things once again. I need to be absolutely certain of the facts and timings and things,' he apologised. 'Now, you ran into Miss Fotheringham just as she came in from her swim, and she was upset about her missing towel . . .'

*

As Martha Van Dyne patiently went over the events of the previous day yet again, on the floor above, Evie Smith, one of the maids, heard the rumble of their voices coming up and through the open window, and paused in her dusting.

She bit her lip nervously, and the duster in her hand stilled.

Should she tell the police about what she'd seen yesterday or not? This was the question that had been vexing her ever since the awful news had spread about the murder, and she simply couldn't make up her mind what to do.

On the one hand, everybody said that you shouldn't get mixed up with the police, and that decent and respectable people should never have anything to do with them. And she knew for a fact that her mum and dad would have a fit if it came to their ears that she had somehow got herself involved in the murder! They were already urging her to quit her job and go back to gutting fish, but she was, so far, managing to resist their demands.

On the other hand, the parson had always said that it was everyone's duty to do all they could to help the authorities, no matter how they felt about things. But what she knew was probably innocent enough anyway, so did she really *need* to bother them with it at all? When all was said and done, all she could tell them was that she'd seen an elderly guest leaving the dead woman's room when she must have been out having her last swim in the sea.

By now, the details of what had happened and when were all over the hotel – with both guests and staff alike discussing it openly. Leading Captain Penderghast to give the staff a little pep talk last night, telling them that if anyone had any information at all they should tell the police at once. And she didn't want to lose her position here by disobeying him.

On the other hand – the thought of talking to the police gave her the shivers. That Inspector who looked so sad and put-upon all the time didn't seem the sort who'd welcome her little tidbit of information. And what if they didn't believe her? What if the old lady denied it ever happened? Everyone knew her memory was unreliable, and she might genuinely not remember the incident. And what if whoever had killed the poor young lady had also stolen something from her room? Might not she, Evie Smith, come under some sort of suspicion if she were to go telling tales?

No. Best to just keep out of it.

On the other hand, it was murder.

And so it went on, with the vacillating maid first veering one way, then the other. Surely, Evie Smith thought hopefully, there must be some middle course she could take that would solve her dilemma?

*

Charles Morris breakfasted early and then left for town again. He cheerfully told Mrs Penderghast that he wouldn't be back for dinner and would find somewhere to dine on the journey back from London, thus giving her one less thing to worry about. As for the party – or the variation of it that was due to take place that night – he had no intention of getting in the way and would simply go straight up to his room on arrival and retire.

Millie watched him depart wishing that all her guests were as thoughtful, then smiled nervously as Mr and Mrs Babbacombe approached the reception desk. She was so sure that the lovely old couple were about to make their excuses and check out and leave, that she almost felt like crying when Jack and Gill made it clear that they were going to stay. And somewhat clumsily remarked at how unfortunate it was that things that were nobody's fault often hurt those who least deserved it. Mrs Babbacombe even went so far as to pat her hand encouragingly.

She was still watching, with sincere fondness, the pair depart on their day's outing when she noticed Mr Swift also leaving through the front door, with a carrot in his hand. She knew from the bemused cook that this had become a daily occurrence, but she was not about to second-guess her most important guest. Perhaps eating a raw carrot was the latest health fad? It seemed every five minutes there was a new health craze that swept over high society, and then fizzled out just as quickly.

She knew an old schoolfriend who insisted on eating nothing but oats, cabbage, fruit and hazelnuts, in an attempt to stay young and beautiful!

When the famous author came back some ten minutes later, sans carrot, she had to admit to being somewhat intrigued though. Perhaps if she hinted about it, he might say just what . . . But then she saw the Inspector come down the stairs after completing his second interview with poor Mrs Van Dyne and promptly forgot about her guest's vagaries as a miserable pall of anxiety settled over her once more.

Telling herself it was no use moping, and that she had to meet disaster head on if she and her hotel were to survive the crisis, she tried to buck up and offered him breakfast in the kitchen, which the Inspector speedily accepted. And when, a few minutes later, his tall Scottish Sergeant arrived, she likewise quickly steered him away from her guests in the dining room and deposited him with his superior. The cook sighed at this infringement on her domain, but obligingly set about heaping more bacon and eggs onto a plate.

*

When Val came down, Arbie was already sitting at the table and reading the menu. She saw Beatrice seated with her parents and her fiancé, and cast her an encouraging smile as she crossed the room.

'Hello, old bean,' Arbie said vaguely as Val slipped into the seat opposite him. 'Had a good night's kip and all that?'

'Arbie, I've been listening to some of the things people have been saying,' Val said at once, ignoring his greeting, 'and some of them aren't at all nice. For instance, did you know about the dead dog?'

Arbie blinked. 'Er . . . Any particular dead dog, or . . . ?'

Val reminded him of the tale of Mona Rice-Willoughby and the tragic tale of Monty the Jack Russell. 'No wonder the old lady has had a positive hatred of Clarice ever since,' she concluded. 'Don't you find that ominous?'

'Not unless you seriously think that Mona of all people could make up a booby trap of such infernal deviousness that it would make even Fu Manchu envious,' Arbie said nonchalantly, helping himself to toast and marmalade.

Val tossed her long blonde hair back with an irritated flip of her hand. 'And that's not all. Apparently Clarice was always snaffling men away from under people's noses. I heard some girl even went so far as to fling champagne in her face at the regatta at Henley.'

'Must have been refreshing for her,' Arbie mused, contemplating porridge or kedgeree. 'But a shocking waste of good champers.'

'So lots and lots of people must have had a down on her,' Val swept on, ignoring his uninterest. 'And as a heartbreaker, there must be any number of men who might have wanted her to get her comeuppance. And who's to say that some of them aren't right here, right now? You know how entangled Beatrice's set are. It's so frustrating not to know all the gossip, but though I went to school with her, after that I didn't exactly move in the same exalted circles as she did. But it seems that half of them have been dating the other half before being thrown over, or doing the throwing over, and then going out with someone else. Arbie, are you listening to me?'

'Hmmm? Oh yes, I'm all ears, old bean.'

'Humph! So, as I was saying, I don't think it's particularly far-fetched to believe that *someone* amongst Beatrice's guest list might have had a motive for doing away with her. Fits of passion and rage and jealousy and whatnot.'

Arbie nodded obligingly – but to his mind, a careful and deadly booby trap didn't really fit in with her theory of uncontrollable emotions running rampant.

'What a pity we can't search all their rooms.' Val sighed, making Arbie almost choke on his toast at this latest example of Val's seemingly effortless effrontery. 'Still, nobody can stop us investigating outside, can they? Oh, do hurry up, Arbie, the sooner we get started on our search the sooner we might find something helpful.'

Arbie masticated then swallowed his toast carefully, smiled at the nearby waitress and deliberately ordered a handsome breakfast.

Val scowled at him, but then ordered one almost as handsome. When dealing with the slackers of the world, she'd found, you needed to keep your energy levels topped up.

*

'Oh, I haven't told you yet about that strange conversation I overheard between Beatrice and Clarice yesterday morning, have I?' Val asked, nearly an hour later.

They were just about to enter a large, ramshackle shed, having thoroughly searched the greenhouse, and much less thoroughly inspected what his uncle would call 'the coalhole' – an underground bunker-type room where the hotel's supply of coke and coal was kept.

Now Arbie, absently brushing coal dust from the right knee of his second-best pair of Oxford bags, wondered how long it would be before he could slope off to the village pub for some refreshment.

'What strange conversation?' he asked obligingly.

Val set out explaining what she'd overheard in the ladies', whilst Arbie opened the door to the shed and ventured inside. It was obviously a cross between a storage place and the gardeners' hidey-hole, for there were spare chairs stacked against the walls, along with some gardening tools, and a workbench. In one section a little spirit lamp had been placed, along with an old biscuit tin containing tea, a can of powdered milk and some tin mugs. A camp stool, folded and put away out of sight under the workbench, was doubtless brought out and used whenever the sons of the soil had their elevenses.

'So what do you think?' Val asked.

Arbie shrugged. 'Well, you know, old thing, you shouldn't ask us chaps about secrets of the feminine heart and whatnot,' he advised blithely, 'because, as you're forever telling us, we have no idea about what's what when it comes to understanding the fairer sex. But it sounds to me, from what you're saying, that the murdered woman was objecting to some proposition or other that had been put to her.'

As he was talking, he moved about this and that and peered into various nooks and crannies, since they were supposed to be searching for some unnamed 'clue' to the murder, but he had more than half his mind on the imminent prospect of a refreshing pint of ale. Listlessly, he moved on to some sort of workbench, which was actually a very old, very overpainted sideboard with a set of drawers, which had at some point been banished from the big house and had been reprieved to be used as a receptacle for garden twine, seed catalogues, potting trays and who knew what else.

Seeing no signed murderer's confession obligingly left lying about in the first drawer, he absently opened another and peered into it, uninspired, as Val sighed heavily behind him. Above him, hanging from hooks near the wooden ceiling, were such lethal-looking garden implements as scythes, shears and various clippers, and he neatly ducked under them to approach a big wooden chest that was overflowing with dirty rags and vast amounts of some sort of netting.

'Well, I was able to work *that* much out for myself,' Val said crossly, absently kicking a sack of what looked like potatoes that had gone to seed. 'But who had propositioned her, that's what we need to find out. And who was she supposed to have twisted around her little finger? And why? Because if Clarice had . . .'

As she said this, Arbie, who was very half-heartedly rummaging about in the wooden box, accidentally knocked over, with his elbow, a large terracotta plant pot nearby, and several things tumbled out of it – including the ubiquitous mud-stained rag and balls of twine.

But what most definitely caught the eye was a simply enormous spider. No mere tame house arachnid this, it seemed to move with a vast, black fluidity that was all legs and hairy-backed body.

It was as big as a dinner plate.

Val shrieked so loudly the glass windows vibrated, and she leapt fully a foot up in the air, whilst at the same time, somehow managing to turn her body almost ninety degrees and catapult herself towards the door. Ordinarily, Arbie would have been most impressed by this gymnastic display, were it not for the fact that he was yelling several decibels louder and had jumped fully another foot higher than his companion.

He was faster than Val too, so even though she was ahead of him, he reached the open doorway at the same time as she did, and for a moment it looked as if they were in danger of wedging themselves together in the egress. Finally, Val gave a massive flex of her tennis-honed shoulder muscles and shot out, like a champagne cork exiting a fine bottle of Moët.

Tumbling and yelping back out on the surrounding path they

staggered a few paces away, then stood there panting at each other, wild-eyed.

'D-d-did you see that thing?' Val gasped.

'Saw it? It almost leapt onto my hand,' Arbie warbled.

'Well, go back and kill it!' Val demanded tremulously. 'At once! I'll never be able to sleep a wink knowing that monster is still lurking about somewhere! What if it leaves the garden and gets into the hotel itself? It might make its way into my room.'

Or even worse, Arbie mused silently, *my* room!

CHAPTER FIFTEEN

Ten minutes later, Arbie, very gingerly, re-entered the shed. He'd spent fully seven of those minutes being logical and reasonable with Val, citing all the reasons he could think of why they should leave things well alone – and things that possessed eight hairy legs, *especially* alone.

The last three minutes he'd then spent resigning himself to the inevitable and convincing himself that, by now, any self-respecting arachnid, on being so rudely maltreated in what had probably otherwise been a perfectly desirable shed, would have taken its eight black hairy legs off somewhere else, and in high dudgeon too. And with any luck was now checking out the delights of the coalhole, or some other homey residence.

He nevertheless hesitated in the doorway and glanced behind him, only to find Val standing, arms akimbo, glaring at him.

He sighed, and went inside.

And instantly saw the spider. It was waiting for him on the floor next to the tumbled plant pot that had been its previous home and was ominously still. As if waiting for him to come closer so that it could pounce.

Arbie thought such behaviour was highly unreasonable.

'Now look here, my good, er, spider, I appreciate the fact that you're a fine specimen and all that. In fact, you may be a veritable prince amongst your kind and so on and so forth, and that, as such, you aren't used to backing down. But don't you think you're taking this rather far? I am after all much bigger than you.'

As he talked he was inching his way slowly forward. 'And, for your information, my friend out there wants me to stamp you into mush.' At this, Arbie looked doubtfully down at his debonair footwear. 'But, to be perfectly frank, I don't much relish the thought of getting blood and g— Oh. Ah.'

The final vowels of this manly speech only came about when he was finally close enough to get a better look at his foe. And several things became simultaneously apparent.

First and foremost, that the spider was, indeed, huge. Far too huge, in fact, to be real. And second, that the thing had been done in some style. No second-rate shiny rubber concoction this; it had been made to look real, right down to the application of napped felt, giving the body a life-like furry appearance, and what looked like strands of animal hair littered about all eight appendages.

Letting out a long, slow breath of relief, Arbie squatted down on his haunches in front of it and regarded it with some respect. He could see his uncle approving of this fake arachnid, and was half inclined to pocket it and present it to him as a gift. Then he thought of the uses to which his relative might put it (and his ongoing feud with the wife of a local JP) and hastily changed his mind.

It had probably been purchased from one of those better class of joke shops that you found almost anywhere, that stocked deplorable balloons that made deplorable sounds, fake noses and various other childish prank-related items.

The light dimmed a little and he could tell by the slight movement of the somewhat rotten floorboards beneath him that Val had stepped tentatively into the shed. 'Is it dead?' she asked warily.

'Oh yes, as the proverbial doornail, old bean,' Arbie assured her. Then the pedantic literary elf in him made him frown. 'Actually, that's not quite accurate. I should more properly say that it was never alive in the first place.'

'What? Arbie, what on earth are you waffling on about? You really are the silliest of duffers when you've got the wind up,' she complained.

Arbie, deciding she would pay for that, nonchalantly reached down, picked it up, placed in on the palm of his hand and turned around. Its long, very realistically hairy legs dangled either side of his palm and Val went pale.

Then red.

Then looked furious.

'It's a fake!' she accused, after having taken a closer peek at it. Then, without a pause for breath, added ominously, 'Arbie, did *you* put it there?'

Arbie's jaw dropped at the sheer calumny of it. '*Me?* Why would I put it there?'

'Because you didn't really want to do this search with me? Or as a way of paying me back for making you actually *do* something?' Val was now well in her stride.

But Arbie had now noticed something else that he hadn't noticed before, and as a consequence, only half-heard her. On the floor, along with the overturned plant pot and its other miscellaneous collection of odds and ends, was a long, new-looking spring. Metal, tightly coiled, it looked as if, when released, it would have a fair bit of force behind it.

'Now that's interesting,' he muttered, and Val, still a little suspicious of his abstraction, somewhat reluctantly joined him and peered over his shoulder.

'What is?' she asked, still not convinced that he wasn't trying to wriggle out from under her righteous accusations by trying to distract her.

'That spring,' Arbie said. 'The other bits and pieces I can understand. A bit of broken pencil, a clothes peg, some string, buttons, I can see how some groundsman might have accumulated those over the course of a few years. But what on earth could he want – or what could anyone want for that matter – with a spring?'

Val stooped down and picked it up. Pulled to its full extended limit, it was more than six inches long. Scrunched down, maybe one inch. It looked, unlike anything else in that place, rather shiny and clean. It was very bouncy, and for a while she held it down and let it spring back. Then shrugged. 'It's just a bit of spring, that's all. Maybe it came off an old sofa or chair or something. Perhaps one of the gardeners found it and just kept it. You men seem to keep the oddest of things. Your uncle, for instance, has so much old junk in his workshop, I bet he has a dozen of these things lying around.'

Arbie nodded. It was perfectly true – his uncle could probably lay his hand on any object you cared to mention, such was his mania for keeping every scrap that he happened to come across. But then, the uncle who had raised him after he'd lost his parents at a young age was . . . unique.

With a toss of her long blonde hair, and a dismissive sniff at the fake spider, Val deposited the spring on the workbench then turned and walked off, stately head held high. As if her dignity had never been troubled in the least.

Arbie, however, was still staring at the spider in his hand. Then his eyes went thoughtfully across to the spring. And for once, the normally amiable and untroubled expression he habitually wore was absent from his face.

*

Mrs Hythe-Gill poured herself a large – a very *large* – sherry and gulped rather than sipped at it. Susan, alone in her room and glad of the respite, slipped off her shoes with a sigh and sat down on the bed.

Ever since that flighty young girl had died, she'd felt as if she'd been living on the edge of some sort of precipice and was now coming to the end of her tether. It didn't help that she was positively dreading the party tonight – which was bound to be a disaster – and, worse still, couldn't help but feel that, as bad as things already were, they were only going to get a lot worse.

A low-level of dread had settled over her and ever-rising panic was setting in, and she suspected that if she once gave in to it, she might well thoroughly disgrace herself.

It didn't help that she couldn't quite pinpoint the exact source of her fear.

She had never liked Clarice and had liked even less the influence she'd wielded over Beatrice. Her daughter, though a good girl in essence, had always been rather easily led. So she'd been glad and thoroughly relieved when Beatrice had taken such a shine to Ernest, who would make a good and solid sort of husband, and had not mimicked Clarice's wayward penchant for older, experienced and more predatory men.

And although she was relieved that Clarice was now gone and her pernicious influence was no longer a source of danger to her, she couldn't help but feel that the dead woman hadn't quite finished with the Hythe-Gill family just yet.

Discovering that her glass had become mysteriously empty, she told herself that she would not pour out another until after she'd had a proper nap. Perhaps a little sleep would get rid of the minor headache that plagued her and help fortify her for the night to come.

She lay down and stared listlessly up at the ceiling for a few minutes, then turned on her side and resolutely closed her eyes.

But it was no use. Sleep just wouldn't come. If only she knew what was going on!

Too many other things seemed discordant and out of place somehow. Oh, nothing as jarring or significant as the murder of course, but still; niggling little things that left her feeling out of sorts and apprehensive. For instance, her husband was suddenly very tight with that nice Mr Harrington, which worried her a little. Although why it should, she couldn't have said, because he was Ernest's greatest friend, and came from a nice family.

According to Beatrice, Randolph had suffered some sort of romantic catastrophe in his life, hinting at an ill-starred romance that had ended in tragedy. Something to do with a young girl he'd always loved from afar or some such thing, who had fallen foul of a heartless roue. This event had left the tall, fair-haired Randolph with an air of quiet suffering which, naturally, made him a magnet for silly young girls with romantic notions.

Not that she had noticed Clarice being unduly impressed by the handsome young man's charms, of course. No, her choice of suitor tended towards the more mature and dangerous. Hadn't someone told her that Clarice had recently been seen gadding around town with some well-to-do gent with connections to the racetrack? That certainly sounded more like the dead girl's forte!

Then, catching herself in such uncharitable thoughts, she gave a small sigh of guilt and rose to pour herself another large glass of sherry.

Well, a little stiffener couldn't hurt, could it? And one thing was for certain, Susan mused grimly. Whenever her daughter had need of her, she never found her mother wanting.

*

Down in the ballroom, the largest room in the old country house, Captain Penderghast was observing his wife in action.

You had to hand it to Millie, he thought fondly, when something needed organising, she was the bee's knees. Already she had the staff cleaning the place, rolling up the rugs to reveal the floorboards, and making sure that the band, due to arrive later, would have an adequate 'stage' on which to perform. She had just made the final decisions on where the floral arrangements were to go, once they were delivered, and was now muttering something to herself about caterers.

To the outside world she looked competent and outwardly confident about the Dashwood's first big event, but he knew she was secretly worried sick about it all. As was he, underneath his own cover of bonhomie and bluster.

This murder couldn't have come at a worse time for them. Getting that nice author chap to come and do a write-up for the place had been a feather in their cap, and their first season had been going so well, with all guns blazing. And now this catastrophe.

He only hoped it didn't ruin the whole show for them. Still, if it did, he knew he could rely on Millie to come up with another good wheeze. He could already hear her. 'You know, George, we should sell this place and try our hand at . . .' Well, something or other. He knew he could always rely on her to steer them through the worst of storms.

Snapping to attention as Millie gave him his orders to make sure the extra deliveries of wine and spirits due in a few hours would have a dedicated space behind the bar, he set to work with a will.

George tended to enjoy life, and why not? He'd always been a lucky sort of chap. He'd come through the Great War all right, hadn't he? And then he'd found his Millie, who understood him and ran his life so splendidly. And if sometimes fellows joshed him about his wife wearing the trousers, what of it? He just laughed and agreed, and life went on in the same, pleasant way.

But Captain George Penderghast knew, as well as the next man, that you couldn't rely on luck to carry you through forever. If only that girl had chosen to make her trouble somewhere else! He'd known from the moment she arrived that she was trouble. That sort always were – good-looking, glamorous, wealthy, able to twist people around their little fingers just for the fun of it. And then laugh at the lesser mortals as if they counted for nothing.

They thought they owned the world. As they probably did. And now, just look at the mess! From now on, George resolved, he'd have to take charge for once in his life, and keep a closer eye on things.

The last thing poor Millie needed now were even more spokes put in her wheel.

*

After their handsome breakfast in the hotel kitchens, Inspector Gormley and his sergeant had withdrawn to the still publicly off-limits writing room, where they were now busy comparing their notes and trying to get to grips with their case. In truth, neither man had much experience of murder, which made them both determined not to miss a trick or make a mistake.

They were expecting the results of the post-mortem on the unfortunate Clarice Fotheringham later that day but weren't anticipating any surprises. The science people had done their own thing, and now photographs were being processed and fingerprints taken and all of that technical stuff. But the Inspector wasn't holding out much hope that any of it would be of much use.

No. This case, Gormley was convinced, would only be solved by observing the dead girl's companions and discovering the motive behind the crime. Once they'd done that, they could then start applying pressure to the guilty party and wait for them to crack.

'So, it seems likely that "chummy" set up the booby trap the night before the lady was killed,' the Sergeant was saying. 'You agree, sir?'

'Ye-es,' his superior conceded, somewhat cautiously. 'Although the hotel was almost empty on the morning of the murder, there *were* still some people about – the staff, the Penderghasts and a smattering of guests who had nothing to do with the Hythe-Gill contingent, like that author chappie. And according to our expert, it would have taken some time for the killer to rig the bureau up, using wood-working tools and electrical bits and bobs and what have you. You'd need to have a strong nerve to have attempted it when someone could just walk in on you at any given moment.'

'Right. Which means the vicar's daughter really *did* hear chummy about his work then?' The Sergeant nodded and sucked his teeth. 'It's a good job she never actually got a glimpse of the character, or else she might have copped it too!'

The Inspector winced at this rather crude observation, but nodded in agreement.

'Which means it definitely has to be someone in the hotel,' the tall Scot continued. 'Which narrows it down for us, so that's one good thing. I checked all the doors and windows, sir, and they're sturdy enough, and Captain Penderghast is adamant that everything is shut and locked up by midnight. Guests who return later than that have to ring the bell for admittance, and again, the Captain is adamant they don't give keys to the main doors to guests, so it's not as if one of them could have lent a key to someone, or had it stolen from them, and a copy made.'

'I agree. No outsider did this,' Gormley mused. 'Has anything turned up in the background checks yet?' he asked abruptly.

'We've only had time to do about ten of them in depth so far, but we should know more about everyone within the next few days, sir. The only news that's come in that might just be significant is that Mr Alexander Hythe-Gill used to own a factory producing electrical products – these new-fangled cleaners that suck up air, and whatnot. But then, he's owned a lot of companies during his career, before he came perilously close to crashing and losing the whole lot a few years back. Mind you, from what I've read in the reports, he was always strictly management. Too lah-di-dah to actually get his hands dirty on the shop floor, I reckon.'

Gormley sighed. 'But it's still conceivable that he picked up enough know-how to set up an electrical booby trap. From my experience, when a man owns a business, he picks up knowledge over time whether he likes it or not. A bit here, a bit more about something else there, until he knows far more than you might think. Even if he never leaves the comfort of his office.'

'Yes, sir,' the Sergeant agreed diplomatically.

With a hangdog sigh to match his hangdog face, the Inspector, with some irritation, relegated Alexander Hythe-Gill to the back of his mind and went back to talking through the reconstruction of the killer's possible timetable. 'So, having set up the lethal trap, whoever-it-is goes back to bed and sleeps the sleep of the just.' He gave an ugly grimace. 'And what does he do the next morning, do you suppose?'

'Well, sir, you can be sure he'd want to put as much distance between himself and the hotel as possible. Wouldn't he?' the Sergeant mused. 'I mean, stands to reason. Human nature, and all that. He'd want to be able to stick with someone else who could vouch for him. And that covers almost all of those attending the young lady's engagement party. We've got all their statements now by the way – and whilst they might have split up into groups, or paired off, not one of them went off on their own.'

'Hmm. Let's not get ahead of ourselves, Sergeant,' the Inspector advised. He might be known for his slow and steady – some might say even *plodding* – approach, but experience had told him that it never paid to rush things. 'For one thing, you're forgetting that warning note. Or death threat, if you prefer. Why bother warning your victim in advance? It makes no sense.'

Sergeant Innes twisted his lips. 'It's a bit of a poser that, sir, I'll grant you. It would put the young lady on her guard for one thing, wouldn't it? Make her feel jittery and suspicious and maybe put her off her normal routine. Which is the last thing the killer would have wanted, after going to all that trouble to set up the trap for her.'

'And yet we know he did. Or *someone* did. Just check that list again for me, Innes. Who were the very last guests to leave the hotel that morning?'

'Er . . .' The Scotsman quickly rifled through his notebook. 'That would be the father of the bride-to-be and the best man. Alexander Hythe-Gill and Randolph Harrington.'

'Hmm. From what we've learned about our victim, she was the kind who liked to have the men dancing attendance on her. I wonder if the young lady had her hooks into either one of those?'

'I haven't picked up on anything like that, sir,' Innes said dubiously, 'and we've spoken to everyone now. It's been my experience that things like that are never as secret as erstwhile adulterers would like to think. I reckon if the dead girl had been carrying on with either of them, one or other of the lasses would have known about it and gossiped.'

The Inspector's mournful eyes actually twinkled a little at this. 'Yes, I agree. Attractive and unpopular ladies are usually very closely watched by members of their own sex – especially those running around in the same set. The married women are worried about their husbands, and the single girls don't like the competition! So – we'll put a question mark against the gentlemen in question, but no more than that. Now, about this death threat . . .'

*

As the two policemen continued to thrash out the whys and wherefores of their case, Arbie and Val continued – rather more cautiously – their hunt around the grounds.

They'd checked out the greenhouses, a now derelict ice house, fished about in both ornamental ponds, and were now about to approach one of the garden's two summerhouses or gazebos.

Arbie paused in front of a fine specimen with a green-painted rotunda. Festooned with the almost obligatory wisteria and clematis, it had a fine elevated view through a gap in the trees to the sea beyond. 'Nice spot this,' he mused, walking up the three wooden steps and into the small interior of the building.

Built in a pleasing hexagon shape, it had bench seating on all but two of its sides. Padded for comfort, they looked the kind that would lift up, providing storage space inside for parasols, cricket bats, towels, picnic accoutrements or what have you.

Mindful of the spider, Val cautiously lifted one of them and peered inside. 'Hmm, nothing much here. A rather battered sun hat, a walking cane and a small chess set. With the bishop missing. Why is it always the bishop that goes missing from chess sets, do you suppose, and not the castle, say, or the knight? Haven't you noticed that?'

'Can't say I have,' Arbie mused absently, lifting up another padded seat and peering fearlessly (well almost fearlessly) inside. 'You'd think, logically, it would be pawns that would end up going AWOL, being more of them, wouldn't you? Hullo, what's this?'

His curiosity immediately brought Val to his side. 'What? Oh, do say it's a clue at last?!'

Arbie shrugged and lifted out his finds. They were not, it has to be said, particularly prepossessing. Several squares of wood painted in bright primary colours, he had discovered them scattered about amidst some spare cushions and a croquet mallet. They had been broken apart roughly for some reason, and in several places had splintered, leaving some small nails sticking out. 'Mind your fingers,' he warned Val, 'there are nails and things.'

Val, rooting about amongst the cushions inside the seat, came up with some scraps of oddly stitched and shaped green and red cloth, which had also been torn apart for some reason. 'Odd,' she said. 'What do you think it could have been? It's too small to be an article of clothing – even the tiniest of tots wouldn't have had much use for this. Although I'd swear that bit almost looks like a tiny sleeve . . .'

Arbie shook his head. 'Beats me, old bean. Though it does remind me of something . . . Just can't put my finger on it. Oh well, best put it back where we found it, just in case the Inspector wants to check it out for himself.'

'All right, all right, no need to be funny!' Val grumbled. 'I know this search idea has been a bit of a washout. We've spent hours and hours, and we've nothing to show for it.' She sighed despondently.

'Never mind, old thing,' Arbie commiserated, but very

carefully put back his finds exactly as he'd found them. 'Let's go and have a drink, shall we?'

'Oh yes! I'd love a cup of tea,' Val agreed. 'I dare say Mrs P. will have elevenses on the go by now.'

Arbie sighed. 'Yes, I suppose she will have,' he agreed fatalistically. And mentally bid a sad farewell to any prospects of enjoying a pint of beer in the village pub.

CHAPTER SIXTEEN

Beatrice's engagement party, as predicted, got off to a somewhat slow start at around eight o'clock. Not being certain of the etiquette in such a situation, no one was quite sure what to do or say or how they should conduct themselves.

Millie Penderghast, as ever, came to the rescue by circulating and chatting unconcernedly, and making sure that the drinks flowed quickly and well. She followed up this good work by encouraging the little band to play the slower dance tunes (as ragtime, jazz or even the Charleston would hardly be appropriate), and slowly but surely, people began to relax and behave more naturally.

By unspoken consent, nobody mentioned Clarice, and out of a sense of loyalty to the obviously nervous Beatrice and her somewhat bewildered and helpless-looking fiancé, the noise level began to rise, and people began to dance. Again, Millie helped spur the process on by encouraging people to start sampling from the wonderful and scrumptious buffet, and by ten o'clock the party was, if not swinging exactly, at least swaying along nicely.

Arbie, having been given 'honorary' guest status by Beatrice, had put on his dress shirt and black tie and was dancing a sedate waltz with a doe-eyed brunette who had snaffled him the moment he appeared, and seemed intent on keeping him snaffled. Arbie had no objection to this, as she looked very fetching in her beaded silver gown and matching headband and was equally happy to be led by this fast-talking siren to the buffet table to put on the old feedbag.

He was just about to bite down into something warm, savoury and delicious, listening with interest to the amusing anecdote his companion had embarked upon, concerning a 'great lark' at 'Lord Binchy's birthday bash' involving a trained seal and a thoroughly outraged baroness who was notorious for lacking a sense of humour.

'And then, the seal tossed his little red ball into the air, and you'll never guess where it landed!' she chirruped, already giggling in anticipation.

'No! Where?' Arbie asked obligingly.

His companion took a sip of her champagne and beckoned him closer. 'I can't say it out loud in polite company. But . . .' She hooked her little finger and beckoned him in, and Arbie, nothing loath, bent his head closer and put his shell-like ear next to her ruby-red lips.

She whispered something and Arbie's eyes immediately widened, as did his grin.

'Isn't it time you started getting ready, Arbie?' The chilly voice asking the question had nothing in common with the dulcet tones of his dancing partner, and both of them sprang apart guiltily.

Arbie looked over his shoulder and saw Val watching him, a rather tight look on her face. She looked lovely in a white gown with multiple strands of different coloured beads hanging to her narrow waist. Her long blonde hair was held up in an elegant chignon, and some sort of feathery plume had been fixed in place on the left side of it. Her blue eyes glittered.

'Oh, er, hello, Val,' Arbie mumbled. He knew from the expression in her eyes that he was in the doghouse for some reason but had no idea why. 'You look smashing, old thing,' he said, warily beginning the process of appeasement.

Val regarded him for a moment, then sighed. Her eyes went over him to the brunette and after some process that totally eluded him, the other girl seemed to wilt slightly, murmured something about having promised a dance to 'Piggy Pomfrey' and slunk away.

Arbie shifted nervously on his feet. Val glanced at the large grandfather clock standing in one corner and said, 'It's nearly ten thirty.'

'Yes, so it is,' Arbie agreed, still baffled.

'Don't you need to start getting ready?' she repeated.

Arbie smiled uncertainly. 'Ready?'

'For our rendezvous with the fierce and loyal steed Stalwart and his less-than-noble rider? At midnight? On the upper road? Remember – the ghost you're here to hunt down for the next edition of the guide?'

As the sentences had whizzed past his ear like a series of sarcastic bullets, Arbie's spirits nose-dived. He'd forgotten, of course, that tonight was the anniversary of the day when the notorious highwayman had been hanged, and one look at Val's slightly amused but still exasperated expression told him that it would be useless to try to deny it.

'Oh, yes. It had slipped my mind, as a matter of fact,' he conceded airily. 'But then, I *have* rather let myself be distracted with all this murder business and your promise to Beatrice that we'd try and solve it.' He neatly tossed a few bullets of his own past Val's admittedly very attractive ears. And was happy to see her look slightly – just *very* slightly – discomfited. 'I've been thinking things over all day, don't yah know, racking the old brains a bit, and you know, Val, I don't like the way things are looking. Not a bit. In fact, I'm beginning to wonder if there might not be—'

'Ah, Mr Swift. I do hope you're having a good time?'

Millie Penderghast, having pulled up alongside him, tempted him with a glass of champagne from a silver tray, an offer that Arbie, of course, felt obliged to accept. With alacrity. Val also took a glass, but barely sipped from hers.

'I'm so glad things seem to be going along all right,' Millie said, casting a look around the room with obvious relief. 'People seem to be enjoying themselves, but not *too* much, don't they?' she added artfully.

But Val and Arbie both understood what she meant and nodded.

'And wasn't it nice of Mrs Hythe-Gill to invite the Babbacombes as well? Strictly speaking, they're guests of the hotel, and nothing to do with their party, but Jack and Gill – such amusing names, don't you think? – have such a lovely habit of getting along with everyone, and really, I'm not surprised that they were invited too. I daresay Mr Morris would have been here as well, had he not had to go up to London again.'

She paused to smile encouragement at Susan Hythe-Gill, who was already on her third G&T (but who could blame her), and sighed. 'I feel so sorry for her. That such an awful thing should happen at what was supposed to be such a lovely time in her daughter's life. And like a lot of us so-called society matrons, there's more to her than meets the eye. Did you know, we both did some similar work for the war effort? Making components for various things in one of those small technical factories that shot up during the early years of the war. You know, when they put out the call for women volunteers with deft hands? Oh, what am I thinking, you were both too young to have anything to do with the Great War, weren't you.' She smiled a vague apology their way, then something else caught her eye. 'Oh, I must just go and see my husband about something,' she interrupted herself to say, and with an all-encompassing smile, passed busily on.

'Bit of a force of nature that woman,' Val said admiringly. 'You have to give it to her – she's determined to make this place a success. And I do hope she succeeds. Oh, Arbie, you *are* going to give the Dashwood a really marvellous write-up in the new book, aren't you?'

'Hmmm? Oh yes, of course I will. Five stars and all the bells and whistles and whatnot,' he said staunchly but rather vaguely.

Val, seeing that his mind was on something else (probably that floozy of a girl he'd been dancing with), fought the impulse to stamp her foot, and remember instead her father's sermons on the virtue of patience.

'So, about our ghost,' she reminded him determinedly. 'When do we need to get off? We've got to change, don't forget, and then walk up there, so we can't be too long if we want . . .'

But yet again she was thwarted in her efforts to get him in hand as, this time, Beatrice interrupted her.

'Ah, Val, there you are. Oh, do you want to dance with Ernest?' Beatrice offered airily, indicating the young man beside her, who beamed obligingly.

'Oh, hello, Bea. Thanks for the offer, but no, I won't borrow him just now,' Val replied. 'We'll have to be off in a tick for our appointment with the highwayman.'

'Oh, yes! Your ghost – I was forgetting,' Beatrice said. Her fiancé blinked a bit at this, alerting Val to the fact that the handsome but not particularly au fait Ernest was unaware of Arbie's mission at the Dashwood. In other circumstances she would have been kind-hearted enough to explain, but right now she had other things on her mind.

'I mustn't keep you then,' Beatrice rushed on, 'but can we meet up again soon? You know, to see how you're getting on with your *other endeavours*?' She lowered her voice to a conspiratorial whisper over the last two words. Which, she concluded, meant that Beatrice had also yet to inform her fiancé that she'd asked them to investigate Clarice's murder.

Val thoroughly approved of this strategy. It was often a good idea, she had discovered, to keep one's menfolk in blissful ignorance. 'Of course. And, Bea, I'm so glad the party is going so well. Chin up, old girl, yes?' She reached out and gave her friend's hand a squeeze.

Beatrice nodded, her eyes suddenly bright with suppressed tears, and began to turn away. As she did so, she almost bumped into Martha Van Dyne, who looked stunning in an emerald green shimmering silk shift that did wonders for her fair skin and red hair. It had clearly been tailored to make the most of her curvaceous figure and Arbie, for one, noticed.

The two women apologised vaguely to each other, and watching Beatrice and her swain walk away, Martha nodded her head in approval. 'A lovely couple, don't you think? And so well matched.'

'Oh yes, absolutely,' Arbie agreed, looking down at her petite form and smiling happily.

Martha flashed her sherry-coloured eyes at him, her own smile widening.

Val coughed. Loudly. 'Hello, Mrs Van Dyne. I do hope your hand is feeling better?' she said solicitously. 'I noticed you were favouring your left hand at breakfast the other day. It's so annoying, as one gets older, to fall prey to arthritis or rheumatism, isn't it?' she commiserated sweetly.

Martha smiled back even more sweetly, her eyes glittering with venom. 'Bless you, *child*, but it was only the result of a clumsy fall in my room on Thursday evening. Luckily it's only a sprain, and whilst it was very painful yesterday, today it's much better. I can wiggle my fingers and everything. See?' And so saying, she held out her hand, which was covered by a matching green silk glove all the way up to her elbow and laid it gently on Arbie's shoulder and caressed the silk of his lapel.

Arbie, like a deer trapped in the headlights of a car, froze.

'Mr Swift, would you do me the honour of the next dance?' Martha asked and gave a small tug. It was just hard enough to shift his centre of gravity and make him take a small step forward to retain his balance. And before Val could say a word, Arbie found himself being pulled onto the dance floor and enveloped in perfumed arms.

Looking down into the smiling sherry eyes of his dancing partner, he noticed that her colour was rather high – which was very becoming – and was aware that she was almost vibrating with some strong emotion or other.

Arbie gulped.

*

'I thought you were never going to leave that dreadful woman alone,' Val said, forty-five minutes later.

'*Me* leave *her* alone?' Arbie remonstrated, with feeling. They were now dressed in their everyday clothes, and carried torches, notebooks and a Thermos of tea, the latter having been provided by the hotel's cook. (The cook, it had to be said, was now not at all surprised by any request of the famous author and had provided the Thermos without a murmur.)

'I like that,' Arbie continued as they tramped their way along the village road, which soon began to climb steeply up one side of the valley. 'I was practically kidnapped and held prisoner on the dance floor!'

'You didn't look to be struggling all that hard to get free,' Val said crossly, lengthening in her stride ruthlessly, forcing Arbie to keep up with her. 'Come on, we're going to be late,' she admonished.

'Ghosts don't run to a timetable, you know,' Arbie, for once, found the courage to answer her back, and then spoilt it rather by adding, 'at least, I don't *think* they do.'

They continued walking, in mutual silent antagonism, until at last the ascent slowly levelled out, and they found themselves on the upper road leading out of the village. Lined with elms, horse chestnut and ash trees, it looked dark and uninviting. But at least it was a cloud-free night, and the moonlight was decent, meaning it wasn't pitch dark.

Beside the road, wide grass verges stretched away on either side. In the village below, a few lights lingered, but these too were soon extinguished. Out in the rural villages, people tended to be abed at a decent hour.

'So, what do we do now?' Val asked.

She'd been on a vigil with Arbie before, but that had been in a house, where they'd sat on chairs in the hall, awaiting the appearance of a ghostly blacksmith.

'We find the spot where poor old Red-Dog Briggs and his ill-fated horse was taken by the King's men, and wait,' Arbie said with a sigh. In his mind's eye he was still back on the dance floor being engulfed by the serious charms of the delightful Martha. That curvaceous figure hadn't been any trick of the dress-designer's art, and he could still feel her contours pressed against his.

'Arbie!' Val hissed. 'Where is this spot exactly? You do *know*, don't you?' she asked suspiciously. 'You *did* ask your sources in the village where this ghost and his ghostly horse appear?'

'Of course I did,' Arbie lied. 'And I know just where we need to be,' he lied again. And setting off confidently he chose a point along the road, selecting a nice spot where they could lean against a large tree trunk for comfort, and where the grass didn't grow too high. Sooner or later, he was going to suggest they sit on the grass rather than remain standing until dawn, and had brought a blanket from his car for just such a purpose.

But he knew Val wouldn't agree to anything so lax until she was thoroughly bored, and the hour of midnight was long gone.

If Valentina Coulton-James knew Mr Arbuthnot Swift very well indeed, then so Mr Arbuthnot Swift knew Miss Valentina Coulton-James equally as well.

*

Down in the village, the church clock began to strike. Silently, the two watchers on the hill counted them down.

'It's midnight,' Val whispered.

'So it is,' Arbie agreed mildly. Over the course of their thirty minutes or so wait, both of them had simmered down, and were now conversing as usual. 'Time to be quiet and alert now,' Arbie added needlessly. And then, he silently added to himself, he might even be able to get in a little snooze if he could fall asleep on the blanket without Val noticing.

As it was, they were both leaning against the trunk of the tree, with Val concentrating on looking in one direction down the lane, and Arbie, a little to one side and behind her, alternately looking both left and then right, ears alert for even the faintest echoes of hoofbeats. But so far, there was no sign of either the highwayman or his horse.

Time passed and Arbie yawned.

A tawny owl called out, and its mate answered, giving the comfortingly familiar 'too-whit, too-whoo' call between them.

Now Val yawned.

Ten more minutes passed. Slowly.

Nothing.

Val shifted a little on her feet. Arbie closed his eyes. A moth fluttered past Val's face and she watched its pale flight through the moonlit-dappled trees until it disappeared.

Arbie was just about to suggest to Val that they spread the blanket on the grass and take the weight off their feet, when something alerted him to movement close by. Moreover, not the quick furtive movements of rodents in the leaf litter or the slinky swish of a passing fox in the undergrowth. No, this was the movement of something more substantial. Something more ponderous.

It was not that he heard anything, because he didn't. Apart from the rustling of a slight breeze in the trees now and then, all was as quiet as before. But he'd been on a fair few of these night-time vigils in the open air before and had now gained some experience of what was – and was not – normal.

'Er, Val,' he whispered nervously.

'Hmm?' Val responded listlessly. She was standing the other side of the tree trunk from him, and was refusing to admit, even to herself, that she was thoroughly bored.

'You've been listening out for the sound of horse's hooves, haven't you?' he asked. Because, naturally, he'd long since ceased to bother.

'Of course I have,' she said, and he knew she meant it.

'And you haven't heard anything?'

'No. I would have said. Why, can you hear anything?' she asked sharply, becoming more alert.

'Er, no,' he agreed miserably. Which meant . . . whatever large thing it was close by hadn't made a sound in its approach. Which was unusual. He tried to swallow and found that a rather hard lump in his throat made the process difficult. 'Listen, old thing,' he began, somewhat shakily, and then abruptly stopped speaking.

Because now he could not only sense movement but could *feel* something else.

Something warm and slightly moist, against the back of his neck. Featherlight, it was not the touch of anything substantial, but more like the movement of displaced air. Like something large that was breathing heavily on him.

Stalwart!

A little too late in the day, Arbie remembered the villager's account of how it was the *horse*, and not the *highwayman*, that was the main focus of the ghostly apparitions on this stretch of the road.

Too petrified to turn around, he felt as if his feet had been cemented into the ground. He opened his mouth to tell the oblivious Val to run, but his lips seemed glued together and he realised his mouth had gone bone dry.

After a moment he managed to pry his lips loose and managed to say her name. 'Val, can you feel anything?' he whispered.

'No,' Val said. Then began to turn towards him.

'NO! Don't move,' he hissed in alarm. Hadn't the villagers warned them that people who were unlucky enough to see the ghostly horse died of fright at the sight? 'Stay exactly where you are, and don't turn around, no matter what. Keep looking forward, just as you are. There's something really close by. Something big – and it's breathing right down my neck.'

As he spoke, he sensed movement again, and this time it made a sound. A sort of soft sighing, snorting sound, that was now definitely and identifiably of the equestrian kind. It was the sort of sound that anyone who'd ever been in a stable would know instantly. Nothing as definitive as a neigh or a whinny, but rather the soft sort of chuffing sound that a horse or pony might make, on spotting its favourite rider.

Arbie heard Val draw her breath in sharply and knew that she'd heard it too. And in the dappled moonlight he saw her fingers, which had been resting casually against the bark of the tree, tense and curl.

'Listen, Val,' Arbie managed to get out. 'When I say run, I want you to run. All right?'

Val, too scared to speak, merely nodded. Luckily, in the moonlight, the movement of her fair head was clearly visible and Arbie felt relief flood through him.

He should have known Val wouldn't let him down and lose her head in a crisis. Good old Val.

'What are *you* going to do?' she whispered tremulously. 'You are going to run with me too, aren't you?'

Of course I am, Arbie thought ardently. Just as fast as my trusty legs will take me. But even as he opened his mouth to say as much, he felt something touch his arm.

It was a familiar gesture – and one he knew well.

And suddenly, Arbie knew exactly who – and what – was standing behind him.

Turning his head to look over his shoulder, his saw his old friend, the donkey from the field next to the hotel. He was looking at him hopefully, his large comical ears flicking in silent greeting. Obviously, he'd got out of his paddock somehow – perhaps the gate had come loose or something, and the old boy had wandered off in search of pastures new. He was shoeless, so they hadn't heard him approach. Also, he'd probably been enjoying himself munching on the lush grass of the untouched swathes either side of the road, and that too, would have muffled the sound of his advance.

Once the donkey had spotted his old friend (he of the delicious carrots and apples), it had been inevitable that he would come over to him in hopes of yet another tasty treat. And he'd taken to giving Arbie's arm a gentle nudge of his nose by way of encouragement ever since his second visit to the paddock.

Arbie let out a long, slow breath and wilted with relief against the supporting tree trunk. He felt the urge to laugh like a maniac and vigorously fought it off.

'Arbie?' Val's voice, quivering with tension as she awaited his answer, brought him back to the present – and alive to the possibilities now presented to him.

'Yes,' he whispered back, already formulating his plans. 'Listen, old girl, about that. I've been thinking. You know what that old chap in the village said – about how seeing Stalwart might, er . . . well . . . be fatal, and all that?'

'Oh, Arbie, don't,' Val moaned.

'We have to face it, I'm afraid, old girl,' Arbie murmured bracingly. 'We might really be up against it this time. It's just not possible to outrun a horse, old bean, we both know that. Right?' he began.

It happened so rarely that he ever got the upper hand over his friend. Now that fate had given him the opportunity to enjoy a taste of sweet revenge, he found it impossible to let it pass him by.

In the dark, Arbie grinned gleefully. 'So if we both try to run, there's a good chance that Stalwart will get us both.' So saying, he reached back surreptitiously with his hand and gave the donkey a friendly pat on the neck. Mentally, he promised to bring this splendid animal as many carrots and apples as he could possibly eat tomorrow.

'And there's no point in both of us copping it now, is there?' he continued nobly. 'So this is what we're going to do. When I say "go" I want you to run, straight down the road, and don't look back. That's very important, Val, no matter what – *don't look back*! This road loops around and returns to the village from the other side, so just keep going until you reach a house, and then seek shelter.'

'But what about you?' Val whispered, feeling sick and a little faint.

'I'm going to distract him,' Arbie said gallantly. 'With a bit of luck, I might be able to keep him focused on me. At least, long enough for you to get safely away.'

'Oh, Arbie, no!' Val wailed. 'You can't! I won't let you! We'll face him together,' she said staunchly, and so saying, and before he could stop her, she took a step away from the tree trunk and turned around.

'Don't look at it, Val!' Arbie yelled quickly, but he was too late.

He could tell by the look on her face that she'd seen everything.

For a moment she simply gaped. And then Val began to laugh. 'Oh, Arbie – it's only a donkey! It's all right, you scaredy-cat, you can turn around. It's perfectly safe. You won't die of fright or anything.' And she began to practically howl with laughter, almost doubling over, her arms crossed around her stomach as she hugged herself with helpless, hysterical mirth.

Scaredy-cat, Arbie thought furiously. As if *she* hadn't been trembling in her boots too! But he knew it would be useless to point this out to her now. Just as it had ever been, since they'd first met as tots and Val had stolen his wooden train from him, the beautiful blonde girl reigned supreme once more.

'It's just a d-d-donkey!' she pointed, tears of laughter now streaming down her face.

'Eh? Oh, is it?' he finally had the presence of mind to say, and turning casually, looked at his large, long-eared friend. 'Oh, yes. So it is. Hello there, er, old boy.' He reached out and patted the donkey absently on his head.

Val watched him, shaking with relief and reaction, then began to feel rather sober. And after wiping her face with the backs of her hands, a thoughtful expression slowly took over her face. It took her a while to understand her change of mood, but after a few seconds, recognised that she now felt rather proud of herself. And that something rather life-changing had just happened to her.

'Arbie, isn't it wonderful?' she said quietly.

'Eh?' Arbie said, his caressing hand stilling on the donkey's dusty fur. And all at once he became aware of an impending sense of doom; indeed, it felt as if it was already upon him; inescapable and unremitting – as if his friend, the donkey, really had been the ghostly, ghastly Stalwart after all. 'Wonderful?' he repeated feebly. His heart quailed, and his blood ran cold. Val's face was now seraphic and serene, and boded no good at all. 'Not sure I'm following you, old thing,' he managed to croak.

'But, Arbie, don't you *see*?' Val breathed, her face radiant. 'We faced down our worst fears. And triumphed!' she enthused. 'If I'd had any doubts about it before, now I know I was right. I'm made of the right stuff to be able to help you properly! If I can face down this, I can face down anything any old ghost has to throw at me! From now on, I'm going to be able to help you with every aspect of your books. From being your literary and research assistant and making sure that you meet all your deadlines on time and whatnot, right down to going on ghost-hunts and vigils with you. Together, we'll make a great team. Don't you agree?'

And as if from some distance away, and with a feeling of horror worse than anything he'd felt tonight, Arbie heard himself say, 'Oh. Right. Er . . . yes. Righty-oh then, old bean. I suppose we'd better get back to the hotel.'

CHAPTER SEVENTEEN

Sunday morning got off to a fairly late start for most of the Dashwood House Hotel guests, which was perhaps not surprising, given the amount of alcohol that had been consumed the previous evening. And when the guests did eventually stagger down to the dining room, they were met with an unnerving announcement from Inspector Gormley that their rooms were to be searched over the course of the next few hours.

This resulted in either nervous silence, resigned acquiescence, or loud bluster and outrage, depending on the personality of the individual guest. As organiser of the engagement party – and therefore the titular representative of the majority of those affected – Alexander Hythe-Gill felt obliged to make a show of protest.

'I say, Inspector, is that really necessary?' he asked, after the initial commotion had begun to die down. 'I mean, I realise you have your duty and all that, but what on earth do you expect to *find*?'

There was a general mumble of agreement and approbation at this, which the Inspector ignored.

'My men will be very respectful of your personal property, I can assure everyone here,' he responded instead, neatly dodging the issue, 'and we won't do more than is necessary. Perhaps, Mr

Hythe-Gill, you will oblige us by setting a good example and volunteering to have your room searched first?'

At this, Alexander threw his rather portly shoulders back a little and looked grim-faced, but nevertheless managed a small smile. 'Very well, if you insist. Go ahead, my wife and I certainly have nothing to hide, and I'm sure that all my guests can say the same,' he added pointedly.

Again, there came another vague muttering of half-hearted agreement from the occupants of the dining room.

'Oh, and we shall be searching *all* the guest rooms in the hotel, sir, not just members of your daughter's engagement party. In fact, Captain and Mrs Penderghast have already agreed to our searching their own private quarters, as well as those of the other live-in members of staff. Indeed, the constables are doing this as we speak. So you can see, sir, everybody's being treated the same.'

Not particularly mollified, Alexander merely shrugged, looking around in a vaguely apologetic manner and clearly washing his hands of the whole affair. As he did so, however, he silently congratulated himself on being careful enough to keep his secrets very close to his chest. His inside jacket pocket, in fact. Which meant that unless this pest of an Inspector insisted on a personal body search (and surely, not even that blighter would dare do such a thing) he would not have any awkward explaining to do.

He only hoped that Randolph had been as discreet, but he dared not seek him out, in case anyone noticed. But Ernest's best man was no fool, he reassured himself, and even if he *had* left discriminating evidence lying around, he'd be sure to get to his room and remove it before the police search made its way to his digs.

A nervous chattering settled over the breakfast tables as everyone tried to digest this latest news, along with the porridge and prunes that were currently being served.

Gill Babbacombe fretfully turned to her husband and said something about some unwashed items she'd left in her suitcase, and how 'dreadful' it would be to have a constable mauling them about. Val, overhearing this, also blanched a little as she too contemplated her 'unmentionables' being the centre of attention (and amusement) for some village bobby. Over at her table, Beatrice looked ready to cry, but was being braced by her mother, who was wondering when the bar would open, and if she could possibly order a large sherry before lunchtime without getting any knowing looks.

*

As the guests picked desultorily at their breakfasts, upstairs, dusting a room that had just been vacated by a rather pink-faced Constable Hubert McGraw (who had, indeed, been obliged to peek under some lady's 'unmentionables'), the young maid Evie Smith finally made up her mind to tackle once and for all the dilemma that had been troubling her.

She knew from the moment she arrived at the hotel at just gone six o'clock that morning that Mrs Penderghast was upset, and it didn't take long to find out why. The news that the police were to search the hotel from top to bottom was little short of disastrous. So far, Evie was aware of only two guests who had left before their scheduled departure date, with everyone else being kind and supportive of the Penderghasts by steadfastly remaining.

But even the most loyal of guests were sure to take umbrage at this latest outrage by the police. How could any hotel survive such a mortifying scandal? One thing was for sure – if there was to be any hope at all of saving the Dashwood, the killer had to be found and quickly. And publicly. Before the damage to the hotel's reputation was irreversible.

And although Evie had no idea who had killed Clarice

Fotheringham, or why, she knew that she had to tell even the little that she did know about that awful morning. But even as she dusted and worked up her courage, Evie couldn't quite bring herself to approach either that sad-faced Inspector or that tall lanky Sergeant with his alarming, rolling Scottish accent. She knew she would just stammer and make a fool of herself.

If only there was someone more approachable that she could talk to instead. Someone who was used to helping people and wouldn't judge her or snap questions at her and make her feel so nervous that she was likely to forget her own name! Someone respectable but clever and . . . suddenly, Evie realised that she had been a bit of a chump, for the ideal person had been right under her nose all along.

In a place like the Dashwood, the maids inevitably learned something of the guests, and everyone knew about the famous author, because Mrs Penderghast had been so cock-a-hoop over getting him to come and stay. But until Miss Coulton-James had arrived, nobody knew that he had an assistant – and the very respectable daughter of a vicar at that. Evie had even heard a guest say that Miss Coulton-James's father was the minor son of a lord or something. A proper lady then, but one who was sure to be kind.

Thinking of her now, with her lovely blonde hair, beautiful manners and air of competence, Evie felt reassured. Yes. She would seek out the vicar's daughter and tell *her* about seeing the old lady leaving the dead girl's room. And then, if *she* thought the police needed to know about it, she could pass it on.

*

Those young scallywags Bill and Bob Sullivan, along with their best friend and constant shadow Ben Sherwood, crept stealthily around the poplar trees that surrounded the tennis courts and found a good vantage point behind a large flowering shrub.

Silently, mostly concealed by foliage and a mass of rather sticky flowers, they regarded the hotel with sombre, excited eyes. 'Enemy camp, three hundred yards, sir!' snapped Ben helpfully.

Bob, who had earned the role of platoon leader by beating his brother at a game of marbles, nodded solemnly. 'Any sign of suspicious activity, Corporal?'

His brother Bill, still inclined to be somewhat mutinous, as he suspected his twin (quite rightly) of cheating by moving his marbles on the sly, said sulkily, 'No, sir. All seems quiet.'

Ben wriggled a bit, having discovered that a dead leaf had somehow migrated from the grass and up one leg of his pair of shorts, and looked around nervously, wondering if he dare remove it and have a good scratch.

It had sounded exciting when his friends had proposed they come up to the big house to see what was going on, what with the murder and everything, but now that he was here, he was having second – and third – thoughts. His dad had given him a right rollicking over that affair of the stolen bucket-and-spade escapade, and his mother had brought out the family Bible, and made him swear on it, in front of PC McGraw, that he had never so much as laid eyes on any fancy towel on the beach, let alone pinched it.

Even more worrying, as he'd left the house that morning, with the whole village still abuzz about the fancy guest who'd got killed up at the now fancy hotel, his mother had told him to keep well away from the big house, and had threatened him with various dire and painful assaults to his person if she was to catch him disobeying her.

'Let's get closer,' Bob suddenly said courageously.

His brother immediately agreed.

Which meant, as ever, that it was up to Ben to be the voice of reason. 'Sir, do you think that's wise? If we're captured, we could compromise the mission. And the enemy's currently swarming all over the target.' And right on cue, and as if to reinforce this argument, the enemy – in the form of a rather dozy-looking young constable – emerged from around the side of the hotel, and retrieved something from his bicycle (probably a packet of sandwiches), before sauntering back out of sight again.

'Hmm, perhaps you're right,' Bob (no fool, he,) agreed. 'Let's look for hidden caches instead.'

'Hidden what?' his brother asked.

'Caches,' Bob repeated proudly.

'What's that then?'

But Bob, who'd come across the phrase when reading a particularly thrilling instalment about the exploits of Handsome Hank, that famous cowboy and all-round hero, didn't know exactly what it meant either. But it had sounded jolly good and whatever it had been, it was something Handsome Hank had been keen to get his hands on. And what was good enough for Hank was good enough for Bob Sullivan.

'Oh, it means we have to search around for anything the enemy might have hidden,' he announced with an airy, superior confidence. 'Come on, men, let's put our noggins together. Now, where should we search first?'

'I know! The coalhole,' Ben said.

'Nah, we can't go home dirty, Mum'll kill us,' Bill said sadly.

'Hmm. What about the summer house then?' Ben offered next.

'Nah. That's a cissy place to hide something,' Bob said in disgust. 'I know! What about Old Glory?'

This met with universal approval, and so wriggling away backwards, stomachs flat to the grass (which allowed something small and possessing six legs to crawl up Ben's shorts to join the leaf already there) the boys retreated from perilous enemy territory and back out to the safety of no-man's land, otherwise known as Jessop's Lane, the rather uneven track running right up against the hotel's eastern border.

Here the boys set off along the tree-lined lane to the ancient oak tree known as Old Glory. This pip of a tree had stood there for centuries, and was possessed of many boles, holes, nooks and crannies, where any amount of treasure might be found.

For a moment, all was silent as the three boys rigorously set about their investigations. From one small but intriguing hole in the trunk, Ben had turned up a very large, very ginger millipede which they had admired for some time. In a V-shaped cleft nearer road level, Bob gave a whoop of delight, and pulled out a packet of cigarettes. For some time, they discussed this booty, and agreed that it had probably been left there by old man Wiggins, whose wife wouldn't let him smoke in the house, claiming it gave her a headache. But apart from the hilarity that this caused, the find wasn't of any use to them, and they reluctantly put it back where they'd found it.

It wasn't until Bill, rooting about in one of the larger holes about three feet off the ground, finally found their treasure. He knew he'd hit paydirt the moment his fingers had encountered something hard and bulky, as opposed to the usual rain-wet and slimy decomposing leaf-litter that had been their lot so far. This hole, however, had kept perfectly dry. And when he was able to bring his hand free, grunting a little for the item had been surprisingly heavy to lift, his find glinted a dull bluish-grey in the sunlight.

'Cooo!' His brother let out his breath in proper reverence. 'Bill! You've only gone and done it! You've only gone and found the spy's gun!'

And the boys crowded around the triumphant but slightly scared Bill, as they all stared down at the large gun in his hand.

*

Arbie was returning from his usual morning visit to the paddock, where today he'd given his friend two carrots and three apples. It was not, after all, the donkey's fault that his nocturnal wanderings had resulted in Arbie's personal catastrophe.

Last night, after leading his amenable friend back to his paddock and securing the gate (which had indeed been left ajar by some careless farm hand), Arbie and Val had agreed there was no point continuing the ghost vigil any longer and had returned to the hotel.

There, Arbie had spent a rather miserable night, tossing and turning, and trying to think of a way of getting himself out of the predicament caused by Val's announcement. Eventually, by the time dawn began to lighten the sky, he'd convinced himself that he was worrying for nothing.

To begin with, there was no way Val's father would allow his daughter to get a job – any job – let alone one working for someone who wrote holiday guides for a living, and would thus require his assistant to travel, unchaperoned, far from home on a regular basis. And if, by some chance, Val was able to get her way, surely his wily and thoroughly unscrupulous uncle would soon come up with a fool-proof way of getting his nephew off the hook. After all, the amount of practice his uncle had had in getting out of tight scrapes was considerable.

Consequently, he was now feeling in a much better frame of mind as he made his way back to the hotel, where the police searches were now well underway. He couldn't help but feel very sorry for the Penderghasts, and the memory of Millie's pale face and brave smile as she'd sorted through the post at the front desk pricked at his conscience.

He not only planned to sing the praises of this lovely place in his next edition but vowed now to devote a whole page to it in the listing. He only hoped it would be enough to help save the place. Soon the reporters in London would latch on to the death of the society girl, and then they'd be down here in droves.

He was just about to start across the gravel towards the front door when the sound of laughter and loud calls of 'Bang! Bang!' reached his ears. Curious, he diverted his direction and followed the sound of childish insults and name-calling, which seemed to be emanating from the tennis courts.

He had yet to fall victim to Val – who inevitably thrashed him on the tennis court – by avoiding this area of the hotel's amenities, but as he rounded a poplar tree, he was amused to see a lad fall to the ground, dramatically clutching his chest, as another boy, who had similar features, shouted, 'Bang! You're dead, cursed villain! Take that.'

Arbie was about to applaud the very dramatic death scene (the lad was writhing around with various shouts of 'aagghs' and 'curse you, Red Baron'), when he glanced at the 'gun' his playmate was brandishing, and saw that it was, indeed just that.

A gun.

A real, actual gun.

In fact, even from this distance, Arbie was pretty sure he could make out just what make it was. Webley Mk VI revolvers weren't exactly uncommon nowadays. After the Great War, demobbed soldiers were supposed to hand their weapons over, but with the sheer volume of troops returning to Blighty, it had been impossible for the authorities to stop the smuggling in of such souvenirs. Arbie personally knew about three people who had German-manufactured guns in their wardrobes, trophies that they sometimes remembered to look at, but were mostly now all but forgotten.

But how in the world had one of these lads stumbled upon such a thing?

And – far more importantly – Arbie thought, breaking out in something of a cold sweat: was it loaded?

*

Not wishing to startle them and have the gun-brandishing 'Red Baron' turn the weapon his way, Arbie approached very slowly and cautiously, calling out softly, 'Hello there, lads. That looks like a good game you're playing.'

The two boys, who looked enough alike to almost certainly be brothers, turned to face him in surprise, and instantly became wary. Then a third individual crept out from under cover of a large bush, and it was this lad who spoke first.

And what he said surprised even Arbie.

'You're famous, sir, aren't you?' the lad asked diffidently. 'My older sister pointed you out to me once when you were in the village.'

Arbie, as he did invariably when asked about his famous book, shrugged modestly, whilst still keeping a wary eye on the young lad holding the gun. He was relieved to see that the lad was beginning to feel the weight of it, letting it drop and hang at his side, harmlessly pointing the gun at the ground.

'Coo, is he really famous?' The one who'd been dying so dramatically had now risen from the dead and was staring at him with intense interest. 'What you famous for then? Can you wrestle tigers?'

'Only on Mondays,' Arbie said airily. 'Other days, I write books.'

'Oh, books,' the one with the gun said dismissively. 'We have to read books at school.' His lower lip, jutting out petulantly, showed exactly what he thought about *that*.

'You'd like *these* books,' the taller one said hurriedly. 'They're all about ghosts and trolls and things. This gentleman is a famous ghost-hunter, aren't you, sir? My uncle Basil has read your book and said it's jolly funny.'

'Oooh, mister, have you really seen a ghost?' The boy who'd

been thrashing around on the ground and dying so spectacularly now looked at him with eyes as wide as an owl.

'That's why I'm here,' Arbie said nonchalantly, still keeping one eye on that alarming revolver. 'To see if I can meet up with Red-Dog and Stalwart.'

'My dad said he heard Stalwart once,' the boy with the revolver put in, not wanting to be left out. 'It chased him down the road, but although he could hear it, he couldn't see it. Mum said he was seeing things because of Mr Sillister's scrumpy,' he added matter-of-factly. But he was clearly won over by Arbie's sudden elevation in status. 'Have you really *seen* a ghost?' he echoed his sibling.

Arbie, whose only concern was to get the gun away from the boy as quickly and safely as possible, nodded absently, his mind racing. If he simply demanded that the boy handed it over, he was pretty sure the youngster would merely thumb his nose at him and run off. That's what *he* would have done, at his age. Which meant that he needed to think like his uncle – and get sneaky.

And after a bare second's thought, he got it. Bribery. That was the ticket. Money usually worked a treat on grubby lads, but he had the feeling that in this particular case, it might prove counter-productive. For so rare a prize, he thought even the lure of a shilling wouldn't tempt them – and might even have the reverse effect. If they once got it into their heads that they had a prize worth having, he'd never get it off them.

No, he needed something more than mere money. Something that would distract them even more than the gun. Something that would appeal to their sense of adventure and . . .

He had it.

Crouching down, and looking around him in a very ostentatious manner, he lowered his voice and said, in his best Sexton Blake imitation, 'Can you boys keep a secret?'

Naturally, every boy's ears pricked up at this. The brothers instantly crept closer, spellbound, whilst the other one – sensible lad – remained cautiously a few steps behind them.

'What?' one of the brothers whispered.

'I'm actually working undercover, with the police. But you can't tell anyone. The killer doesn't know, you see, and mustn't find out,' Arbie said, 'or I'll be for it!' And so saying, he ran his finger gruesomely across his throat. 'The fishermen will find my body floating in the sea.'

'Oooooh,' he said, entranced, and swiftly held up a finger and crossed his heart with it. 'We won't tell a soul, will we?' His brother fervently repeated the action, as did the taller lad.

'Now, it looks to me as if you've found the killer's gun,' Arbie said, hoping and praying this was going to work. Even as he spoke, he saw the lad with the gun look down at it, as if surprised he was still holding it. 'Well done – clever work, chaps,' Arbie put in, before the lad could start to get proprietorial. 'And you know what? I bet the *Inspector*,' Arbie did his best to invest the word with an air of majesty and magic, 'will be over the moon. In fact, it wouldn't surprise me if he doesn't give you a medal.'

Arbie had been hoping for a better reaction to this than he actually received, for instead of looking thrilled, the three boys looked at each other rather uncertainly, until the taller one eventually spoke. 'We don't like the police, mister. They think we pinched a towel and a bucket and spade. PC McGraw is very cross with us.'

'Ah. Well, that *is* annoying,' Arbie said, at a bit of a loss. But his brains were nothing if not agile. 'But PC McGraw is just the village flatfoot,' he said scornfully, mentally apologising to the good constable for the slur on his character. 'It's the *Inspector* who is the real brains behind the outfit. He's got the face of a sad dog to look at him, but don't let that fool you. That's just his cover, see? So that nobody suspects him of really being a mastermind of Scotland Yard.'

He doubted that Gormley had ever crossed the portals of Scotland Yard in his life – or would ever want to – but Arbie wasn't about to let trifles like that stop him now. He had the boys hooked. 'He's here after a notorious killer and jewel thief, er, One-Eyed Clarence, the scourge of, er, Bristol.'

'And One-Eyed Clarence did the murder?' the gun-less brother said, breathless with excitement.

Solemnly, Arbie nodded. 'Pinched her jewels, and she found him out, so he had to . . . you know.' Again he ran his finger across his throat. At this, the lads looked even more thrilled. 'Now, if I'm not mistaken, the Inspector is going to be very impressed with what you have there. He'll want to know all about where you found it, and everything.' Which, Arbie thought with an inner smile, was something of an understatement.

'You'll be his star witnesses,' he carried on enticingly. 'So why don't we all go and see him? I'm sure he'll soon put PC McGraw in his place,' he added, by way of further incentive. And it was indeed the prospect of seeing their nemesis thwarted and publicly shamed that turned the tide in his favour.

'Okay, mister, if you say so,' one of the brothers said. Then added slyly, 'You will make sure that the Inspector tells Constable McGraw off where we can watch and listen, won't you?'

Again, mentally apologising to the blameless Constable McGraw, Arbie nodded solemnly. 'I give you my word. I say,' he added, super-casually, 'that gun looks rather heavy, old man. Want me to carry it for you?'

'Sure,' the lad said, and with a careless shrug, raised the gun and waved it up at Arbie who, having gone rather pale, carefully relieved him of it. A quick check showed him it was not loaded, for which his blood pressure was most grateful.

Together, with the three boys chatting excitedly, they went

boldly up to the big house, and confidently swept through the front door with a swagger and a swank that made Arbie want to applaud. No doubt they'd never been allowed through the portals before, and their glee at being free to be 'naughty' but without any of the consequences quite warmed Arbie's heart.

Captain Penderghast, spotting them as he passed through the hall, halted abruptly, and the boys wilted under his outraged gaze like deflating balloons.

But Arbie became their hero all over again by coming up behind them and saying cheerily, 'Oh hello, Captain. Is the Inspector around? Would you be so kind as to tell him I have some important witnesses for him? Tell him we'll be in the lounge, would you? Oh, and would you mind asking your excellent cook to provide us with some of her excellent cakes? And scones – with cream and jam, I think.'

CHAPTER EIGHTEEN

News that a gun had been found nearby swept through the hotel like wildfire. As a number of guests got ready to go to church, in private rooms, out in the gardens or where they congregated in the public rooms, everyone spoke in rushed, heated, worried whispers.

In the kitchen, Evie saw Mrs Penderghast come in to discuss the lunchtime menu with the cook, but her shoulders were slumped, and you could see by the dull look in her eyes that the mistress of the new hotel looked ready to throw in the towel.

And who could blame her? Evie had already overheard several guests saying that they didn't feel safe in the hotel anymore and would leave that very day – no matter what the police said about them staying. The pervading public opinion being that if the police had done their job properly, Clarice's killer would now be behind bars, not out there, making preparations to commit another murder with a gun.

With a heavy heart, Evie couldn't see any other immediate future for herself other than going back to cleaning fish, because once her parents heard about this latest scare, she could see her father putting his foot down and forbidding her to come back to the big house tomorrow. Unless, by some miracle, someone was arrested and taken away in the next few hours.

Well, Evie thought determinedly, she would at least do her

bit to try to help make that wish come true, and after peeling the last potato, set off to find the vicar's daughter.

*

Martha was not one of those intending to go to church and had risen that morning positively looking forward to the day ahead. She had gone into breakfast with a fine appetite and was on good form – dressed in a becoming shimmering grey summer dress that set off her colouring to perfection. But news of a gun being found had clearly shaken her. More than one person noted how pale she now was, and was so nervy she tended to jump at the least little thing.

But in that, she was hardly alone. Both Beatrice and her mother looked to be in similar states of high tension, whilst the menfolk did a better job of looking sanguine; but even they tended to smoke more than usual and talk either too loudly or too quietly. The growing air of uneasy expectation that had settled over the Dashwood House Hotel was infectious, and nobody was immune to it.

On the reception desk in the front hall, Captain Penderghast was doing his best to make light of things and reassure everyone of their safety, pointing out that the police were everywhere and had things under control. But already the Babbacombes had, somewhat shame-faced, notified him that after attending church and lunching at the hotel, they would then be leaving, a few days earlier than planned. And the other guests who were not members of the Hythe-Gill engagement party were also making clear their intention to leave, and for once Millie seemed too despondent even to try to talk them into staying.

Whenever the Inspector or his Sergeant appeared, going here or there about their business, worried eyes watched them. Many of the guests had seen three boys leave the grounds, chatting excitedly, and rumour had it that it was the author fellow who had found them with the weapon. So now, whenever Arbie appeared, he too found himself uncomfortably the centre of attention, but since the Inspector had forbidden him to talk about the incident, he was forced to fob everyone off with vague comments and unsatisfactory mumbles, which did little to endear him to anyone.

A little after eleven o'clock, the pretty Miss Coulton-James was seen to intercept the tall Scottish Sergeant and say something to him that seemed to startle him. The police had been allocated a small private study for their use, and when she disappeared inside with him, and remained there for some little time, speculation only increased.

Many eyes watched as the trio emerged. The blonde girl sought out her beau, the writer, but the two policemen mounted the stairs with a portentous air. Where were they going? Were they going to arrest someone? What information could a country vicar's daughter possibly have of any use? Gossip and speculation spread and became ever more feverish.

*

Oblivious to the growing angst going on downstairs, Inspector Gormley tapped on the door of Mona Rice-Willoughby and waited patiently for it to open.

When it did, the small, slightly stoop-backed woman stared at him and his sergeant with rheumy grey eyes that looked slightly perplexed. 'Yes?' she said severely. Her white fluffy hair had yet to be brushed properly, and the Inspector could see that she was still wearing her slippers.

He cleared his throat uncomfortably. 'I'm sorry to disturb you, madam, but would you mind answering some questions for us?'

Mona craned her head to look up at the tall Sergeant, who instantly felt, as had his superior, as if he was being a bit of an oaf, disturbing a little old lady like this.

'Who are you?' Mona asked, making the two policemen exchange rapid glances. For the Inspector had, in the past few days, spoken to her once or twice, and the Sergeant had taken down her statement, spending at least ten minutes in her company doing so.

'I'm Inspector Gormley, madam, and this is my sergeant. Remember us?'

The old woman suddenly nodded. 'Oh yes, I've got you now! Well, come on in then.'

The men stepped through the door, Gormley instantly aware of lavender talcum powder scenting the air and noticing, at the same time, a rather complicated-looking corset that had been tossed carelessly over the back of a chair.

Both men instantly looked away from the whalebone article, dull colour staining their cheeks. 'Come and sit down, won't you? I was just attending to my toilette,' the old lady said, baffling them once more by plunking herself down at her vanity unit and staring a little forlornly at the mirror. 'Used to be a pretty little thing in my time. Wouldn't think so now, would you?' she muttered darkly.

Gormley said something that he hoped sounded gallant, and got down to brass tacks quickly, before things had a chance to deteriorate into downright farce. 'Mrs Rice-Willoughby, a maid says that she saw you coming out of Miss Fotheringham's bedroom on Friday morning. Is this true?'

'Was it Friday? What's today?'

'Sunday, madam.'

'Ahh. Is it? I suppose I've missed church then. What a pity. Still, I'm sure the Almighty didn't miss my company.' She gave a sudden cackle, then went back to frowning at her reflection.

'Too early for face powder, I think.' She ran her fingers lightly over several pots of creams and lotions and took the stopper off one, to sniff it cautiously.

'Can you tell us what you were doing in Miss Fotheringham's room, madam? She wasn't in, at the time. The maid who saw you states that Miss Fotheringham had gone to the beach for her swim some time before.'

'Had she? Thought herself a mermaid that one,' Mona snorted.

By now, both policemen were getting the feeling that this interview was going to be rather tricky. But Gormley was not the man to give in easily. Slow and steady, that was what won you the race, he reminded himself. 'Why was it you wanted to see Miss Fotheringham?' he tried next.

'Now why would I want to see *her*,' Mona asked, breaking off her study of her reflection to cast him a puzzled glance. 'That vain little heartless murderess was somebody I was quite happy to avoid, I can assure you.'

The Sergeant, who had been taking down her words in his notebook, jerked his head up to look at her, and noted that the Inspector too was staring at her in consternation.

'I'm sorry, Mrs Rice-Willoughby, did you say *"murderess"*? I think you may be getting a little confused. It was Clarice Fotheringham who was murdered,' Gormley explained kindly.

'Oh yes, I know *that*,' Mona said airily, waving a somewhat swollen-knuckled hand vaguely about her head. 'Serves her right too. She killed my Monty, you know.'

'Monty?'

'My dog. With her motor car. Just ran him over and never cared a whit. Oh, she said she was sorry and all that, but I could tell. She just didn't care. I'd had him for so long . . .' Two fat tears ran down her face, and the Sergeant, hideously embarrassed, quickly bent his head back down over his notebook.

'I see. I'm very sorry to hear that, madam. It's heartbreaking to lose a pet, I know. They become one of the family, don't they?' the Inspector said gently. And added craftily, 'That must have made you angry.'

'Oh it did,' Mona agreed willingly enough. And making her selection of lotion, she poured a tiny amount into the palm of one hand, pressed it against the palm of her other hand, then raised both hands to her face and began to work the cream into her cheeks.

'Did you leave a note on Miss Fotheringham's bed, when you went to her room?' he asked casually.

'I did indeed,' Mona agreed crisply. 'Warning her what happened to heartless people. I hope it gave her pause for thought,' she continued, her voice going hard and cold. But then she shrugged, and said in a more even tone, 'But I daresay it didn't. Heartless young hussies have no moral fibre.'

'Miss Fotheringham never got to see the note, Mrs Willoughby,' the Inspector said, his voice no longer so gentle. 'She was killed before returning to her room.'

Mona shrugged. 'Yes. I daresay some man did it. Girls of that type are always getting mixed up with men, aren't they? Who did you say you were again?'

'The police, madam,' Gormley said. 'You don't seem to realise, madam, the severity of your situation. You admit to leaving a threatening anonymous note in a woman's room, and hours later, you are nearby when that same young woman is killed. You *were* on the stairs in the hall, merely yards away from the doorway of the writing room when Clarice Fotheringham died, weren't you?' he asked carefully. 'Mr Randolph Harrington states that he saw you there.'

'Oh, him,' Mona said, with a smile. 'Rather a handsome chap, isn't he? And he's quite right too – I was coming down the stairs and he was in front of me, watching that floozy like a hawk. Well, being dressed only in a swimming costume and wrap and nothing else, who can blame him. Shocking!'

'Is it fair to say you hated the deceased, madam?' the Inspector asked casually.

'The who? Oh, the heartless hussy. Oh yes, she killed my Monty. Did I tell you?'

'Mrs Rice-Willoughby, how often have you used the writing room since coming to the hotel?'

'Hmmm? Oh, not once. I left my reading glasses behind – that damned fool of a maid forgot to pack 'em for me. Can't see a blasted thing close up,' Mona said tetchily. 'Now, where are my shoes . . . ?'

*

'Well, that seems to let her out of it, sir,' the Sergeant said ten minutes later, emerging from Mona's bedroom. 'Even if by some perishing miracle the old girl knew anything about electricity, she wouldn't have been able to see what she was doing, fiddling about with wires and things anyway.'

'Not to mention that she has arthritis in both her hands,' Gormley put in. 'Even if she'd had the know-how to set up the booby trap (and let's face it, that's about as likely as my putting a tenner down at the derby on a 100-1 shot and it romping home), she wouldn't have had the physical ability to set it up.'

As they spoke, Beatrice Hythe-Gill appeared at the head of the stairs and began making her way towards them uncertainly.

'Good morning, miss,' the Sergeant said smartly.

'Hello, er, Sergeant. Is it all right if I talk to Aunt Mona? Someone told Mother that you were interviewing her and she was getting rather worried. You see, what you have to understand is that Aunt Mona is . . . er . . . well, she tends to be forgetful and somewhat . . . er . . . vague,' she said unhappily, her pretty face tense and pale. 'We don't want you to get the wrong idea if she says anything . . . well . . . a little strange. Or odd. Sometimes, she might not be . . . er . . . as discreet as one might hope. She wasn't always like this,' she added hurriedly, biting her lip. 'She used to be such a nice old thing . . .'

'It's all right, miss,' the Sergeant said kindly. 'And not to worry. We've cleared up one or two things that had been brought to our attention but we shouldn't have to bother her again.' And so saying, he knocked on the closed door behind him then opened it up for her to pass through. 'You'll see for yourself, she's perfectly fine and happy.'

Inside, Mona looked up from her chair and spotted her. 'Ah, Beatrice, just the girl I wanted to see. Why don't you come in and help me put on some lipstick?' But as the Sergeant began to close the door again, both men heard her say chidingly, 'Now, don't you go frettin' yourself about all this nonsense. Your future will be very happy *now*, you just wait and see.'

As the door closed, the eyes of the two men met. 'And just what do you suppose she meant by that, sir?' the Sergeant asked nervously. The emphasis on the word 'now' had been too striking to miss.

But the Inspector had had enough of Mona Rice-Willoughby for one day, and refused to speculate.

As the two men began to walk down the landing, a young constable rushed up the stairs to meet them. 'Sir, sir! The courier has just been in with more reports.'

'At last. Well, let the dog see the rabbit, Constable,' Gormley said, and the youngster flushed and thrust out the envelope he'd been clutching possessively to his chest. The Sergeant winked at him and jerked his head indicating that he could go, and the youngster gratefully scarpered back down the stairs.

For a while the Sergeant waited patiently as his superior scanned the contents of the various reports before stopping at one in particular, and nodding. 'Now, that's interesting. I think we'd better have a word with Mr Morris.'

Sergeant Innes, for a moment, had to think who that was. 'You mean the antiques chappie, sir? But he isn't even a member of the engagement party.'

'No, I know. But he's been telling us lies nevertheless, Sergeant.'

*

'But I *did* have to go up to town on business, Inspector,' Charles Morris said, five minutes later. He'd been called into the small study after the PC sent to find him had discovered him just about to head off down into the village.

Now he sat on one of the padded armchairs in the office-like room, one leg casually thrown over the other. He was fiddling about with a cigarette case but had yet to light up.

'According to our colleagues in London, sir, you never went into your office on either of the days you left the hotel,' the Inspector said mildly, making a show of consulting his notebook. 'On either, er, last Thursday, early in the afternoon, or yesterday morning. They checked with your secretary and one of your clerks.'

'Well, there's no mystery there, Inspector, I assure you,' Charles said with a smile. 'As a dealer, work doesn't always mean going into the office, you know. Antiques are found out in the world, not in a filing cabinet. You have to chase down rumours of Chippendales, or sightings of rare porcelain wherever they may be. Now, let's see. Thursday, one of my barkers (that's a chap I pay to keep his eyes peeled for such things,) tipped me the wink that a house clearance was scheduled, and there might be some nice Regency snuff boxes in the offing. That was out near Kew way. And yesterday it was some really dirty Continental silver that had been mis-identified and stashed amongst a box of pewter in a junk shop that was closing down and holding a sale. That was in the East End and, once again, a long way from the office.'

'I see, sir. And did you get your hands on the silver?' Gormley asked blandly.

Charles gave a rueful laugh. 'Not the silver, no. Some hawk-eyed so-and-so had got there ahead of me. I did pick up the snuff box collection, though,' he added, with a grin of satisfaction. 'And have high hopes of making a good profit on them, too.'

'So, if I were to send some of my officers scouting around some of the hardware shops near the railway stations you might have used, they won't find any shop assistants who might have sold you some pliers, or electric wires, or some such things?'

Charles, who had finally decided he was going to smoke after all, paused in the act of flipping his lighter and gazed at him fixedly. 'Good grief, man, no. Why on earth should they?'

'Someone must have gathered the equipment to make the booby trap that killed Miss Fotheringham, sir,' Gormley said mildly.

Charles finished lighting his cigarette and then smiled. 'Go ahead and check away, Inspector, if it pleases you. Though why on earth you think I would want to kill a good-looking young woman that I'd never clapped eyes on before coming to this hotel, I don't know.'

*

'He's quite right, you know,' the Inspector said as the door closed behind Charles and he was left, once more, leafing through the rest of the latest reports for any other useful nuggets of information.

'Unless he's lying and they *did* know each other before,'

Innes said, playing the devil's advocate hopefully. 'Everyone agrees she was a bit of a flirt, and we've being hearing that our antiques dealer had an eye for the ladies. Who's to say they weren't old flames?'

Gormley shrugged. 'So far, there's been no suggestion of it. We've gone over the victim's history in some detail now and have a list of young men she's been associated with as long as your arm, with some horse trainer bigwig being the current flavour of the month, but Mr Morris isn't on it. Besides, even if they *had* had a liaison and it has slipped through our net somehow, do you really think they'd have been able to fool everyone here that they were strangers?'

'No, I reckon not, sir,' the lanky officer agreed.

The Inspector sighed and looked even more woebegone and hangdog than ever. 'Which means we can cross off the old aunt who's going a bit ga-ga, and, without a motive, Mr Charles Morris. Let's just hope there's something else in these reports that might help us. The Superintendent is getting restless and wants results.'

*

As the two policemen pored over the latest information on the lives and doings of everyone currently resident at the hotel, Arbie and Val were sitting under an apple tree, listening intently to Beatrice Hythe-Gill.

Val had sought her out so they could get to the bottom of the incident in the ladies' lavatory, and now Beatrice was looking at Val wide-eyed. 'You mean to say that you were in the cubicle all the time, and never let us know? A bit below par, wasn't it, Miss Valentina Coulton-James?'

Val flushed at the reprimand. 'It was rather, Bea, and I'm so sorry, but I was too embarrassed at first to come out and declare myself. And you were already chattering away as you came in, and well . . . But that's not the point! Just what on earth was it all about, Bea?' Val said hardily. 'You can't keep secrets when someone's been killed.'

Now it was Beatrice's turn to look a little flustered. 'Well, it was all a bit silly,' she said, looking at Arbie uncertainly, then appealingly at Val.

But Val was having none of it. 'Oh, you can say anything in front of Arbie,' she added, dismissing his presence airily. 'And whatever you have to say, poor Clarice is past caring. And if you expect us to clear up her murder, Bea, you simply have to tell us everything.'

Beatrice gave in with a shrug. 'Yes, I suppose you're right. Well, it's all a bit complicated. See, it turns out that poor Randolph was in love with this girl who had her head turned by an older man. He was a bit of a rotter, and, well, you can imagine how that turned out.'

Val shook her head sadly. 'Oh no. Left her holding the baby?'

'Not quite. The poor girl threw herself into the river,' Beatrice said grimly. 'It was awful. Her family was devastated. Randolph lived almost next door to her, apparently, and had loved her always, but being the chump he is, never really had the gumption to step in and sweep her off her feet.'

Arbie, wisely, said nothing to this. The minefield of masculine behaviour, when discussed between women, was nowhere he would ever voluntarily tread. He was no chump.

'Anyway, after she died, he felt guilty as anything and went about moping and whatnot,' Bea swept on, somewhat heartlessly, Arbie thought. 'So when he saw this Casanova-type right here in the hotel, he—'

She broke off abruptly as Val started violently, 'What? Here at the Dashwood? Who was it?'

'Can't you guess? Charles Morris.'

For a moment, Val had to struggle to place him, and it was Arbie who said helpfully, 'Handsome fair-haired chap, mid-forties, semi-retired and playing about in the antiques trade.'

'Oh, him,' Val said. 'He gave us a lift into the village once, didn't he? Kept staring at my legs?'

'That's him,' Arbie agreed woodenly.

'Ugh,' Val said with a shudder. Then frowned. 'But I don't see what this sad story has got to do with Clarice? I wouldn't have thought she was the sympathetic type. Sorry, Bea, that was tactless, I know she was a great pal of yours,' Val said, reaching out to put a hand on her friend's knee.

'No, that's all right. I know Clarice could come across as . . . Oh, let's not pretend, shall we?' The young girl sighed heavily. 'Clarice had a hard side to her that could be very unattractive. But it was just that hard, calculating side of her that made Randolph approach her with a proposition.'

'Now, we're getting to it,' Val said eagerly. 'What was this proposition?'

At this, Beatrice couldn't help but smile. 'Oh, Val. The man only wanted her to vamp Charles.'

'Eh?' Arbie said, wide-eyed, and unable to help himself from butting in. 'I say, that's a bit thick. Asking a lady to, well, er . . . That's really beyond the pale.'

'Oh, Arbie, don't be so wet,' Val said with an air of sophistication that fair took his breath away. Beatrice merely looked on him kindly.

'So what was his plan?' Val mused out loud. 'He couldn't really expect someone like Charles Morris of all people to fall headlong in love with Clarice, then throw *himself* into the river when she threw him over, surely?'

'Of course not,' Beatrice said scornfully. 'No, what he wanted was for Clarice to get close to him and find anything that Randolph could use against him. You know – old love letters from married women, or better yet, some sort of proof that he'd seduced the dead girl. But not for blackmail,' Bea added hastily.

'No, no,' Val agreed. 'It was so that he could disgrace him and ruin him publicly, yes?' She began to nod at her own hypothesis, then stopped and frowned instead. 'But I don't think a man like Morris would care much what people said about him, would he?'

'Oh, I don't know,' Beatrice argued. 'A man's reputation, once ruined, can't be reprieved. And men like that can't afford to have society turn its back on him altogether. Think about it – no decent woman would have anything to do with him, and nobody of quality would ever sell him even the most beastly of their antiques – let alone buy anything from him.'

'Yes, I suppose that's so. Arbie,' Val said, suddenly turning her shining blue eyes his way. 'Do you think Charles found out what Clarice was going to do and killed her to stop her?'

'Oh, hold hard a bit, Val.' It was Beatrice who responded first. 'Clarice had no intention of doing any such thing. There was nothing in it for *her*, you see,' the young girl added sadly, showing Arbie that Beatrice had a much better understanding of her friend's character than he might once have supposed. 'Charles was good-looking enough, but not really her type. And although he was wealthy, her family had oodles more money. She might have done it just for a lark, but in the end she decided she couldn't really be bothered.'

'So bang goes that motive then,' Val said sadly, shoulders slumping a little. 'Oh, well. Thanks for clearing that up anyway, Bea. Oh – I've just thought of something,' she added, her blue eyes once more beginning to shine. 'What if *Randolph* was upset with her for not falling in with his plans? That would make him as mad as a hornet, wouldn't it? And maybe want to pay her back? I mean, if he was really off his head about the dead girl, and maybe a bit off his head generally?'

'Sorry again, Val, but it's no dice, I'm afraid, old thing,' Beatrice said, shaking her head. 'For one thing, the idea of Randy being a killer is simply absurd. The man just doesn't have it in him. But apart from that, Clarice never got around to telling him it was no go. She told me she'd told him she would think it over for a few days and then let him know. I think it amused her, to think of him waiting for her decision, all on tenterhooks. And I know she hadn't got around to telling him yet, because on the morning she died, I asked her, and she said she hadn't.'

'So another suspect drifts by the wayside,' Arbie said, somewhat sardonically.

'I think Daddy would like to blame it all on poor old Mona,' Beatrice said, and seeing Val's admonishing glance had the grace to look a little shame-faced. 'Well, she *is* the limit. Her latest gaffe was to tell poor old Martha that she would never hook the wealthy chap she was after, even though she now had a clear field.'

At this even Val gulped. 'No! She didn't? How awful.'

'We could all have dropped through the floor,' Beatrice agreed. 'You simply never know what she'll come out with next. I say, Val, this business about the gun,' she said, changing the subject nervously. She turned to Arbie and asked intently, 'Do you have any idea what that's all about? Are we in danger?'

Arbie thought that one person was very much in danger but couldn't see the point in scaring Val's friend unnecessarily, so he merely smiled at her affably. 'Oh, don't you worry about that – Inspector Gormley won't let anything happen now. And the place is fairly swarming with police. No killer would risk anything now.'

Somewhat reluctantly, Beatrice nodded at this reasoning, and after begging them to inform her the moment they solved the mystery, trailed disconsolately back towards the hotel patio.

Arbie saw her pause at the top of the patio steps to let Jack and Gill Babbacombe pass by her. Arbie watched the old couple's progress down the steps and through the garden casually at first, then straightened up a little as he saw that they were heading directly towards the apple tree.

'Hello, Mr Swift, I'm so glad I spotted you,' Gill said earnestly as the pair arrived in front of them, and Arbie rose to offer her his seat. Gill sat down gratefully. Her husband leaned against a section of garden wall surrounding a sumptuous rose bed and smiled on them genially. 'We've just come from church, and then we're heading home. All this business with the gun has really upset me, I don't mind saying. And I so wanted to say goodbye before we left. And wondered if I could really be the limit and ask if there's any way I could get a signed copy of your new book, when it comes out?'

'Oh, I'm sure that'll be easy enough to arrange,' Arbie assured her. 'I'll have a word with my publishers. If you can let me have your address, they can send it on.'

'Oh, how marvellous!' As Gill fished in her handbag for her little notebook and pen, she sighed and shook her head. 'We were having such a nice holiday before all this happened. It's Captain and Mrs Penderghast I feel most sorry for. Oh, and that poor woman, Mrs Van Dyne, naturally. I saw her in the hall on the morning that poor girl was killed you know, and she looked simply dreadful! Pale, and trembling a little, and even from a little distance I thought her lips looked rather blue-ish. So when someone told me last night the poor lady had a heart condition, I wasn't surprised. Oh, where is that dratted pen? Ah, here it is . . .'

Arbie obligingly took the torn-off page containing the Babbacombes's address with only half his mind on the job. And as Val chatted with the couple, flirting very lightly with Jack – much to his and his wife's delight – the people and the chat around him faded even further away.

By the time the Babbacombes finally took their leave, Arbie still hadn't fully returned to the present, and watched them walk away with only half-seeing eyes.

'Arbie, are you all right?' Val asked him sharply, finally bringing him out of his reverie. 'You've got that dopey expression on your face that tells me you're not paying attention,' she admonished.

'Hmm? Oh, sorry, old thing,' he apologised. 'I just . . . You know, Val, I think I need to have a quick word with the Inspector.' And so saying he set off so abruptly that Val, after a startled pause, had to run to catch up with him. And when she did so, a quick look at his tight, worried face told her that now was not the time to find out what was biting him.

A decided chill settled over her that had nothing to do with leaving the bright, sunshine-filled garden, and walking into the large, cool hall, where Millie had now taken over from her husband at the reception desk.

'I say, Mrs P., do you know where the Inspector is?' Arbie asked her, forcing his voice to sound urbane and casual.

'In the study, I believe, talking to Mr Hythe-Gill and Mr Harrington.'

But even as Arbie turned to head towards the study door it opened, and Alexander Hythe-Gill and Randolph emerged, each one looking rather pale and deflated. With their tails between their legs, both men headed off towards the bar, where a steward could be seen getting ready for the lunchtime trade.

The tall Scottish Sergeant watched them depart with a little smile playing about his lips.

'Ah, Sergeant, is the Inspector in? Can I have a quick word?' Arbie asked, coming up alongside him.

Innes hesitated visibly. They'd just had a very interesting talk with the two gentlemen who had left, after the latest police reports had informed them that both men had been up to some interesting tricks in the city's financial circles. And he rather thought the Inspector would prefer to be left unmolested to digest what it all meant. Although, as far as Innes could make out, the activities of the two men could have little to do with the murder. Unless something else was going on at the Dashwood hotel.

But after glancing at the author's face, he could see that Mr Swift felt the matter was urgent, and abruptly changed his mind. 'Certainly, sir, won't you come in?'

Val, having no intention of being left out, followed closely on their heels. Alas, she was not to hear what Arbie might have to say, for even before the Inspector could rise from his chair and ask what they wanted, and before Sergeant Innes could close the door behind them, they all heard hurrying feet crossing the hall, and a moment later, Captain Penderghast burst into the room.

'Inspector, it's happened again,' George Penderghast exclaimed. He was breathing hard, pale of face, and sweating visibly. He was feeling so weak-kneed that he had to cling onto the doorframe for support.

'What has?' Gormley barked.

'Someone else has been murdered!'

CHAPTER NINETEEN

'*What? Who?*' the Inspector yelped.

'It's not Beatrice, is it?' Val wailed at the same time.

'Oh no, it won't be Beatrice,' Arbie said with certainty.

This last comment had the Inspector's eyes swivelling his way. 'Oh? You sound very sure of that, Mr Swift, if I may say so.'

Arbie, catching the gimlet eye of the law upon him, gulped like a goldfish. 'Yes. Sorry,' he said inanely.

'Arbie, who is it?' Val said, a little beside herself, and clutched his arm like a vice.

'Well, I rather think . . . I mean, I'm not sure, I don't have all the pieces put together just yet, but there's really only two people that it *could* be,' he said miserably.

'Two?' she squeaked.

'Yes,' Arbie said, trying not to lose his head. But everything was happening too quickly, and he was reeling a bit. He dragged in a deep breath, straightened his shoulders then looked at George Penderghast, who was staring at him with fascination. Mentally tossing a coin, he said flatly, 'Is it Charles Morris?'

The Captain's jaw dropped. 'How the hell did you know that?' he gasped. 'Because you're right. It is. I've found him just now, in the doorway of his room. He's been bashed over the head with something.' Dragging his eyes away from Arbie with some effort, George turned to the Inspector. 'You've got to come quick.'

The Inspector, though, needed no urging, for he was already heading for the door. 'Sergeant, find a constable to stay here with Mr Swift and see that he doesn't leave the premises, then come and find me,' he ordered sharply, and disappeared into the hall.

Val sat down abruptly, all the strength leaving her knees.

Arbie sat down just as abruptly and stared miserably at his hands. He'd been too late. If only he'd put it all together sooner! And yet – until that last bit of information had dropped in his lap only a few minutes ago, he couldn't see how he could have.

*

It was nearly half an hour before Gormley and Innes returned to the small study, during which time Arbie and Val had sat in relative silence. Although Val was itching to ask Arbie to spill the beans, the presence of the silent, watchful constable unnerved her. And Arbie was too deep in thought to notice his friend's unusual reticence.

As the door to the study opened, it was clear that news of the latest tragedy was now rife in the hotel, for many guests were 'casually wandering' about the hall, awaiting developments.

Gormley stood in the doorway and regarded the author thoughtfully. He was not unaware that, in the Cotswolds last year, this young man had helped one of his colleagues to bring a murderer to justice, but had, hereto, believed that it must have been a sheer fluke. It had certainly never crossed his mind that this affable, pleasant young wastrel would be of any use to him in his own murder case.

But now he was by no means so sure. The fact that Mr Arbuthnot Swift had predicted the identity of the latest victim had shaken him. Even more so because, although he'd now had half an hour in which to do some serious thinking, he still couldn't, for the life of him, see how the two murders could be connected. And yet common sense told him that they must be.

Within the last hour, it appeared that Charles had been hit over the head with something like a poker, and a search for the murder weapon was now underway, although he doubted the killer would have conveniently left their fingerprints on it. Morris had been hit from behind on entering his room – which all suggested to him that this crime, unlike the meticulously planned first, had been a much more hurried and spontaneous affair. But he simply couldn't believe that the crimes had been committed by two different people.

But what on earth connected the victims? And just what had been gained by the death of these two people?

'All right, Mr Swift,' the Inspector said with heavy sarcasm. 'You seem to have some insight into what's just happened. Care to share your thoughts with the rest of us?'

Before Arbie could speak, however, Captain Penderghast spoke over the Inspector's shoulder. He had stuck by the policeman closely, determined not to miss anything. 'Is this right, Mr Swift? Do you know who the killer is? Because if you do, I have a right to know as well.'

His voice carried clearly to those behind him, and within moments, Beatrice and her father, too, were crowding around the open doorway. 'Is it true, Arbie?' Beatrice called. 'Have your investigations turned up trumps?'

At this, the Inspector turned a beady eye on the young man, who uncomfortably loosened his collar with one of his fingers, and turned an imploring eye towards Val.

Val, naturally, came instantly to his rescue. 'My friend, Miss Hythe-Gill asked us to see what we could do to help find out about Miss Fotheringham's murder, Inspector. And we could hardly refuse to help, could we?' she asked reasonably, her big blue eyes turned appealingly his way.

'If you have information, I demand to know what it is,' Alexander insisted peremptorily, adding his voice to that of his daughter.

This seemed to rile the Inspector even more, who turned his beady eye from Arbie and fixed it upon the older man. 'Do you really, Mr Hythe-Gill? I would have thought that a man in your precarious position would be the last one to stick his head above the parapet. I've half a mind to arrest you, sir, right now.'

At this Beatrice gasped, and cried, 'Daddy! You didn't kill Clarice, did you?'

Behind her, the milling guests seemed to hold their collective breath.

'Of course not,' Alexander said, appalled. 'Why should I want to kill Clarice, for pity's sake?'

'But you *were* actively engaged in trying to bankrupt Mr Morris, sir,' the Inspector put in, losing his head a little. Normally, he wouldn't be bandying information about, but he was feeling at the end of his tether. 'You and Mr Harrington have both admitted that between you, you were buying up certain stocks and shares and persuading various financiers to come into a venture with you that would almost certainly have wiped our Mr Morris's investments, had he lived. Not an hour ago you were in this room,' he waved a hand around him at the study, 'and confessing that you both had good reason to want revenge on the man. And now he's been killed. I've half a mind to ask my sergeant to arrange a warrant for the arrest of both of you! Now then!'

At this, Arbie coughed loudly, and when the Inspector's mournful visage turned his way, he saw the author give a slight warning shake of his head.

The beleaguered Inspector drew his breath in sharply. 'Look

here, Mr Swift, do you know something of use about this wretched business, or don't you?' he demanded wrathfully.

'Oh no,' Arbie said, then seeing Val shoot him a horrified look, added hastily, 'that is to say, I don't *know* who did it – if by that you mean that I can prove it or anything. But I *think* I know who killed Clarice and Morris. And I think I know why – well, some of it anyway. Although I'm pretty sure I'm still missing pieces of the puzzle.'

'I'm not interested in the speculations of amateur detectives, Mr Swift,' Gormley said bitterly. 'Any Tom, Dick or Harry can spout theories at me!'

'Well, *I'm* interested in what he has to say,' George Penderghast said bitterly. 'This affair has all but ruined our lives. My poor Millie is beside herself. If he knows something that can clear this mess up, I for one want to know about it!'

'And I want to hear it, too,' Beatrice said firmly.

'Hear! Hear!' A voice from out in the hall added its own general encouragement to the motion. 'Let's hear what the chap has to say.'

The Inspector shook his head wearily, but fearing there'd be a riot if the guests didn't get their way now, he heaved a sigh. Besides, he mused, the local doctor was now examining Charles Morris's body, and it would be some time before reinforcements arrived, so there was nothing urgent to do. And with everyone who needed to be questioned right here in the hotel, it would keep his suspects all in one place if they were gathered together out of the way and listening to fairy stories!

Besides, a little voice piped up at the back of his head, it wouldn't hurt to let the man have his say. No doubt it would all be hogwash or pie in the sky. But it was just possible that this relaxed author might have stumbled upon a few morsels that could prove useful to him.

'Very well, sir,' he capitulated graciously. 'I suggest we all retire to the lounge, and Mr Swift can give us a lecture,' he agreed drolly.

At this, Arbie flushed, Val glowed in anticipation, and everyone eagerly began to make their way to the lounge. Along with the Penderghasts, the Hythe-Gill family, Martha Van Dyne, Mona Rice-Willoughby (who was looking thrilled) and Randolph Harrington, there were perhaps another dozen or so party members who quickly settled themselves into various chairs, and then went curiously and somewhat eerily quiet.

Arbie, unhappily finding himself on his feet and the cynosure of all eyes, wondered how on earth it had come to this. But there was no time to bewail the fates now. Hoping that he wasn't about to make an utterable ass of himself in front of everyone, he took a deep breath, and then felt a moment of panic.

'Well, it's hard to know where to begin really,' he said helplessly.

'Begin with the booby trap,' Val said encouragingly. 'Do you know who made it?'

'Oh, yes. And why,' Arbie began, confident of that at least. 'He was very clever about it, too, I must say. Given that he had to think it all out in barely a day or so, he kept a cool head and planned it brilliantly. Of course, in spite of all that, right at the end it all went catastrophically wrong for him, though.'

'What do you mean?' Val asked impatiently. 'It worked, didn't it?'

'Oh, yes. It was just that it worked on the wrong woman,' Arbie said simply.

There was a collective gasp. Then silence again.

Val ignored it all, her eyes remaining fixed on Arbie, who she noticed was sweating rather visibly. She felt a wave of empathy for him wash over her, and smiled encouragement at him. 'Who was supposed to die then?' she asked calmly.

The onlookers, who were turning their eyes from Val to

Arbie then back to Val again, rather like people watching a tennis match, stared expectantly at Arbie.

Who smiled uncertainly. 'Well, old bean, ask yourself. Who else, besides Clarice, regularly used the writing room?'

There was a moment of confusion, then slowly, the people in the room began to turn, seeking out the redhead in the room.

Martha Van Dyne, dressed in a powder-blue outfit, put a hand to her chest and licked her dry lips. 'Do you mean me?' she asked. Her voice was so quiet it was little above a whisper, but such was the silence in the room, that everyone heard it.

Inspector Gormley, prepared to be entertained, was leaning against one wall, arms folded across his chest, content simply to watch and listen. And he was not the only one who was watching things closely. Mona Rice-Willoughby was on the edge of her chair, eyes darting here and there. And a few feet away from her, sitting half-concealed in a wing-backed armchair, Susan Hythe-Gill was tense and watchful. Millie Penderghast reached out and clutched her husband's hand compulsively.

'I'm afraid so, Mrs Van Dyne,' Arbie said, not quite meeting her eyes. 'The killer knew, as we all did, that on that morning practically everyone was going to leave the hotel. Only a few had stated they had no intention of leaving the hotel that morning – and one of them was you.'

'But why would anyone want to kill me?' she asked faintly.

But before Arbie could respond, Beatrice – who could stand the suspense no longer, burst into voice. 'But who *was* it, Arbie?'

Again, Arbie shrugged helplessly. 'Well, who else was *here*? That's the first thing I asked myself. Who made a point of talking about a fabulous mink coat that could be won in a newspaper competition, knowing that Mrs Van Dyne would be unable to resist entering?'

'Mr Morris?' Millie Penderghast burst out.

Arbie inclined his head in acknowledgement. 'You were here that morning, Mrs P. Charles, despite usually heading out sometime in the mid-morning, remained stubbornly on the premises that day. He had no other choice you see. He had to make sure that Clarice, who was by then the only other person who might use the writing room, didn't do so. In fact, I've often wondered if he hadn't come up with some way of ensuring she didn't. Because, of course, she was always writing . . .'

'*The letters!*' Millie suddenly cried out, making everyone in the room jump in their seats like scalded cats. 'I *knew* there was something odd about the post that morning!' she breathed. 'After the post had arrived, I saw there wasn't much of it, and assumed most of the guests had come down and picked up their mail early. Then, not long afterwards, it seemed to me there was *more* post than there had been before, not less, which made no sense.'

But Arbie was already nodding. 'Ah yes, so that's how he did it. Clever.' And then, as if aware of all the accusing eyes levelled on him, he gulped a little. 'He must have removed all of Clarice's mail when it first arrived, so that she'd have no reason to postpone her swim and answer them, then replaced them once she had left for the beach and was safely out of the way.'

Arbie looked around and saw mostly still blank faces looking back at him, but his jumping nerves settled a little as he saw Val give him a small nod and an encouraging smile.

'With both the booby traps now in place in the bureau, he retired to a garden bench that gave him a good view of the back patio and the French doors leading into the writing room and waited. He needed to be on hand in case anyone entered the writing room other than Mrs Van Dyne, to prevent them from going anywhere near that deadly bureau. He must have been heartily relieved when Martha finally arrived there to try and come up with a winning entry for that mink coat – although

I daresay he had some sort of plan B as back-up to ensure she used the writing desk.'

At this, Martha Van Dyne flushed a little, and demurred. 'I only went in there to write some postcards. I wouldn't demean myself by entering some ghastly newspaper publicity stunt.'

At this, a few sly and knowing smirks passed among some of the women, and Martha's colour ran even higher.

'Wait a minute. Did you say both booby traps?' Val asked.

'Oh yes,' Arbie said. 'Charles set up the deadly one connected to the electricity, but we know he did a second one too.'

'We do?' Val blinked.

'Yes. The police found evidence of two sets of holes and scratches at either end of the top bureau drawer, remember?' Arbie said, then shot a horrified glance at the Inspector, who had stiffened at this blatant proof that they'd been ear-wigging outside on the patio on the morning of the murder. 'And of course, that explained the jack-in-the-box,' he swept on quickly.

At this, everyone in the room turned from looking at the bridling Inspector and back again at Arbie.

'Jack-in-the-box? Did he say jack-in-the-box?' Arbie heard someone – he thought it might have been Randolph Harrington – whisper to the person sitting beside him.

'Sorry, yes, you don't know about that yet.' Arbie felt compelled to apologise – but whether it was to the room in general, or the two policemen, he wasn't quite sure. 'Val and I found some colourful bits of square wood and some scraps of material hidden in one of the summerhouses. I knew it reminded me of something, but it took me a little while to remember what it was. They were the remains of one of those colourful jack-in-the-boxes you can find in any nursery. You know the kind I mean – you open them up and a little puppet springs up, scaring the kiddies into hysterics.'

'Hold on, Arbie,' Val said uneasily. 'You're losing us now. Why would Charles make up two booby traps?'

'Well, isn't that obvious?' Arbie asked and was once again uncomfortably aware that he was in danger of making himself very unpopular as around twenty people glared his way.

'Not to us,' Val gritted. 'Oh, do get on with it, and *explain*, Arbie,' she chivvied him on.

'Right. Sorry, old bean,' Arbie said, trying to pull himself together and marshal his thoughts into some sort of order. 'Alrighty-then, his plan was this. Martha would enter the writing room, and at some point go to the bureau for stationery. She would open the drawer and, er . . . well . . . be killed.'

Again everyone, fascinated, turned to stare at Martha, who went as pale as milk.

'He, having put himself in the right place to see it happen, would then dart in and remove the deadly device, leaving only the jack-in-the-box set up in place. That way, when someone found her, they'd find her dead on the floor, apparently the unlucky victim of a practical joke. By then, we all knew about her heart condition, didn't we, and that a severe shock could bring on an attack.'

'Not much of a shock though, sir, I'd have thought,' Sergeant Innes felt obliged to put in. 'A jack-in-the-box would hardly frighten an adult that much.'

'The spider!' Val shouted, and again everyone in the room jumped like scalded cats. 'Sorry,' she instantly apologised, glancing around, red-faced. 'It's just that we found this enormous and very convincing fake spider and a strong spring in one of the sheds. Obviously, the "jack" was discarded, and this awful spider added instead. Now *that* would have scared anybody, I can assure you,' Val promised, with a shudder. 'Opening a drawer and having a huge spider jump out at you – Ugh! I can tell you from my own experience, just the sight of that thing would give *anyone* palpitations.'

Almost as one, everyone turned to look at Arbie. Even the Inspector, who was beginning to look less entertained and much more thoughtful.

'So, er, where was I?' Arbie asked.

'Charles has just rushed in, removed the fatal electrical booby trap, and scarpered,' the Sergeant said helpfully.

'Right. Yes. Well, that's what he *thought* would happen,' Arbie said slowly. 'But as we all know, things didn't work out that way. What he didn't realise was that Mrs Van Dyne had hurt her wrist the night before, and so couldn't use both hands. And unless his victim used both hands, one on each metal handle to complete a circuit, the trap wouldn't work and she wouldn't be electrocuted.'

'But why would Charles want to kill you, Martha?' It was Susan Hythe-Gill who dropped the inevitable question into the tense silence.

In her chair, Martha stirred. She looked frightened and uncertain, but with everyone waiting expectantly for her answer, had little option but to tell them.

'I recognised him the moment I arrived here and saw him,' she admitted, her voice fluctuating and weak. Hearing it, the Inspector hoped she wasn't about to have another 'episode' and was glad the doctor was back on the premises, just in case.

'You'd met him before then?' Gormley asked her gently.

'Yes. Oh, many, many years ago. He married a friend of mine, thinking she had money of her own, then deserted her when he realised that she hadn't, and that her family weren't going to be generous with her allowance. Only he wasn't called Morris then,' Martha added, gulping in air and looking rather like a fish that had been taken out of water.

'Please, don't distress yourself, Mrs Van Dyne,' the Inspector said quickly. 'Just take deep breaths. I take it the blighter changed his name so that he could marry again. Was there a divorce, do you know?'

Martha shook her head. 'My friend was a Catholic,' she said simply.

'Which would have made him a bigamist,' Susan Hythe-Gill said, and shuddered. 'At least his poor second wife died and was spared the shame of it all.'

'So that's why he wanted you dead, because you knew he was a bigamist,' the Inspector said, watching Martha closely, and didn't miss the flicker of her eyes as she nodded.

Gormley caught Arbie's eye, and wondered if the author, too, strongly suspected the redhead of trying her hand at a bit of blackmail. It was obvious the lady liked to live the good life, and the idea of having a rich man paying her regularly to keep quiet must have been tempting. For if Morris was not legally married to his late, wealthy wife, then he might just have to give back his inheritance. And Morris was not the kind of man to take that lying down.

Yes, Gormley thought. She told him he had to pay up or be exposed, and he decided he wasn't happy with either option and elected instead to kill her. It fit all right. Except . . .

'Hang on a moment, Mr Swift, if Mr Morris tried to kill Mrs Van Dyne, and poor Miss Fotheringham ended up dying by mistake, who killed Mr Morris?'

But even as he spoke, he was turning to look at Martha, who gasped, her hands clenching spasmodically into fists, her eyes shimmering with unshed tears of fright. 'Mrs Van Dyne?' he began grimly. 'Can you tell me where you were about forty-five minutes ago?' This was the time that he had estimated Charles Morris must have been killed.

'Now hold on a moment.' It was Alexander who came to his relative's aid. 'Martha, don't answer that without a solicitor present,' he advised crisply. 'Isn't it apparent to everyone by now that her life was in danger? And that she must have known it! First the booby trap, and then the discovery of a gun! You're not trying to say that the gun that was found by those young lads didn't belong to Morris, are you?' he demanded scornfully.

To the Inspector's chagrin, this question was fired at Arbie, not at him, and Arbie, caught off guard, responded automatically.

'Oh no, it was his, all right. He went up to town for the second time to get it, after his first murder attempt failed. The first time he went to buy up all the doings for the two booby traps, of course,' Arbie said. 'It was one of the things that put me on to him as a matter of fact – all those so-called work trips he began making. When, the very first time I met him on the day I arrived here, he said to me that when he went on a holiday he liked *to be* on holiday, and not have anything to do with work. So why, I asked myself, the sudden volte-face?'

'And that's all you had to go on to connect Charles's murder with Mrs Van Dyne?' the policeman asked doubtfully.

Arbie shrugged. 'I admit it's all been sheer deduction on my part. But once I was satisfied that only Charles could have set the booby trap, then it stood to reason that only Martha had a reason to kill Charles – knowing that he'd tried to kill her first and was about to try it again. Er . . . if you see what I mean?'

He shrugged then glanced around. 'Sorry, where was I? Oh, yes – the gun. No doubt he had the gun in his room waiting for the opportunity to use it, but when the Inspector announced they were going to search all the rooms, he had to nip out pretty quick and find another hiding place for it.'

'Which makes it as near to damn it as self-defence,' Alexander swept on, looking around him for support – and mostly getting it, if the many nods were anything to go by. 'Damn it all, it was obvious the blighter was going to try and kill her again. Maybe that's what happened? He attacked her again this morning and she managed to fight him off. What do you say, old girl, is that what happened?' Alexander asked craftily, nodding at his relative and willing her to go along with this explanation.

At this, there was a general sense of relief in the room and many sympathetic glances went Martha's way. But the lady herself seemed to have turned to stone, sitting so pale and still in her chair. Only her eyes looked haunted and terrified.

'No jury in the land will convict her,' Mona Rice-Willoughby averred stoutly, nodding sagely. 'You can trust twelve good men to show common sense.'

Val noticed that Arbie had begun to hop from foot to foot, a sure sign that he was very unhappy about something.

'Arbie, what is it?' she asked, and instantly the room fell silent again, and everyone looked to the oracle to speak.

Arbie shook his head miserably. 'I'm afraid it doesn't matter. I mean, whether or not killing Charles could be argued to be a form of self-defence or not.'

'But why not?' Val demanded indignantly. 'You didn't expect her to just let herself be murdered, did you? Good grief, once she heard about a gun being found, she must have known it would be only a matter of time before he tried again. But Martha, why didn't you just go to the police?' Val said, the rather obvious question only now just occurring to her.

But Martha Van Dyne merely shook her head, as if unable to speak.

'But, Val, don't you see, she couldn't risk it,' Arbie said miserably. 'Her only chance was to lie low and hope like blazes she was never suspected. She might have got away with one murder, but not with two.'

For a moment, it was as if time stood still. Then Val frowned uncertainly. 'I don't understand. What do you mean, two murders?'

'But don't you see, Val,' Arbie said helplessly. 'She killed Clarice. She might be able to concoct some story about fighting off Charles when he tried to kill her again. But there was no way she could explain away killing Clarice.'

'But you said it was Charles who set up the booby traps,' Val cried.

'Yes. He did. But it was Martha who made sure that it was *Clarice* who was killed.'

The entire room seemed to draw a quick, sharp breath at this.

'No, hold on, sir, that doesn't follow,' the Inspector felt obliged to say. 'If Mrs Van Dyne never used the bureau she'd have no way of knowing it contained a deadly trap.'

'But she *did* use the bureau,' Arbie insisted. 'Who do you think removed the spider-trap, somewhat awkwardly being only able to use one hand, and then later hide it in the outhouse once she knew the police search of the grounds was over? Not Charles – he was still on his bench, waiting and hoping for Martha to die.'

'Wait a minute,' Gormley put in. 'Just what are you suggesting happened?'

'I think Martha opened the bureau drawer using just one hand – her uninjured hand – by pulling on first one handle then the other. It would have been awkward, but you can get a drawer to open that way. I know, I once broke my arm as a little nipper, and had to find out ways to do most things one-handed. And once she had got it open far enough, the spider shot out and no doubt scared her silly, but the deadly booby trap didn't engage.'

'But that's sheer speculation,' Alexander said furiously. 'You have no proof any of that happened!'

Arbie nodded. 'Oh yes, sir, I agree. And until the Babbacombes spoke to me just an hour or so ago, I was still in the dark about so much. Oh, I had the outline of the thing clear enough, but no real direction in which to take it.'

'Jack and Gill?' Val said. 'But, Arbie, what have that nice old couple got to do with it?'

Arbie looked at her sorrowfully. 'Val, didn't you hear what

Mrs Babbacombe just told us? How she saw Martha the morning Clarice died and how she looked as if she was about to collapse? Blue in the face, and shaking?'

'Anyone would be shocked after seeing someone die,' Alexander thundered.

'Yes – but nobody *had* died *then*,' Arbie said quietly. 'If you remember, Mrs P, Jack and Gill left fairly early that morning to go on a day's outing,' he said, turning to look at Millie Penderghast, who nodded at once.

'Yes, that's right. They left not long after breakfast.'

'Exactly. So when they came across Martha, it must have been when Clarice was already on the beach or swimming. So why should Martha look as if she'd just had an enormous shock? Because she had! She'd just been in the writing room – and had opened that bureau drawer.'

'That's very astute of you, sir,' Sergeant Innes felt compelled to say, with admiration. 'And very well thought out, I must say.'

Arbie appeared nonplussed by this unexpected approbation, and cleared his throat, even as the Inspector looked daggers at his underling.

'Er, yes, well, thanks, old sport,' Arbie muttered. Then braced himself to get across the finishing line. 'Now, put yourself in Martha's shoes for a moment,' he swept on, and everyone in the room seemed to straighten a little and pay attention, like children in the classroom. 'She knows Charles is sitting on the bench in the garden watching the room, because she must have seen him through the windows when she approached the bureau. If *he* had a clear view of the room, then it must be that she had the same view of him.'

'Granted,' the Inspector agreed cautiously. 'Go on.'

Everyone in the room was now hanging on Arbie's every word – except, curiously enough, the lady concerned. Martha seemed to be staring down at her hands and oblivious to what was being said about and around her.

'Well, just think about it for a moment. She knows someone has played a trick on her. Her heart is probably still racing from the shock of the spider. And she knows that there's one man who has reason to fear her, and she knows he's sitting not far away in the garden. And then she sees the other contraption in the drawer. A thing with wires. And she starts to wonder. Charles Morris made no secret of the fact that he was a sapper in the Great War and so would know all about fatal devices. She might not know exactly what that second whatsit is, or what it does exactly, but she must have had a pretty good idea that it had been designed to kill.'

'But surely she'd march out and confront him,' Val couldn't help but put in. 'I know I would!'

Arbie couldn't help but smile at this. 'I know you would, Val, and probably box his ears too while you were at it. But I think Martha had a better idea. It was not only Charles Morris who could think quickly. She could too. And after a bit, she realises how she can turn everything to her own advantage.'

He paused, as if waiting for Martha to make a comment, but she remained silent.

'She makes sure to show herself to be still moving about the room, so that Charles knows his plan hasn't worked yet,' Arbie continued, painting the scene. 'And then at some point, she must have left to go back to her room to fetch a manicure set or some such thing as she'd need some kind of implement to help her remove the non-fatal booby trap. After using the scissors or files or whatever, she takes the fake spider and spring, and once again leaves the room. By now, Charles must be waiting feverishly for his trap to work but has no other choice but to be patient and wait it out. Martha hides the second, harmless booby trap in her room, to be disposed of later in the shed.

Coincidentally, Charles had already hidden the unwanted bits of the jack-in-the-box in a different location.'

Arbie paused to take a much-needed breath, and unable to bring himself to look at the silent red-haired woman in her chair, glanced out of the window instead. 'Now, all she has to do is wait for Clarice to come back from her swim. And when Clarice comes back to the hotel, she's livid about the theft of her towel. But of course, Martha already knew that she would be, because she'd not long taken it herself. Don't forget – she already knew about the local children pinching things off the beach! So now what does she do? She oh-so-helpfully tells Clarice all about it, and encourages her to write to the parents then and there. Clarice is already wet from her swim, which, for those who don't know, makes electricity even more dangerous, and . . . well . . . there you are. Clarice opens the drawer with both hands and . . . there it is.'

'But she was genuinely shocked and distressed.' Randolph finally spoke into the appalled silence that followed. 'I'd swear that she was. Miss Coulton-James, you saw for yourself the state she was in.'

Val nodded, but now she, too, couldn't bring herself to look at Martha Van Dyne.

'Oh yes, I'm sure she was,' Arbie agreed hastily. 'After all, it must have been a terrifying thing to witness. I doubt Mrs Van Dyne would have known or understood just how terrible it would be. And don't forget, she'd already suffered one shock to her system already that morning. This second one would knock even the most hale and hearty of us for six.'

'But why would she do it?' Beatrice wailed. 'What had she got against Clarice?'

'Yes, that has been stumping me too,' Arbie said. 'It's one of the main reasons I was reluctant to go to the Inspector with my theories. It's a big missing piece that still needs to be fitted in to place. But then something Beatrice said gave me pause to think. She said that Mona had taunted Martha about not hooking a wealthy man *"even now the field was clear"*. Well, that implied to me that somebody else had been after this well-heeled chap, and now wasn't. And who did Mona know had just been removed from the scene? Clarice. Of course, I might be wrong . . .'

'Oh, I think I can help you out there,' Susan Hythe-Gill said sadly, reaching across the small gap between their chairs and taking her daughter's hand in her own and squeezing it. 'Clarice *was* after Martha's chap, I'm afraid. Some of us suspected that Martha was hoping to marry Michael Tanter, the millionaire racehorse fellah. But we didn't like to mention it.'

Here Mona let out a wild cackle which discomfited everybody.

'But recently there were rumours going around that he was being seen about town with Clarice,' Susan continued firmly. 'And you know what Clarice was like, Bea darling. She probably wasn't even all that serious about him. But then again, she wasn't getting any younger, and would have to marry eventually. And someone rich but slightly unorthodox, who made his money from racing, was just the sort she might choose. And poor Martha knew this, and could see herself about to be robbed of her much-needed second husband. The pity of it is, I don't think Martha would ever have even *thought* about doing anything so drastic about it, had she not stumbled upon a murder that had already been set up and was ready to go. So to speak. As it was – well, the temptation to get rid of her rival must have been just too much.'

'Is this right, Martha?' Alexander asked querulously. 'For pity's sake, woman, say something. Defend yourself!'

For answer, Martha Van Dyne gave Arbie a bitter and reproachful look, tears pooling in her eyes. 'You don't understand! None of you do. I had to do it . . . She was trying to steal the man I love. But I didn't know it would all be so . . .

so . . . aw-awful . . .' Remembering again the moment Clarice had died, she went as white as a ghost, put a hand up to her heart and gave a pitiful moan. Her eyes rolling up in her head she then slid out of the chair and onto the floor.

There was a disconcerted movement from almost everyone in the room but it was the Inspector who got to her first. Kneeling over the prone woman he put a hand to her neck, and then shouted to his sergeant to run and get the doctor.

But it was too late.

By the time the doctor arrived, Martha was dead, and the shadow of the gallows no longer loomed.

And for this, everyone in the room was profoundly grateful.

*

With the Inspector's permission, the sad little wedding party left en masse the next day, but Val insisted on helping Arbie type up his notes for the second instalment of *The Gentleman's Guide to Ghost-Hunting*, so he delayed their own departure for another day.

Now, after stowing away their luggage, Arbie helped Val into the passenger seat of his Alvis and was about to get behind the wheel to commence the long drive home, when he suddenly checked himself.

'Hold on a mo', Val, won't be a tick,' he said, and sprinted back into the hotel. Emerging from the rear exit by the kitchen he trotted over to the paddock, where he fed the donkey his farewell gift of an apple and a carrot.

When he returned to the car, Val gave him an odd look. 'You and that pesky donkey seem to be the best of friends all of a sudden,' she said suspiciously.

'Hmm? Oh, no, wouldn't say that, old thing,' he said carelessly. He had hoped that she wouldn't notice what he'd been up to but should have known better. 'It's just that you can't blame the old moke for giving us a scare, can you? It wasn't his fault, after all. Live and let live and all that sort of rot, what? Anyway, all set for the off?' he finished breezily.

Val settled herself more comfortably into her seat and sighed. 'Yes, I suppose so.' She glanced out at the hotel. 'You know, I do hope the Penderghasts don't lose this place. Wouldn't it be awful if nobody comes here again?'

'Oh, I shouldn't worry about that. The place will probably be packed next season. The murders will be old news by then, and besides, people are morbid,' Arbie said airily. 'They won't be able to resist telling all their friends they stayed here – and each and every one of 'em will have claimed to have slept in a "haunted" room,' he predicted cheerfully.

'Oh, I do hope so,' she agreed. 'The Penderghasts are due some good luck for a change.'

And as the car began to climb up the steep valley side, towards the upper road, she added, 'And we are going to give it a good write-up in the next edition of the guide, aren't we?'

Arbie pretended not to hear the 'we' bit and nodded. 'Oh, yes – *I'll* be sure to sing the praises of both the hotel, the Penderghasts and even old Red-Dog to the rafters.'

'Huh, not sure the highwayman deserves any gold stars,' Val said crossly. 'He never even bothered to show up! Him or his dratted horse.'

Arbie smiled. 'Ah yes – true; but thanks to the donkey, the entry for Galton-next-the-Sea will at least have an amusing anecdote to entertain and amuse *my* readers.'

Val nodded and pretended not to notice the use of 'I'll' and 'my'.

'Any idea where we're going next?' she said instead.

'Oh, I don't know,' he said, vaguely. 'I've got wind of a ghostly train in farthest flung Yorkshire somewhere. All brooding bleak moors and lashing rain and whatnot. Definitely doesn't sound like much fun to me. And no place for a lady,' he added firmly.

Val merely smiled.

The weather had finally turned autumnal, and there was no longer any sign of the bright sunshine that they'd enjoyed for so long. Instead, the day was overcast and cloudy, and the breeze carried with it a definite chill in the air.

As the car passed along the tree-lined upper road, in the dense shade cast by a large elm tree, a sturdy, large black horse watched the Alvis disappear with uninterested dark brown eyes. It had gone unseen and unnoticed by the two occupants of the car, but the horse didn't mind that. He was used to being overlooked. He'd just wait there patiently for his master to return and ride him once more . . .

Discover Val and Arbie's first mystery

MURDER BY CANDLELIGHT

'CHARMING AND CLEVER' SARAH YARWOOD-LOVETT

'THE PERFECT VILLAGE MYSTERY' J.M. HALL

SOMEONE IN THIS HOUSE WILL BE DEAD BY MORNING...

FAITH MARTIN

THE MULTI-MILLION-COPY BESTSELLING AUTHOR

Oxfordshire, 1924. A scream rings out across the village of Maybury-in-the-Marsh. The lady of the house has been found dead at the Old Forge. But with all the windows and doors to her room locked, how – and by whom – was she killed?

Arbuthnot 'Arbie' Swift, author of *The Gentleman's Guide to Ghost-Hunting*, is investigating a suspected spectre at the house, and now the more pressing matter of murder falls to him too.

With old friend Val, he uncovers a sorry tale of altered wills and secret love affairs. When events take another sinister turn, Arbie must use all of his sleuthing skills to catch a killer and crack a most ingeniously plotted crime...

Discover more gripping mysteries from Faith Martin with the Ryder and Loveday series.

Coroner Clement Ryder and probationary WPC Trudy Loveday form an unlikely duo when they team up to solve crimes in 1960's Oxford.

DON'T MISS THE LATEST NEWS,
RELEASES AND EXCLUSIVE CONTENT
FROM FAITH MARTIN

SIGN-UP TO HER NEWSLETTER AT
WWW.FAITHMARTIN.CO.UK

Dear Reader,

We hope you enjoyed reading this book. If you did, we'd be so appreciative if you left a review. It really helps us and the author to bring more books like this to you.

Here at HQ Digital we are dedicated to publishing fiction that will keep you turning the pages into the early hours. Don't want to miss a thing? To find out more about our books, promotions, discover exclusive content and enter competitions you can keep in touch in the following ways:

JOIN OUR COMMUNITY:

Sign up to our new email newsletter: http://smarturl.it/SignUpHQ

Read our new blog www.hqstories.co.uk

https://twitter.com/HQStories

www.facebook.com/HQStories

BUDDING WRITER?

We're also looking for authors to join the HQ Digital family! Find out more here:

https://www.hqstories.co.uk/want-to-write-for-us/

Thanks for reading, from the HQ Digital team